EYE
of a
ROOK

First published 2021 by
FREMANTLE PRESS

Fremantle Press Inc. trading as Fremantle Press
25 Quarry Street, Fremantle WA 6160
(PO Box 158, North Fremantle WA 6159)
www.fremantlepress.com.au

Cover images: *Rook*: Illustration by Edward Lear from John Gould's *The Birds of Europe*, vol. 3, 1837. *Flower*: Illustration by Pierre-Joseph Redouté in *Les Roses*, vol. 3, 1824. *Other botanical elements*: Illustration by Jacob Sturm in Johann Georg Sturm's *Deutschlands Flora in Abbildungen*, 1796. *Map*: London by Edward Weller, FRGS, 1868, Mapco, london1868.com.
Cover designed by Nada Backovic, nadabackovic.com.
Printed by McPherson's Printing, Victoria, Australia.

A catalogue record for this book is available from the National Library of Australia

ISBN 9781925816716 (paperback)
ISBN 9781925816723 (ebook)

Fremantle Press is supported by the State Government through the Department of Local Government, Sport and Cultural Industries.

Australia Council for the Arts

Publication of this title was assisted by the Commonwealth Government through the Australia Council, its arts funding and advisory body.

JOSEPHINE TAYLOR

EYE *of a* ROOK

Josephine Taylor is a writer and editor who lives on the coast north of Perth, Western Australia. After developing chronic gynaecological pain in 2000, she was forced to surrender her career as a psychotherapist. Years later, research into the condition made its way into her prize-winning PhD thesis, an investigative memoir. Josephine is now Associate Editor at *Westerly* Magazine and an Adjunct Senior Lecturer in Writing at Edith Cowan University. She teaches in literary fiction and creative non-fiction, and presents on disorder and creativity. Her writing has been anthologised and published widely, including in *Australian Book Review*, *Axon*, *Southerly* and *TEXT*. *Eye of a Rook* is her first novel.

For Dad

Chapter 1

Perth, May 2009

It hurts.

It hurts like a toothache that pierces the bones of your face and shoots through your thoughts, scattering them like frightened birds.

What else? Alice opened herself to her body, registering the sensations she usually fled.

It hurts like an earache that squats in your skull and scrawls graffiti on its walls, trashing the house that was once your home.

She wished she had brought pen and paper. Yesterday's decision to write differently about the pain had brought a rush of words and images. She wanted to fix them in writing, shape them into some kind of new understanding.

Inside out. Lashed to a rack. Glistening innards and frayed nerves, ratcheted around my body. Prisoner. Torturer. Which am I? Where am I?

She pulled herself back from a brink, took deep, long breaths until her thumping heart slowed, shifted cautiously on the horseshoe cushion as scraggly wattle whipped past the window. Only ten minutes now. She must hold on.

How hard it was to describe the sensations to someone who'd never known such pain – pain without sense or logic, pain that ate away at all that was good in you, pain that might never go away. Especially there.

Alice wanted to speak the terrible words to Duncan. Press them upon him so that he too was scored by their jagged edges, make an offering of them so he could help her bear their weight. But she wasn't sure his idea of sharing could stretch that far. *For better, for worse, for richer, for poorer, in sickness and in health*. The words had come so easily then, the feelings too. But now? She looked at his hands on the steering wheel; there was no room for error. She took in his certain profile and knew it would not be softened – not today, anyway.

Perhaps it was enough that he was with her. Taking charge. Accelerating through amber lights, swinging the car round the bend, up the ramp and onto the freeway, and shooting that same, same question at her: 'Tell me again why we're doing this?'

Alice swallowed a sigh. 'Because he seems to understand the pain – it feels like he can work with it.' She chose her words carefully. Tried to speak calmly. 'Some of the others in the support group have taken along their partners. It seems to help.' She waited. But he was not going to make this easy for her. 'It would be great if you could watch, cos I can't see what's happening. Then maybe we could try it the same way, at home.'

'How do you feel when he's working on you?'

Was she imagining the suggestion?

'It's scary ...' Duncan stared doggedly at the road. Alice held her words until he glanced at her. Only a second, but it was enough. 'And it's weird. Feeling another guy's hand, for a start. Then what he's doing ...'

'And how is it better than working with the female physio?'

That sharp clip to his voice. Maybe a casual approach would help, a conciliatory tone.

'Mainly the way he uses breathing, I guess. It's not better, just different. Contracting with the inhalation and releasing with the exhalation – you know. So I'm breathing out and he's pushing and stretching at the same time and that, that ... barrier? I can feel it relaxing.'

Alice wished them away from this speeding car with its difficult thoughts, its tactical parleys. She wanted to place her husband's arms around her, recreate the comfort and pleasure of the past within the circle of their bodies.

'It almost sounds like you enjoy it.' This time it *was* an accusation.

'No – no, I don't. But when he massages and stretches the muscles inside it feels better. Like when you have a headache and I give you a neck massage.' How to both soothe and persuade? 'It's a relief because of the release, but it's bloody painful.'

Alice knew she was telling half-truths. That hand hurt enough to make her cry, but it also coaxed moments that reminded her of what pleasure used to be, before this strange pain lodged in her undefended body.

She rested the side of her head against the window. The Swan was empty of boats today, the water dismal, the sky leaden. So different to that summer's day when they'd hired kayaks and paddled through a blue so dazzling it was hard to imagine it any other way.

'Fuck! Arsehole.' Duncan's gaze was trained on the tinny old Cortina blocking his way. 'Get in the left lane, idiot.' Duncan swerved to the left himself, accelerating past the car. The driver – a young bloke with messy hair – didn't notice her frowning husband. He was laughing with an invisible companion and gesticulating expansively, dangerously, in the air.

On the phone, she thought. Carefree.

Through the keening ache of her body, she reached out and touched Duncan's thigh, rested her hand there. 'Babe. What's going on?'

'Do you really want to talk about it?'

Was it a warning? 'Of course I do.' She silently urged him to look at her, to place his hand on hers in reassurance.

'I'm just really sick of this. And I'm wondering how much you want to get better.' His voice inflexible. 'Maybe that doctor was right.'

The shock jolted her hand back against her belly. She remembered coming home crying, repeating the gynaecologist's words to Duncan: *Do you think you might be dragging this on a bit?* She remembered Duncan cradling her. Seven months ago; what had changed?

She heard his voice, and there was something different now. 'If it keeps going on like this,' he said, 'I'm not sure if I can handle it. It's been a year and a half now. Unless you can try …'

'But I *am* wanting to try. Why do you think I'm putting myself through these appointments?'

She heard his sigh. 'I don't know, Alice.'

'But I thought you believed me – that you understood. You've been okay with it all this time. You're pushing me now, when I'm almost ready!' Her throat clenched with the refusal to cry.

Silence formed a wall between them. Alice fixed her eyes on the arrow of the freeway. The burning had flared but they were almost there. Soon she would be able to stand and find some relief.

She wondered if asking him had been a mistake. Maybe she should continue the appointments alone. Permit this different man, this stranger, to enter her body. Encourage the sensations on the wavering border between pain and pleasure, build the trust that helped her open to him a little more each time, endure the stabbing and searing so she might 'get better'. So she might, one day, be able to reach for her husband again.

Was it too late to turn back?

Off the freeway and Duncan's lips pressed closed. He seemed uncertain of the way now. Would she wait for him to ask? Force him to need her?

She felt hollow with the concessions she'd already made, but it was her body, after all; her fault, if no-one else's. So she offered the words. 'Turn right, here.'

Duncan cornered hard.

Just the small street now. The white building. And soon, the white room. She pictured them, her husband and her physiotherapist, meeting over her body. Felt the impossibility of negotiating the demands of the two. Imagined closing the door on her awareness as she pulled down her skirt, then climbed onto the bench.

London, February 1866

Emily makes herself seemly.

Arthur imagines it thus, sitting in the adjoining room. But the particularities of her actions are obscure to him. Was his wife made to remove her crinoline for the examination? Her chemise? Is anyone there now to help her robe—to pull the laces of her stays tight, sculpting that biddable waist? He has not been privy to these intimate moments for some time, but still he remembers, and hopes.

Arthur pictures Emily. The milky skin where the sun has not touched; the smooth slope of her buttocks, which has been solely his province. He sees the grey-blue of her eyes. Strokes the side of her face, with its sprinkle of light freckles. Scoops up her hair, red-gold and silky in his hands.

He wishes he could be with her so she is not left undone, shamed by all she has endured.

Instead, here he is, listening to the surgeon scratching notes at his stately desk, trying to fool himself that he is in a drawing room—because, look at the ornaments cluttering the mantel; and there, the heavy sofas illuminated in the light sidling past velvet curtains. But the certificates above an elaborately carved cabinet remind him otherwise. Arthur peers through the hazy air. *President of the Medical Society of London 1865*, announces one. Another gilt-edged document proclaims an opening: *The London Surgical Home for the Reception of Gentlewomen and Females of Respectability suffering from Curable Surgical Diseases*. He can just make out the year: 1858. How many gentlewomen have been brought here in the intervening years? Have their husbands or their fathers sat in this same overstuffed chair? Were their thoughts as his: addled with concern and suspicion; terrified of consequences this man might not disclose? Though spare of figure, Mr Isaac Baker Brown has the look of a large horse harnessed to a plough. Is he as solid and unstoppable?

"Now, Mr Rochdale." The surgeon leans back in his leather chair. "Before I give you my diagnosis, I require some facts from you about your wife. Is she restless—perhaps, excitable? Or is she of a melancholic disposition? Even ... shall we say ... withdrawn from you?"

What can he say, when the questions are so weighted with authority?

"She manifests these qualities in turn." It seems disloyal to talk about Emily in this way to a stranger, but even as he speaks, Arthur feels the burden of his wife's peculiar malady shifting. "Sometimes she has such nervous excitability she is unable to sleep and paces restlessly by day. But then she is prostrated by nervous exhaustion and weeps and sighs ceaselessly."

The steel nib of Baker Brown's pen scrapes at paper. Arthur imagines other instruments this hand must hold: a caustic compound, surgical scissors—

His mind shies away.

"Does she complain of various affections?" The man's question returns him.

"She is always ailing but has become silent in my presence, where before she confided eagerly." He should have removed his frockcoat; the tweed is heavy in this close room. "Recently she has become indifferent to the functioning of the home and fanciful in her food."

"Does she speak of pain in the head or down the spine?"

Baker Brown is, it seems, working his way methodically through a list. Arthur wriggles ineffectually against the stuffing of his seat.

"We have purchased a spinal couch that she might rest comfortably, as she has always pain in the lower back."

The surgeon frowns. "It is in these cases of spinal irritation that we observe functional derangements. These are very likely to pass into actual organic diseases."

Arthur's belly twists.

"Does she have distaste for the closeness incident upon marriage?" The question more direct this time.

"At first our relations were ..." Arthur's lips close on this intimacy. He has to force them open. "Relations were natural and pleasurable for us both. But then she began to complain of a burning and stabbing in her private parts, such that she must pass her water every half-hour—this for nigh on a year now." He is dismayed at the tremor in his own voice; newly perturbed at the disordered woman revealed by his account. "She has pain on visiting the water closet, pain with our congress, pain when walking. It seems her life has been reduced to suffering."

Baker Brown's full mouth purses and releases as he writes. Arthur looks into the small fire crackling in the grate, its smoke the memory of roasting chestnuts, its gentle staccato a childhood lullaby. He remembers the voice of his wife as it was when they first met: eager, musical—the cadences weaving around him, as his evening brandy clings to its snifter when swirled. And he remembers her lovely intimate voice, lost nine months into their marriage. She still spoke, but in a faltering tone. He no longer heard her cries of pleasure, twined with his, only this new, bewildered voice in the night; nor could he speak in return, when compassion, embarrassment, helplessness, rose up and stopped his throat.

Baker Brown sets down his pen. "When I examined your wife," he says, steepling his hands, "she admitted to frequent periods attended with pain. There are further indications of nervous disturbance: her eyelids quiver and her gaze will not easily meet my own. Upon a personal examination I also noted peculiarities typical in such cases …" He hesitates for a moment. "A certain coarseness …"

A certain coarseness? To what is the man referring, when Emily's skin is so soft, her nature so sweet?

Baker Brown releases his fob from its pocket, fingering it deftly. "In conclusion," the man pronounces, "there is evidence of persistent excitation of the pudic nerve. Nerve power has been exhausted through overstimulation. Your wife"—he falters—"your wife herself …" He looks at Arthur suggestively. "Do you understand my meaning?"

Arthur does not wish to understand. To what strange desires and unnatural behaviours has his Emily been made to confess? Arthur would like to strike this interloper. Rescue his wife and never return. He has to remind himself of her unaccountable suffering and the surgeon's reputed skill.

"We are both learned men, Mr Rochdale." The voice smooth and assured now. "Hysteria is established in your wife and maintained by this continual irritation. The operation I am suggesting destroys the nerve, excising the cause of excitement, so that hysteria is halted before it progresses to epilepsy and idiocy. Even death."

A sharp tremor seizes Arthur's body. *Death*, the man said, his face implacable. And those other words, like an assault: *epilepsy*, *idiocy*. Arthur sees his wife pulling herself close and quietly retreating to the spinal couch in her bedchamber. He hears her small voice, diminishing further as she withdraws from her family, her friends, and then, finally, from him.

She could not have brought this on herself, surely? This sick and troubled woman who is his wife?

"Judicious aftertreatment is critical to the success of the operation." Arthur marks the surgeon's words now, and feels their terrible gravity. "The continuous observation and moral influence of the nurses helps to prevent further … shall we say … unnatural practices."

Unnatural practices. Is this possible? How has he not noticed? Arthur feels admonished along with his wife. But he also has the impulse to take up a pistol and defend her honour; the urge to clasp hands in solidarity with the surgeon and castigate her wantonness. The elements are capricious and he a weathervane.

"I should warn you that aftertreatment requires perseverance. Not only on your part, but on the part of your family and friends. However"—Baker Brown's mouth curves into a shape resembling a smile—"your wife is anxious to be cured, which is a favourable sign. I would advise her prompt admission to the Surgical Home. Here, I will note the address." He scribbles, then holds out the note. "And a date: two weeks hence."

The details sprawl confidently across the page. February 26th: so close, so utterly … chilling. Arthur imagines Emily lying unrobed in a narrow bed at this "Home", her eyes wells of despair and accusation.

"The operation is radical. I am concerned that my wife's pain might have another cause—that we may unnecessarily expose her to increased suffering." A surge of protective unease gives Arthur the courage to challenge this unsettling man; to speak for Emily, who seems no longer able to speak for herself. "Might not this operation take from my wife the seat of her womanhood?"

"No, no. Nothing of the sort. Rather than interfere with marital happiness it may enable procreation. Surely that is what you wish?"

"Yes, of course, but it seems somehow … immoral, to be acting so."

The man's smile is conspiratorial, unnerving. "It is our moral duty," he says, "to protect the weaker sex from indulgence in unnatural venereal pleasure. We must consider the facts."

Arthur hesitates. "Perhaps," he says faintly.

"Many of my former patients go on to bear numerous children. They become in every respect good wives."

Children. They had wanted children, he remembers. In their marriage bed, in the dark—where they'd discovered each other's bodies and shared their most precious dreams; when it seemed that everyone else in the world must be asleep—they'd whispered their imaginings. Would their children have Arthur's glossy brown hair? Emily's broad brow? What little ones might chase each other through the delphinium bed at Hierde House and pluck the peaches from their espaliered wall? Longing is a pang in Arthur's chest.

What if Baker Brown is simply trying to help?

"Your wife has asked for assistance. We need to make the right decision."

How can Arthur be sure? He feels the heaviness of Emily's life in his hands. Sees again her journal page, glimpsed before she snapped close the cover. *It is like a brand searing my flesh, inside and out. How can I continue?* The naked plea: *Oh God, please help me!*

How can he hesitate?

Sudden sunlight shafts the room, catching Arthur in its glowing bar. He feels transparent: as if Baker Brown can see, through his translucent skin, his confusion, his reluctance—his antipathy.

"Yes," says Arthur, the word anchoring his sliding world. "Yes."

Chapter 2

Rugby, June 1853

"*Omnia vincit amor.* Construe. Harris?"

"I … I don't know, sir."

Arthur Rochdale listens intently, biding his time. He knows the master will turn to him, if it comes to that.

"Rowlands?"

"Something about armour … and fighting, sir?"

"Not everything is about fighting, Rowlands." The master's admonishment is softened with a smile. Encouraged, the boys laugh. "Though in this case, you might be stumbling blindly onto the right path. Lawler?"

"Love, sir? And violence? Or victory?"

"Boys, boys—look to your Virgil. You should be able to translate this one in your sleep." The tolling of the bell sounds through the room and the boys nudge their graduses and dictionaries and shuffle their feet. The end of second lesson. Their form master sighs. "Rochdale. Put us out of our misery."

"Love conquers all things. Sir?"

"As always. Try and drum some sense into these friends of yours, eh?" The master waves a hand towards the door, releasing his students. "And try not to get into too many pickles before Monday!" His voice is lost in oaken scraping.

Students jostle as they funnel through the door and into the quadrangle. A small group surrounds Arthur, eager puppies ready for play, all shining eyes and bouncing bodies.

"To the Close!" Arthur sets the pace as they run through School House and then out, out, into the startling green. They pause, momentarily blinded, then strew books and bags on the grass. The windows glint with sunlight and the great flag on the tower ripples in the breeze. Rooks caw raucously from the treetops. Some younger lads begin to pelt each other with old acorns.

It is Saturday and lessons are over for the week; apart from Sunday's chapel services and lecture, till Monday the time is Arthur's to spend as he pleases. He turns and gazes with satisfaction upon the Close. The fields lie gently rucked before him, a long swathe marked only by the three great elms with a scattering of sheep beneath. In the distance, set alight by the sun, Bilton spire pierces the woods.

Arthur longs to pull the boots from his feet and the schoolboy armour from his chest. He imagines the tickle of grass between his soft toes and is taken back to another day, where he lay between Mother and Beatrice on a green carpet, their nestled bodies and faces turned to the sky.

A princess rides on a stallion.

Bea had gone first, that day, weaving a story from the scattered clouds beyond their hollyhock frame, then Mother had continued the tale, on into distant inky mountains. And what had he said? Something about trolls and a curse, his body held firm and safe by the warm earth and the hands of Mother and Bea.

He remembers Mother's hair tickling his cheek as she leaned her head to his. *What about this one?* The whites and greys had shaped themselves into fantastical beings. *Ummm. I know! Beetles and elven folk host a midsummer ball,* he'd started. Then Bea had squealed something about the guests, their own Hierde House flowers, while Mother's hands drew a dance of violets and bluebells in the air.

The memories and longing still grasp at him, still carve a hollow in his core.

Arthur chases the pictures from his mind. He is Rochdale of the lower fourth and he has friends to lead and masters to impress. He sighs quietly. It is nearly the end of his first year at Rugby School House and he is beginning to understand that he will not make this place home by prattling about faeries and buttercups.

Bill Rowlands shoves the other boys aside. "Rochie, where's the cricket ball?"

Rowlands has become his friend through wet months of kicking the puntabout and playing in little-side football matches in their School

House scarlet and gold. They've worked well together—Bill throwing his body against boys like a bulky sack of potatoes, Arthur dodging and weaving, fleet-footed, both swaying shoulder to shoulder in scrummages that held the menace of an angry bull—but they've strived to outdo each other in tries and drop-punts at goal, the tally measured in mud and bruising and the admiration of their School House friends. Arthur remembers the last match. His knock against one of the trees on the pitch and that dizzy run with the ball. The sore glory of the team's victory and Bill's bruising clap on his shoulder. The smile like a scowl.

At the edge of his vision, Arthur sees Edward Harris stepping into the Close. He holds his breath; turns, as if his own eyes have been caught by something in the distance; intends distraction. But it's too late. Though Harris swivels away, Rowlands strides into his path. Arthur's breath quickens at the sight of Bill's puffed-up body shadowing the lad.

"*I … I don't know, sir*," stutters Rowlands, mimicking Harris's soft Scottish burr. Arthur wonders at his friend's pleasure, this malice a new sport—one that shoots queasiness into his throat. Can Bill be drawn away?

Arthur mock-punches the mottled arm. "Come on, Rattlin, we've better games to play."

The nickname suits Bill perfectly: once Rowlands hit someone so hard the lad said he felt his teeth rattling. Rattling Rowlands. Apart from close friends, the remainder of the lower fourth have begun to draw wary circles around Rattlin.

"Better games? But I like this one." Bill's smile is tight.

He is mean, thinks Arthur. The protest is unbidden and unwelcome; he does not want to make an enemy of his friend. But his mother's voice comes to him as he stands, wavering: *Sometimes, Arthur, we must fend for those who are not able to fend for themselves.*

"Leave him alone, Rattlin."

Arthur sees his friend's surprise and then his new appraisal of Harris: the small boy's hunched shoulders and his white face, turned to the ground. Arthur notices a hesitation; sees Bill's eyes flicker uncertainly.

He presses his advantage.

"Come on, let's see who can throw the ball furthest."

Rattlin was the first in their form to throw a cricket ball over the rook trees to the headmaster's wall. But challengers are already nipping at his heels.

"You're right, Rochie; he ain't worth it." Rowlands turns to their group. "Come on, lads. Just try and beat me!"

*

Arthur walks up the spiral staircase behind the praepostor. Why has he been fetched? He only sees the headmaster at assembly and chapel service and knows boys are not brought to his study without good reason. Perhaps it is to do with Smyth's pea-shooting raid, or the slipper battle that spilled into the corridor and neighbouring dorms in a jumble of arms and legs and hot boy bodies. Arthur joined in both capers. But why would he alone be in trouble? His tummy growls and squeaks.

Hetherington is silent as they climb. Arthur wondered at the praepostor's shifting gaze when he came out into the Close and fetched him from morning break, and now he is not sure how to break the strange quiet. Of the sixth form leaders, Hetherington is one of the best. He looks out for young'uns when bullying draws blood and acts the boss when fifth or sixth form fellows become loutish. He is also, usually, a man to give advice to the smaller lads, especially about fags' duties. How to know when to fetch hot water. Where to escape from brutish fifth-formers. But, today, it seems, he has no counsel to offer.

Arthur wishes Mother were here, her steady tread beside him, her eyes reading his secret fears. Seeing him. Not popular Arthur, but the Arthur he tries to ignore when hemmed in by the boys and men of Rugby School.

He spoke of it to her—that tearing inside him, the two Arthurs pulling him apart—on that precious morning in the last break. Beatrice and Cecilia at Herdley Hall, playing with the squire's daughters; Mothering Sunday, and a morning spent with Mother all to himself. And at Hierde House for a change, not smelly London, where Father is busy and important—"hectic politicking" his parents call it, in a way he understands is a joke.

On that day, Mother had been drawing a portrait of herself for him to keep at school. *So I will always be with you, wherever you are*, she'd said, smudging the charcoal image, those blackened fingers and their rounded waltz on the paper like a caress. Drowsiness had him sinking into the sofa. But then a strange pressure in his chest, that hard lump in his throat, snatched him back—back into wakefulness. And then he'd heard his own voice, like a stranger's, speaking of who he must be at Rugby School. Telling his mother of the fags who cower at the demands of older fellows. Confessing his silent fury in the face of bullies and his pity of the weedy, who make him want to shield them. And when he does not? The disgust at them. At himself. And, oh, how he wants to be a simple Rugby cock: funny, clever and strong.

He can feel it now, the tearing. An Arthur who cares and an Arthur who does not, not at all. But she helped, didn't she, just as she always does. Wiping her hands on a cloth and seating herself next to him. Lifting his hand and squeezing it with her long fingers. *Sometimes, Arthur, we must fend for those who are not able to fend for themselves.* A sweep of her hand through his hair. *And sometimes we must listen for the quiet voice that tells the truth.*

Arthur can hear her saying the words to him as he climbs the staircase, trailing his fingers against the stones of the wall, *tha-dub tha-dub tha-dub.* He imagines her beside him, her feet on the same cold steps, and feels her hand clasp his. Then, without warning, they are on the landing. He comes up hard against Hetherington's dandruff-speckled shoulders and tightens his lips against a nervous giggle.

Hetherington's knock is hollow on the heavy door.

"Come."

Faces of past headmasters peer down at Arthur as he enters the study, but the only one he recognises is Dr Arnold. His father often speaks with fondness of the great man and his own years at Rugby School, but something in his voice reminds Arthur of the mummers at Christmas, their masked words and waving arms. What does Father really feel?

"Here is Rochdale, sir."

"All right, Hetherington. Just wait outside, will you?"

"Yes, sir."

Dr Goulburn—"Old Ghoul", the boys whisper at night, shuffling cold linen—takes no notice of Arthur. He frowns and pushes his pen at the paper on his desk, then sets to work on a fresh sheet.

The study window is placed too high for Arthur to see his friends, but he pictures himself still with them, hitting the cricket ball in the Close. Wishes himself at Hierde House, feeling rested and right. *The summer holidays are only short weeks away,* Mother reminded him in her last letter, *and then the whole family will be together.* Soon he will race with the village gang to the marketplace, the thought of spiced pie lending wings to his feet; stride through the Herdley hills and over the craggy slopes of the Peak District, Taffy panting at his side; chase Bea and Cissy around the delphinium bed, his sisters screeching and giggling; hide in the elm thicket by the village path, losing himself in the trees' green embrace. Finding himself in another world.

The headmaster harrumphs and mutters a couple of words, then scribbles again. Arthur can only see the wide brow. He has to picture the boxer's nose and long, downturned mouth, the pouchy jowls that shake when boys are in trouble. Arthur imagines all the lads who have stood here: proud, relieved, terrified. Wondering, will it be the birch? Arthur knows his own fear but he cannot read the mood; the air is as clotted as Hierde Farm cream.

Tap tap. The head manages his papers into a neat pile. He takes off his spectacles and rubs at the crease over his nose. Only then does he look at Arthur.

"Well, Rochdale, I'm afraid I have some unfortunate news." His eyes like pebbles. "Your mother has died. Right now, I believe your father is attending her funeral."

Arthur's body sways, punched. A cold swing of weight.

"I am addressing some correspondence to your father now, expressing the school's regard."

Desk, chairs, headmaster—they rush away as he reaches for them. Flat. A picture.

Who is it that feels the cold prickle sweeping from foot to head, scalp tugging at face? Who is it that senses the tight eyes, the thudding heart?

"Sir?" Is it his voice?

He is beside himself.

Crack of ball on bat. Harsh caws that swell and recede, swell and recede, as rooks circle the tree beyond the window. He is outside with them, a bird flying towards white clarity. The air opens beneath him …

"Right, Rochdale. I'll let Hetherington take you to your dorm. Matron is waiting for you there. I expect your father will be in contact soon."

Golden pudding steams gently in the bowl. Dead Man's Arm is Arthur's favourite but today his stomach tips at the cloying smell. To his right, Lawler's shock of hair bobs as he and Smyth scoff their pudding; to his left, Hodge, Greenwood and Rattlin argue in whispers about cricket between great gulps of food.

Arthur swallows against his knotted throat. If he does not eat the pudding, his friends will begin to wonder.

He wants to disappear. He wants to flee his body as he did so briefly, days before. He's not invisible, but maybe he can avoid talking to Rattlin and the others if he keeps his eyes lowered, gets the sticky mass past the rock lodged in his throat. His tummy heaves and for a moment his grip loosens. At the clatter of the spoon, Lawler turns, face concerned, eyebrows lifted with enquiry.

Father's brow had wrinkled that night before the new term, when he saw Arthur picking at the turkey on his plate. What might have been a treasured time, all of them together at Hierde House, Father up from London at the end of the last short holiday, Mother quietly beaming at her family around the dining room table, but for his own roiling thoughts: the return to Rugby School on the morrow. The bubble and churn of his gut had been the same, then, but Father's frown had told him he must eat. And after that silent mealtime battle, after he'd cocooned himself in bed, he'd imagined the days to come and the pictures had drifted him slowly towards sleep: his Rugby friends' eager faces and the excited slaps on his back; the pleased expression of his masters; the glower of fifth-formers ordering him to fetch food and books and balls and ... Then he came back to himself—he, Arthur: this boy who must prove himself over and over; this boy he wants to shove away like a stranger. And though his talk with Mother had eased him, he felt newly clogged with it all, full to the brim with things he couldn't name. He sat up in bed, supper's turkey and bread rising sour in his throat.

Arthur digs his spoon into the Dead Man's Arm and pushes the red ooze about. Tries to recollect the rest of that last night, even if it hurts, remembering Mother.

He'd pulled his eiderdown aside and slipped into the soft leather slippers by his bed. He'd slid along the edges of the squeaky corridor to the top of the stairs. Felt the deep rumble of Father's voice through the wood.

—and let him grow up, Louise. After all, he is almost twelve.

How can I not be concerned, when he speaks of ... Mother's voice had faded here, hadn't it? Anyway, he'd slipped down the flight of steps to his favourite corner. Heard her say something about him growing bigger, stronger, but somehow less than he was. Heard Father using hard words in a harder voice: *confides, indulge*. Then Mother again, talking about him not eating—and he'd tasted the sourness once more, clasping his bony knees under his nightgown, while Father talked about his own time at Rugby, saying, *I know what it is to be sick for home.*

And now he wonders: did Father also have two selves? Did he leave one George Rochdale behind, then? Back at his old school?

Have you not heard him talking about the football matches? his father had continued that night. Something about *a scholar*, and *an athlete—*

and the form master's praise: *a future leader*. But Mother's voice, too, had been clear and certain, and she'd talked about love and power in ways he didn't understand, though he remembers her saying it was the greatest men who love and protect those in need. And he remembers the smile in Father's voice as he replied, *Ah, Louise. Louise. It took your love for me to realise that caring is not weakness, but strength.*

Are they right, these memories? One thing he does know: something settled inside him then, only short months ago, at his parents' words; scattered things found some kind of home.

But now? Now, he has never felt so uncertain, or so lost—as if he is adrift in the dark; as if there will never be anything, *anyone*, to draw him back to the light.

He lifts a spoonful of the pudding. Opens his mouth.

Gentle breaths and occasional rustles come from the beds lined against the dorm wall. Arthur swallows, then swallows again. If he could just dislodge that rock ...

He still hasn't cried. He feels numb and cold, yet on the verge of explosion. As if someone has placed gunpowder within him and lit a fuse that travels from his feet, up, up, through his legs and torso and into his throat and head. He imagines himself exploded—bits of skull and brain on the ceiling, intestines slapped against the wall with mushy Dead Man's Arm seeping from the mess.

He quietly pulls his mother's drawing from where it is folded in tissue paper under his pillow. In the dark of the dorm he cannot see her features, the details she has drawn herself, but he pictures her face in his memory and traces it with a finger: the fine hair, drawn back smoothly over the ears and into a heavy braid that haloes her head; the angles of her face, softened by large brown eyes that dip gently at their outer corners.

How can he go on without her?

He swallows. And then, slowly, with care, he begins to tear bits from the charcoaled sketch and place them in his mouth. He nibbles and chews piecemeal, tasting the gritty residue of the cooled hearth, the image of his mother transforming into a soft pap that he swallows. He wonders where within him Mother might lodge and thinks, for a moment, of his classes on ancient Greece, the writers and physicians he loves. The tragedies of Euripides, the sound of them like music, and his prized volume of tales by Herodotus. The humours that ebb and flow beneath the skin. He imagines Mother seeping into his mouth and throat, his tummy, legs and arms, hands and feet. Into the organs his master told them make up their sad bodies. Lungs. Liver. Kidneys. Heart. She knits herself softly into the fibres of his being. Lights a flame in the hollow below his chest. Speaks calmly to him: *So I will always be with you, wherever you are.*

He swallows. And swallows. Mother washes at that rock in his throat, softly, lovingly, until he feels it dislodge and, finally, dissolve, somewhere deep within. Tears begin slowly to slide from the dipping corners of his eyes.

Chapter 3

Perth, September 2007

'Let's find spring,' Duncan said.

They packed up the SUV – 'Finally, some off-road driving,' Alice teased – abandoning half-reworked stories and conference papers, student essays and crisis emails, and set off at once. A rare stab at spontaneity, a week away from the madness.

They drove northward through the rain, singing along to old Radiohead CDs, slowly rousing from their urban stupor. The clouds cleared and the wind blew the wild scent of the ocean through the car, and the world came to life again. They exclaimed at the massed pinks, yellows and whites of everlastings swathing their route. Shared gossip about their colleagues at uni, laughing at the burdens that seemed less weighted now. Swapped jokes and lollies, searching for their favourites in the jumbo bag they'd bought at the service station, nudging each other like excited children.

Alice drifted into sleep smiling, and when she woke saw the tutor she'd fallen in love with years before. She watched the movement of his wide mouth and heard anew the deep voice. When his spiced freshness came to her, she inhaled it greedily. And when they stopped for petrol she stayed in the car so she could observe the slow roll of his hips. It made her want to hold him, her hips stilling his. She felt intoxicated. Predatory.

Then off again, Duncan still driving – 'You relax,' he said indulgently – and her mind free to wander, empty for just one single moment before it filled itself, crammed itself, with writing – the last few hectic years of writing, writing, writing ... mind dashing round and through the stories – those weird, sometimes startling mutations of family – the essays to submit ... the tutorials, whipped up and delivered on the run. She let her mind spin all the thoughts, twirl about half-formed plans and ridiculous ambitions until finally it was done, her mind, it had released her. Emptied, she floated over the scrubby dunes and wind-blasted trees that passed them by like scenes in a movie.

In the warmth of the coastal town Alice felt herself further loosen and unfold. Though she and Duncan talked about swimming and fishing and dining out, protective of their recovered easiness, they barely left their room. On the queen-size bed – so much smaller than their king-size in Perth – they pressed and rolled, sweated and laughed. There was something illicit about the room and their privacy that reminded Alice of the time she was Duncan's student. He became as he was once, too, back in their delayed coming together, their sex-glutted days and nights: not the middle-aged man who these days, it seemed, no longer really wanted sex, but the lover who wanted to push himself inside her, over and over. Whenever they felt they must leave the room – to eat, to breathe fresh air, to stretch their surfeited bodies – they rushed back impatiently, and with each passing day he seemed more assured. She began to understand how much of his potency was connected to her desire for him. Her encouragement, even praise.

On the evening before the day they were to return to the city, Duncan brought a gift to the bed. 'An early birthday present,' he said. They sat naked next to each other as Alice turned the tissue-wrapped oblong in her hands. She was used to receiving gifts from him: prized books – he gave her a first edition when she graduated from her bachelor's degree, and then again to celebrate her PhD – and sometimes tasteful pieces of jewellery. She sensed from his nervous hands, though, that this one was different, so she drew out the unwrapping, forcing the pleasure to linger. When she had removed the final piece of tissue, she thought that the gift was itself further wrapping. Until she really saw it.

'Oh, Duncan. It's lovely!'

It was a silk purse, intact but very old. She could tell this by the metal frame with its embossed flowers, by the tattered remnants of lining when she opened the 'kiss' lock. She looked more closely at the embroidery on the front panel and saw an image of courtship: a gentlewoman reclining slightly on a garden bench, red rose in hand; a gentleman inclining towards her, his hand covering hers. Her peach gown, his hose and ivory robe, and behind them a woodland, above them a small cupid. Alice looked even closer, saw expressions of tenderness in the young couple's faces. Enquiring, perhaps; flushed by love or desire. The perfect pastoral, she thought.

'It's a reticule. An evening purse.' Duncan's voice brought her back. 'Nineteenth-century. Mum thinks it was made in France – maybe the 1870s or 80s? We could get that checked if you like.' His face, too, was flushed. 'Apparently it's been in our family for generations, but she isn't sure of the original owner.' Duncan was delighted with her, the gift, himself. It was a success.

She brought the purse to her nose, not knowing what to expect. What does age smell like? She was surprised by the sweet, musky scent.

'Mum stored it with sandalwood. She said, *A thing of beauty should also smell beautiful*.'

Dear Ena. Alice could hear her saying the words, the slight lilt a reminder of her Scottish childhood.

Who had cared for the purse over the years? Had it been used, or kept for show? Alice saw that it was slightly faded down one gusset. She imagined it sitting in a lady's bedroom in a country manor, maybe on a dresser ready for use, the sun through the window falling always on the one side. Perhaps her husband had given it to her when they were courting and she had used it, when they went visiting, to hold her coins, handkerchief and smelling salts.

Alice wondered what items she might secrete within its small pouched form. She let her fingertips probe textures and ridges, squeezed the body of the purse to see where it resisted and where it surrendered.

'You know, when I first saw you, I was reminded of this purse.' Duncan's hand rested on hers, an unconscious echo of the courting couple. 'Something about you …' His eyes moved upward, recalling. 'A self-containment. You hadn't been discovered yet; what was inside you hadn't been brought out.' A smile. 'And I wanted to be the one to do that.' He leaned back against the pillows and pulled her towards him.

With her free hand, Alice placed the purse carefully on the bedside table. 'And have you?' She lifted her leg over his thighs and rubbed herself against him.

'I'd like to think so.' He pushed her onto her back, then traced his finger around her belly and slowly down. Tickled at her and sampled her wetness. 'Sometimes I feel that I will never reach to the bottom of you.'

'You're getting pretty close right now.' But he was too focused to laugh. She felt his fingers, slippery now, moving lower, circling her anus. The involuntary pucker. He brought his fingers to his mouth and licked them, his tongue a small triangle, like a cat's. Then he tweaked and pulled at her nipples with his fingers and mouth. His penis moved against her.

It was too much. 'Duncan.' That intolerable pleasure. The ache inside.

'Not yet.' He lowered his head between her legs and lapped at her with that delicate tongue, teasing the small hardness. He put his fingers beneath her buttocks and tilted. Brought his hands to the outside of her thighs and pressed her legs against his ears, till all she could feel was his mouth. Drawing it out.

'Oh, Duncan.' But she pulled away. 'Wait – wait.' He read her intent and lay back, passive. 'That's it.' When she straddled him, he began to move. 'No.' She stilled his hips with hers. Looked into his eyes. Found that place where they could meet. She began to rock against him, choosing the pressure, that elusive feeling coiling. Then slowing the pace. And stop, suspended. She leaned forward and kissed him, open-mouthed.

His voice against her cheek. 'You are mine, aren't you?' He turned her onto her front and before she had settled was inside her. 'You are mine.'

She felt his penis pushing deep, and herself stretching, expanding. He lunged further, into her belly. Stroked her, his fingers following the rhythm of their bodies. The sway and plunge. The quickening thrust.

Oh, God, the joy. It was upon her. So deep. Wide.

I cannot. I cannot.

And, oh, I will, I will.

Now. Now. Splitting into light. Cracking open. Now. Into the white.

Gone, gone.

Gone.

She returned to herself reluctantly, holding his hand against her, squeezing herself around him in diminishing spasms, eking out the pleasure. Sinking into the languid heaviness of her body, her thoughts dormant.

Then slowly, in the pool of her mind, lines and colours swimming, weaving, threading, finally coalescing – a different kind of desire in her chest and in her belly. She saw a baby, and felt it moving; witnessed its translucency and helplessness.

Duncan's stance on children came to her – how could it not, when they'd talked it through so thoroughly before marrying? – but there was something about this moment that made the thought natural, the idea possible. For her, at least. Should she broach the subject or hold it to herself for now, a delicious secret?

She turned her face and saw the evidence on his. How much he loved her.

She listed them, her post-PhD plans, from least to most important, and clearer now after the oceanside break from their confused, chattering demands.

1. *Update CV – short fiction publications & sessional teaching at uni*

2. *Publish from thesis exegesis*

3. *Submit more stories from thesis – competitions? journals?*

She'd need to look for academic articles relating to her thesis. 'Representations of Family in Contemporary Western Australian Fiction': it sounded boringly pragmatic, when really it was a wonderful opportunity to re-read her favourite authors, to write about them. But it had been a while since she'd been on top of journal publications, what with the frenzy of thesis submission and examination. She'd need to see if the topic had any traction, identify the best journals to submit to.

And the stories … They were lodged in her, these tales of modern families: the harried single mum with fourteen kids, the bloke lavishing care on his cabbage-patch-doll children, the same-sex couple meeting a potential surrogate, the family that knitted disparate ethnicities together with urgency, with care – all the adoptive, half, step, part, foster, de facto, in-law mutations of kinship that wound their way through the pages of her collection. The characters were as familiar as friends or enemies, and she loved her tales, was proud of their success – the PhD award; three stories finding quick publication – but their creative heat had dissipated since the heady days straight after graduation. Maybe it was down to the barrage of teaching, all the other perks and demands that came with being 'an academic'.

Dr Alice Tennant: it still felt like she was pretending. Bluffing away as the months passed, as her confidence in these tales of strange families seesawed, as she re-edited scenes and fussed about with fine details, as she hummed and hawed about where to send the coll–

The phone. And, damn, she needed to go to the loo again.

'Happy birthday, Alice!'

Her mother. What time was it in Melbourne? Five-ish. Joan must be finished for the day, though Alice knew she often saw patients in the evening. She caught herself: analysands.

'Hi, Mum.'

'Have you had a nice day? What are you doing tonight?' It was her birthday congratulations voice, especially excited because of the figure: thirty.

'We just got back.'

'What – today? How was the drive?'

She could hear a second voice behind her mother's, the low hum of conversation in the background. Andrew. Her mother's second marriage, the one that had pulled her from Perth to Melbourne. Soon Joan would sit down to one of his famous meals – stroganoff or sushi; he was versatile. Then they might recline on the leather sofa and share news with their guests, or with one of Andrew's adult children, 'just popped in'.

'Alice?'

'It was fine. Fine. The day was great. And we had a fantastic break. But we're going to have a quiet one tonight.'

'You're not being taken out for dinner? No party?'

'No. I'm not feeling so good. I think I've got a urinary tract infection.' She wouldn't usually share the information, but there was a certain satisfaction to be had. 'I'm just going to lie low and drink plenty of water. Maybe see a doctor if it hangs around.'

'What brought that on?'

'Mum. Holiday. With Duncan. What do you think?'

The pressure in her bladder was a strange relief, mixed as it was with rawness and satiation. Lust had overcome them; they still found each other desirable.

'Oh!' her mother exclaimed. 'You must have been at it like rabbits.'

Alice chuckled smugly. 'Yep. Still going strong.'

But then she had to run to the loo. Cut off the conversation … had she overstated things?

Alice returned to the sofa and tried to relax, but her bladder called out its constant message: you need to pee. You need to pee. You need to – Maybe if she lay down … No. What about on her side? That was better; less pressure on the bladder.

Duncan's voice drifted from the shower. That beautiful baritone. She remembered the moment when her allegiance had shifted irrevocably to him. A conversation with her mother in 2000 that was the final in a series lasting several years. Her mother's concern; her own defence. Also conducted by phone, while she sat in the corridor of the share house where she lived then, though Joan was still in Perth. Just beginning her psychotherapy training.

Twelve years, Alice. It's a big gap at your age.

She'd snapped at her mother to let it go, rushing to Duncan's defence … how they'd been together for three years, for Christ's sake, how he loved her and she loved him and what did age even matter? And then her mother snapping back, yes, but Duncan was in a position of power ... and Alice feeling the anger rising, rising inside her.

Mum, please. You don't think I have my own thoughts? My own ideas?

Of course you do. But it remains that you began a relationship with him when you were an undergraduate and he was your tutor. Your much older tutor.

Alice had made her voice dry, demanding her mother give her some credit, stating coldly that they'd managed to hold off.

This was debatable, the holding off, but she'd maintained the fiction. To protect their mothers, and themselves. The reality? Only the one unit with him – English to top up the writing degree – but the rush in her gut each time she walked into his tutorial room not open to mistranslation, unlike his response, which, perhaps, could have been. And then the coffees on campus – perfectly innocent – and the charged phone calls – not so much – the end of the unit, the end of the year, the end-of-year party. The lift home and then, yes, the knowing.

You understand what I mean, Alice. She remembered the desperation in her mother's voice, as if she knew she'd gone too far but couldn't hold back, saying *Duncan took advantage ... nineteen ... someone his own age ... worried about his hold over –*

Enough, Alice told herself. It wasn't as if they were a proper family anyway, her mother an occasional fly-in fly-out visitor, her father living in a haze of hippiedom in Nimbin, Daylesford, Eumundi ... somewhere that was just a name to her, anyway – and no cute brothers or sisters to pull the scattered 'family' together, when she alone had never been enough, or so it seemed. It was Duncan who'd been there when it mattered; Duncan who was her family. And she didn't want to think about the hard words she and Joan had flung, her mother's judgement on Duncan, her own sobbing drive to Duncan's house – into his arms and then straight into his home. The new divide separating daughter from mother. It was the jagged words that diagnosed Duncan like he was some kind of illness, the words that came to her whenever she had doubts about her husband, that played in her –

Stop.

The sharp twinge behind her pubis was proof of their desire. Desire and love. Sometime soon she would share her new feelings with Duncan. Describe that translucent image and how it called to her. Persuade him.

And tomorrow morning she would go to the doctor. Antibiotics should fix this bloody problem.

Chapter 4

Herdley, December 1857

Forms slide through the mist: the Naze above and, when he swivels, Hierde Farm below. Arthur can see his home beyond the farm; can just make out the village path and the bare branches of the elm thicket beyond that and, further north, a few of the scattered cottages of Herdley. His family will be nestled in Hierde House, behind its low wall. Father, Beatrice and Cecilia. And Mrs Malley, who has managed the household ever since …

An indistinct Old Susan bustles across the Hierde Farm yard like a busy hen. A second after each step comes the faint *clack, clack* of her pattens. She disappears into the dairy.

Is he the same person who teased Old Susan, scoffing a handful of stolen curds as she chased him from the farmyard—*Hoy, Master Rochdale! Stop there, you young scoundrel!*—the fierceness undercut by the smile in her voice? Is he still that boy who fled through the gorse spinney to Hierde House? Who ran, giggling, between the lavender beds, through the garden entrance, across the lower hall and into the morning room where Mother sat sewing? Who knocked Bea sideways on the rug and slid on her jigsaw—*whoosh*!—into his mother's lap? Is he the boy who was scolded by Mother, then held in a laughing embrace as she wiped his grubby mouth? Who she held …

The girls will be in the kitchen now, making the Christmas pudding with Bess and Ellen under Mrs Simpson's watchful eye, then, when the cook's back is turned, cramming sticky raisins in their mouths, the air warm and spiced. Father will be addressing Christmas correspondence and planning the next year—*parliamentary hijinks*, he used to wink, once, and, *my man, Gladstone*, he would smile—maybe in the library, rather than shut away in his little study. It is almost Christmas, after all: village carols and the annual Herdley pantomime; the yule log burning in the open hearth.

But Arthur wants no part of such rituals now. No role in this hollowness he feels at their heart. Family lost its claim on him four years ago at his father's, *We'll jog along comfortably enough together, eh, old chap?* The sole reference. Grief measured by the new lines on Father's face and the silent spaces in their home.

Damp has seeped into his boots.

"Taffy!" The terrier is nosing busily at the stone wall over which they've just clambered. "Come on, then."

Arthur's legs swish through the wet heather. His feet are chilled and his calves ache; he is used to the gentle undulations of Rugby, not the dips and highs of the Peak District. As he nears the gritstone outcrops of the Naze, the slope becomes steep and slippery. He takes his time skirting the rocks on the kinder south side, Taffy at his heels, and comes out on the ridge that runs east, above the Naze. The mist lies heavy on the village of Herdley, but he looks over it, north to Kettle Peak and its surrounding knolls: Wight Hill, where he climbed with Taffy last year; lofty Dungast; and Crag End, grim and grey.

An uplift of air hits the ridge and nudges Arthur. He sucks it in and feels the bite in his throat and chest. Looking to his left he can see the top of the Naze and, to the right, much higher, the crest of Hierde Hill. Father traced the giant form for Arthur when he was a boy, as they climbed south together to the Naze, the son straining to match his father's stride.

It is Old English for guardian, or shepherd, "hierde", Father had said. Then he'd pointed to the guardian's nose, *There's the naze and above that—see?—the top of his head.*

When they'd reached the Naze, they had stood, hands on hips, and he'd felt as if he could scoop up the world around him and hold it to his chest.

A baronet is a little like a guardian, Mother said once, when he'd asked what his father did. She told him that, along with the squire in Herdley Hall, Father looked after everyone in Herdley, *just like his father, and his father before him.* They owned Hierde House, she explained, and Hierde Farm, and a little more property that was rented from them. Then she went on to tell him more: that Father stood for the people in the House of Commons and that was why he was so busy, why they could not be more in their beloved Herdley. And though they weren't quite aristocrats, she said, *nevertheless, as a politician and a baronet, your father serves his country and its people with unswerving dedication.* She'd swept her hand through his hair and smiled down at him. *And you, Arthur, are the heir to the baronetcy. What do you think of that?* She wrote the strange words—baronet, estate, tenant, constituent, Parliament, heir—and tried to make sense of them for him.

Arthur looks back at the proud and craggy nose, then trains his gaze along the ridge, up, up, to the rounded lift of the skull.

How had their guardian slept as the world turned upside down?

On the moorland plateau just below, a grass owl swoops, claws outstretched. A vole? Hard to tell from here, but the bird has something in its grasp as it flies north. Arthur pictures pink bodies, pulsing in the dark, waiting for their mother. How is this different from egg-collecting? Are the mother birds ever puzzled at their empty nests? Other lads at Rugby leave only one or two eggs, but he only ever *takes* one, telling himself it won't be noticed; reassuring himself it won't be missed.

He gathers the eggs alone, blows each until his cheeks are sore, and nestles the emptied shells in straw. His remaining schoolfriends think he collects them to compete with other students, or to admire his bounty. And it's true he finds the eggs beautiful. He likes to take them from the shelves of his tiny study to cradle them, his breath slow, feeling their curve soft against his skin: smooth olive-toned nightingale eggs, the brown-spotted kestrel egg found in an abandoned crow's nest, lustrous white kingfisher eggs, sedge bird eggs, pale brown, mottled darker. And his prize, the rook egg. When he holds it, that egg, marvelling at its glossy green-blue wash, the dark tracings like a language he cannot quite understand, he is again in the elm thicket against the path to Herdley, digging irons into bark, clinging to the giant tree's branches as if he were a rook himself.

One day returns to him now: a day that was different to the rest, a day when he'd had to think things through. He'd hoisted himself past clusters of crimson flowers, he remembers, lifting his head above a branch, coming suddenly face to face with something he could not make sense of. It took a full moment to understand it as the eye of a rook, and in it the reflection of his fragmentary form. He'd backed away from the bird as she hunkered down on her eggs and made his way down the trunk, vowing he'd leave this family, at least, alone.

It was deference he'd felt then. The sense of an abiding love and dependence. An intimation that it was more, much more, than contesting or possessing, this climbing of trees, this immersion in a world without people: it is something he must have. The buds swelling on dog roses. Tiny golden-crested wrens nesting in a stand of firs, their multitude of even tinier eggs. Wild hedges, with their unkempt tangle. Soft catkins, drooping gently. All these would go on, if he did not.

No, nature does not ask of him all that people do—all that everyone did, more than four long years ago. He pulled away from the village lads then, their holiday scraps and antics. His school results dropped and he slid into the background of big-side football matches. Old Ghoul wrote, *Arthur must apply himself*, and his form master, gently, *Arthur seems lost*. But Arthur cared for neither sternness nor compassion, as long as everyone left him alone. And yet, strangely, the boys still looked to him for leadership.

Since autumn, their respect seems to teeter on fear.

He remembers September, when the weather was hot and clammy, thunderheads swelling in the sky. Day after day, Arthur and Rattlin Rowlands—uneasy pals now—and their friends in School House making their way to the lazy Avon, over the Planks and past the holes where the smaller boys sported: Sleath's, the beginner's pool; and Anstey's, deep but small. Then Wratislaw's, the first of the larger holes, and older lads pitting themselves against each other, faces sly, and finally Swift's, where only the sixth and fifth forms were allowed to swim. Shining bodies writhing and splashing and duck-diving, down to where the warm pool shifted into depth.

Then the sight of Fish. Edward Harris, who'd earned the ironic moniker because of his ineptness in the water. Arthur remembers wishing the lad back to Wratislaw's that day—even Anstey's, where the weaker swimmers in the fifth flailed about, convincing each other of their prowess. But Harris was stubborn. The lingering summer had seen him at Swift's in every spare moment, struggling with the water and the taunts of housemates, paddling the thirty-odd yards over and over, eyes glazed. Arthur had found himself admiring the scrawny lad.

On this day, though, the thunderheads had clustered and the air was electric. Ominous. Almost-men jabbered at each other and jeered viciously at Fish.

He remembers shutting out the cruel voices. Swimming back and forth, back and forth, in long, slow strokes that drew him under the surface, then up for air. Back and forth, back and forth. Trees and boys fading. The chattering in his head slowing, stilling, absorbed by the rhythm in his arms and legs and the power running through his torso. Back and forth, back and forth. Finally he'd stopped at the centre of the swimming hole and looked around. Harris was still paddling laps nearby, though he was low in the water, his face tilted skyward, gasping quick breaths. Other lads were noisy around the springboard, waiting to bellow and leap.

Then, his favourite time, repeated on each visit to Swift's. Drawing air and diving deep into the cold. Relaxing. Hanging, a suspended moment. Unburdened. Water a cocoon, muffled voices tuneful. Soft, soft, the waving motion over his skin, the liquid press and embrace. Still. Still.

Finally, the need for air pulling him to the surface. His return to the world—swimming to the bank and climbing, feet slipping on the muddied steps, onto the grass.

But then, the shouted alarm: *Where's Fish?*

He remembers the lads at the board, still and tense, their bodies turned to the ruffled surface at the deep heart of Swift's. Then, himself, arrowing into the water and towards the telltale ripple. Diving, fingertips piercing the cool, groping through the murk that pressed his open eyes like a bandage. Nothing. Swiftly up again. Gulping at air. Voices a babble.

Is he—

—his hands—

Fish ain't—

No! No—

Down, down. Silty mud through fingers. Chest bursting. To the left. Nothing. Right. Nothing. Around, around, limbs sweeping. Nothing. Nothing. To air! But wait. Something there. What? An arm! Quick. Grasp and pull. Quick! Solid from liquid, embraced. Up. Quick. Up. Up.

Hard light. Air, sucked hard.

Harris's form had been quiescent against him, eyes shut, face bluish-white and inscrutable, like a creature from the deep. Boys tugged at the body and Arthur surrendered his light burden. Reluctant. Relieved. He'd swum alongside them to the water's edge, where Harris sputtered, then spewed a thin brown mess, his inert body coming to life in a sudden rosy flush.

In the twenty minutes it had taken them to walk back to School House—Harris stumbling at first, then coming slowly back to himself—the group had recovered their cruelty.

Trying to be a fish, Fish?

No, he's pretending to be a mermaid! Ain't that right, Fish? A wee mermaid! The boys jostling Harris, jabbing at him with sharp fingers. Hot drops of rain spattering against them all. Harris dazed—almost … absent.

Got to move those arms, Fish. Here, I'll show you how. Rattlin. Arthur remembers feeling drained yet alert. Sensing the old queasiness rising up his throat. What now?

What now? Why, Rattlin grabbing Harris's arms and pumping them up and down. *See? Like a dog, not a fish!* Harris trying to pull his arms from Rattlin's great paws. Rattlin snapping, *Hold him, lads.* Hodge and Greenwood moving towards Harris, the others looking down—save for Lawler, who'd stood next to Arthur, shoulder to shoulder.

For goodness sake, Rattlin. Leave over.

Arthur knew his weary tone would irritate Rattlin even as he spoke, but he was sick of his old friend's petty meanness. Worried, too, as he watched Rattlin become the bully they had both once despised.

Drops of rain struck heavily at the group.

What are you going to do about it then, Rochdale? Rattlin had pumped Harris's arms. Harder, this time.

He couldn't ignore it. *Why, stop you, of course.*

Arthur returns to himself. Crouches at Taffy's head, tugs his ears and cradles the eager snout. Taffy gazes at him hopefully.

"Come on, Taff. Let's take on the Hierde."

Up the ridge he strides, Taffy busily scouting the way ahead and racing back to him. Then, off again. It is open moorland along the pitched ridge, save for a short gritstone edge and a solitary stack of stone that squats like a mushroom. Elf Tor, they'd named the miniature crag, he and Beatrice, years before. When faerie rings were as real to them as their Hierde House dinner.

His feet move steadily up the incline until, near the summit, the ground shifts to an outcrop of gritstone. He has to work to gain the crest, clambering over and through the rocky tumble, while Taffy squeezes through gaps and crannies, panting happily up at him. Arthur smiles at the dog's pleasure and the honest ache of his own muscles.

Then, the summit. The skull. He turns a circle for the familiar view of distant hills and shires—even North Wales. Below, Herdley is a mist-scattered play-time village with Herdley Hall and the church sitting prettily at its eastern edge. To the west, cotton mills are plonked like toy blocks on the silver ribbon of the river. He rubs his chilled leather-clad hands together and stamps his feet to bring feeling to the numb toes.

Taffy hears the guttural *buck buck buck* first. The terrier's keen snout whips towards the slanting south face of Hierde Hill, then he circles Arthur, barking sharply.

"Aye. It's not views you're wanting, is it, my boy?"

Taffy yaps, expectant, then leads the way towards the stone wall that marks the edge of Farmer Hayes's property. Arthur's feet run away with him down the slope.

They stop, panting. On the other side of the wall, the ground is thick with heather; Arthur scans the moorland and the pasture that lies beyond another stone line, further down the hill.

"Where is it then, lad?"

Taffy follows his nose along the ground. Ten yards or so into the property, Arthur glimpses movement. He carries the muscular little terrier over the wall and puts him down with a calming stroke. Taffy stills obediently, small ears raised.

Red-brown colour shifts through a curtain of heather and coarse grass. Arthur treads carefully with Taffy at his side, the dog quivering but quiet. There: a plump red grouse. It scratches at the ground with its pale-feathered feet and struts around a shallow scrape, giving an important *buck buck* now and then. A male. Arthur wonders whether Taffy could take it, if they drew close enough. After several days hanging, it would make a tasty roast. "Red game", he's heard the hunters call it when they descend on Hierde House for grouse season, their voices greedy with blood.

Taffy whines softly. "Taffy!" he whispers. They are within striking distance now and the grouse could lift out of reach quickly, if alarmed. Yards. Now feet.

Wait. It has seen them.

He expects a sudden whirr of wings, but the moorcock surprises him. It puffs its feathers and bobs its head. Steps from side to side, giving its guttural bark and eyeing them all the while, combs bright red. Then, a sudden rush at them, the *buck buck* shifting to a loud *yow r-yow r-yow*. Taffy's thighs flex, but Arthur quickly grabs at his terrier. He squats, hesitating. Watching.

Plucky little cock.

And it comes to him again, that sultry day at Rugby. The fight that had begun in a civilised enough fashion. Removing their jackets and waistcoats and placing them, folded, under the chapel railing. Rolling up shirtsleeves. Shaking hands. School House students—and students from other houses now too—forming a large circle around them, and a School House fifth-former keeping a lookout from behind the chapel. For masters, but also for fellows in the sixth form, who might halt the fight.

Arthur had been determined to give his old friend a beating. Not just to revenge Harris and to stop Rattlin's bullying ways, but also for some other inchoate reason that beat at his mind.

He remembers looking at the looming sky, the clouds a heavy mass that irregularly shook the air and earth with thunder. Large raindrops hitting the group, stopping, then starting again, a solid downpour surely near. His gut churning and bubbling as he drew deep breaths and sized up his opponent. Other fellows doing the same, pointing at Rattlin's bulky shoulders. *Peels well,* from one. Another's appraisal, *Aye, but a tad too much tuck.*

Arthur can still see Rattlin's thickset body—the same height as him but much heavier. The boy's belly slinging downward, and solid thighs and legs rooting him to the ground, while he, Arthur, had felt lithe, hard and fit. All that swimming and tree-climbing. Still, though, his legs had quaked at his opponent's presence. How had Rattlin become his enemy?

Then that blast of white hair—Lawler stepping up to be his second. He wasn't sure why; he hadn't been much of a friend to anyone in recent years. But there was Lawler, armed with wet sponges and advice—*Use your speed … Save your punches till he's lost his wind*—and Smyth hovering, with a few other School House fellows backing him up. And, across from them, Rattlin standing, legs wide apart, chest thrust forward and arms crossed, conferring with Hodge and Greenwood. Several other School House students giving him their tuppence worth, the rest uncommitted. Keen for entertainment, perhaps.

The details hold a crystalline clarity: a timekeeper volunteering—Foster puffed up with importance—round times decided, thirty-odd lads encircling them—he can remember each excited face. No Edward Harris, though, for he himself had already sent the lad to Matron, worried about the effects of the near-drowning. They might have scuttled away from the word, but that's what it was, in truth. And Rattlin wanted to keep needling the poor boy? Well, he'd have to think twice.

Then a rush of energy surprising him, bouncing him to his feet, moving him around and through the blasts of rain, his steps loose and springy. Like at Herdley dances when he was a boy. Rowlands was up, too, his step menacing, and Arthur raised his fists, felt readiness sweep through his body.

Rattlin's first jab had been ill-timed and Arthur skipped around it with ease, smiling at his old friend.

You'll have to do better than that, my lad.

Rattlin's rush at him with a heavy right-hander. Deflect and dance.

Deflect and dance.

Again.

Again.

And again.

Then a loud crack of thunder travelling through the ground and up his body, and he was springing into the air now—tuned to the darkening elements; aligned to some kind of justice.

Time.

How could the first round be over?

Lawler mopping at him with the wet sponge, his wild fuzz of hair coated by rain. Rivulets running down inside his own shirt, mixing with sweat. The air and his body hot and steamy.

Stay focused.

What?

Stay focused. Lawler commanding him. *He ain't done with you yet.*

Then more of Rattlin jabbing and punching. Arthur skipping away, taunting and laughing. One or two punches catching him now. Blows glancing off lightly, but registered. White shirts gleaming in giddy rings around him.

Come on, Rattlin!

Hold your nerve. From Lawler. *He's slowing.*

Rattlin hadn't looked like he was slowing. He looked solid and brutal.

When the call came the second time, it had been a relief. Arthur remembers leaning against the rails and the wash of rain on his upturned face. Were the elements still on his side? He'd felt the energy of the day's drama ebbing, the weariness in his legs.

But Lawler had read his discouragement. *He's slowing, I tell you.* Lifting his chin and sponging his forehead, making it sting. *Now you can attack.*

Time's up!

Arthur saw himself in that moment, turning towards Rattlin, aiming for a jaunty air. Saw, too, that Lawler was right, with Rattlin plodding forward, raising his fists as though they were lead weights. So he'd rushed him, punching toward that round face, feeling the jar in his hand and the tearing at the root of his thumb, seeing blood on the big man's mouth and rage in his eyes and feeling, for the first time, terror. Wrestling with the impulse to run.

The thunder had stopped and the rain set in, properly now. Spectators running for cover. They were—

The crunch as his nose was punched. The backward wrench of his head and the grab of his neck muscles. Trying to steady himself, resume his springing dance, but the pain … Shaking his bleary head to clear the ringing of his ears and Rattlin coming at him again through a wall of rain. Feinting to the side and landing a desperate punch to Rattlin's head that had him on the ground, his own hand lanced with fire.

Looking down at Rattlin, whose eyes were open but briefly unseeing. He supposed he'd won, but the grass had turned to mud, the heat to cool and still he'd wanted to put his foot on Rattlin's neck and press down hard. Feel bone give way beneath him.

Rochie. Rochie. Lawler had squeezed his arm, covered his head with a jacket—*It's all right. You can stop*—and still he'd shuddered. Cold and scared—not, now, of Rattlin, but of something in himself.

Was this what he'd wanted?

A piercing note in his ears. His thumb aching and stinging, his eyes too. A throb shooting through his nose and across the bones of his face. He'd reached down and shaken Rattlin, then turned away. Hodge and Greenwood could look after him; he'd had enough of the man. And of himself, when he saw the fear in Smyth's face.

What had he come to, that day?

He still didn't regret it: Rattlin would never again hold the same sway or torment younger students. And he and Tom Lawler had formed an unspoken, unbreakable bond that day, too, so he is no longer completely alone. But he'd felt ashamed somehow, himself muddied—still feels that taint.

Who was he fighting for? Harris? Future victims of school bullies? Himself?

Is there a right kind of fighting?

Arthur looks at the little moorcock, puffed and proud, at his mercy. Thinks about what men defend and protect, what they fight for. Other people. Memories. Love.

He makes his decision. "Don't worry, my lad. You can keep your patch of turf; you've won it. And your mate. Where is she, anyway?" He swings an arm while holding his wriggling dog tight, not trusting the terrier to leave the bird be. "Off, then, off. Bring her here. Make your nest, raise your young. I won't be back to bother you for the eggs." He pictures the grouse eggs already in his collection. Their muted pink, mottled with crimson-brown. "Whoosh, whoosh—away! Away! These monsters will leave you in peace, bless you."

The moorcock launches itself with a loud whirr. Arthur hopes he hasn't scared it off for good. He looks down at the terrier's face and laughs. "Why, Taff. If you were a man, I'd call that disappointment." He bends down and scruffs his dog. "Come on then. Back to Hierde House. They'll be wondering."

Chapter 5

Perth, October 2007

They couldn't go on like this. Duncan puzzled and wondering; herself, miserable and awkward; their strange new politeness unable to bridge the space that grew between them.

Maybe if she could open herself fully, sex might be okay. After all, it seemed to be mainly on the outside – as if someone had thrown scalding water between her legs.

It was a mystery that had not been solved by several visits to the local GP. The one who'd diagnosed the urinary tract infection and prescribed a repeat antibiotic. Who'd taken fresh samples that yielded no answers. Instead, he'd offered her vague reassurances: residual soreness; mechanical urethritis that would ease. And the dismaying suggestion that she had brought this on herself: *Maybe the sex could be less rough*.

But perhaps she was being oversensitive.

Why wouldn't it go away?

She'd thought about setting to work on the internet, typing in symptoms to see what came up. But the thought provoked a definite refusal each time. Was she reluctant to accept that this strange pain was real? Resistant to confirmation that her problem was serious? Whatever the reason, she ignored the online search for now, didn't demand an answer for that instinctive refusal, kept assuring herself this weird collection of sensations would disappear as quickly and mysteriously as it had arrived.

She looked over at Duncan, absorbed in a documentary. American fiction writers. Steinbeck, Faulkner ... his favourite, Hemingway. The subject of his biography. Duncan watched the screen jealously, as if his ideas were under threat. The biography was close to completion and a tender subject. Usually Alice would reassure him in these moments of uncertainty, but her mind and nerves were fizzing, preoccupied with this strange, disordered self. She held her body still, leaning back against the cushions in the corner of the sofa to reduce the pressure on her bottom. Wondering how she might prepare herself for him. For them.

You need to pee. You need to pee. You need to – Alice closed her ears. It had been a month now. Her body could not be trusted. Urine that felt about to burst from her was usually scant and brought with it fiercer scorching and the reinstated demand: you need to pee. You need to pee … And was it her imagination, or had the strange rawness spread? The urgency and frequency seemed to have become a continuous burning, stabbing ache that the term 'UTI' could surely not account for.

'How are you doing there?' The show was finished. Duncan was smiling: his critical perspective on Hemingway must be safe. He shifted on the sofa, then put his hand on her leg and began rubbing it. Her knee dropped away from his touch before she could countermand it. She had to will her body closer to him. Ask her mouth to kiss him. Tell that sensual melt to spread and take hold. It feels good. It hurts. Which to listen to?

'I'm okay.' She smiled at him – fuck this thing – and gave the invitation: 'Let's go to bed, hey?' No toilet; ignore the bladder. Maybe it would be alright this time. The week's lectures were already sorted, so worst come to worst, Sunday could always be spent recovering.

The doona was humped at the end of the bed and their pillows were askew. Clothes a messy shape in the corner. Damn, the washing. Penny would be surprised at this new, cluttered Alice when she came. But it would be good to confide properly in her friend, to share what she'd only hinted at on the phone and through hurried emails. The sudden stinging of her eyes prompted Alice to scrub at her teeth with gaze averted. Then off with her clothes, into that tangled pile, and quickly into bed, leaving the bedside light on and herself curled around the doona, the silhouette a delicate solicitation.

She must not listen to her body. She could do this. Duncan would be relieved and grateful, this problem would pass, as these things always did, and they would return to their lives and their recovered love. She focused on the sounds of his preparation. The bristles against his teeth, the gargle and splash. The piss hitting the back of the toilet and then tapering. The pause and short jet. Then the click of the switch as he left the bathroom.

She opened her eyes to lamplight and his form standing over her. The bigger shadow looming on the wall behind him.

'Are you up to this?' The concern undermined by the bob of his penis.

'Let's try, hey?' She pulled him onto the bed. 'Maybe we just need to get past this thing.'

He lay down next to her and lifted a hand to her breast. Gave the tweaks and squeezes he knew she loved. Desire spread, molten, through her gut and flowed into her groin. Ow! An answering lance, quicker than thought, shot to her nipples. Her body tensed instantly. No, she ordered herself. You will not pull away. She lifted her hand to Duncan. Stroked his face, chest and belly. They must hurry, before her determination lapsed. She licked her fingers and gently touched herself, right at the front. Still exciting, and further from the core of the hurt. She willed the pleasure. Felt moisture and blood gathering and building. The hardness growing.

'You look wonderful.' His voice anticipatory. But also hesitant.

'It's okay.' And, yes, it actually was okay; the craving now was stronger than the spasms of pain. She reached out and drew him onto her, wrapping her legs around his back.

The blind pushing was at first blunt. Exciting. Then it shifted. Became piercing. Scorching. Quickly, now, while she still could. Was he inside her? She couldn't tell through the burning. Oh, no. No. The freezing. Oh, God. Duncan's head buried into her shoulder. The tears threatening. No. She pushed her feet hard against his buttocks, forcing him in. A knife. A slash. A wound, gaping. Bleeding. Weeping. Open more, let him in. *Let him in.* An iron, branding. Oh, God. It *hurts*.

'Alice.' She could hear the love in his voice. 'You feel so good.'

The sway and plunge. The quickening thrust. The blade that had become all that she was.

So deep. Wide.

I cannot. I cannot.

Splitting into light. Cracking open.

'Duncan. No!' Pushing him backwards and rolling to the far side of the bed. Curling tightly round herself. 'Oh, fuck. Oh, God.' The searing between her legs. Embers flying, settling in bursts of fire over her buttocks and down her thighs. Her body aghast.

Not again. Never again.

'Alice.' His hand on her shoulder. 'Alice.'

Salty mucus in her mouth. Cheeks wet. Oh God, please take it away.

'Alice.' Duncan's body against her back, curving around hers. 'Baby.'

Her sobs harder now, racking her body. An ugly wailing. 'I wanted to do it so much.' She couldn't turn to face him.

'I know you did.' His words vibrating. A fleeting memory: her aching ear against her father's chest. The dependable thud and soothing warmth. The resonating voice. The honest comfort. 'Alice, it's okay.'

She rolled over and pressed her face against his chest. 'No, it's not. It's not okay.'

'How bad is it?'

'It's really … fucking … bad.' She sobbed the words out. 'Oh, Duncan, I'm so sorry.'

'Baby, you mustn't do it if it hurts. You have to tell me. I don't want to make it worse.' He stroked her back.

'But it always hurts.' Her tears were slowing. The searing had calmed to a hot, dull ache. 'This can't be just an infection or bloody residual soreness. It's way too bad for that.' His fingers on her back, stroking. 'I'm going to have to see someone else. Maybe a female GP, or a gyno. This guy hasn't a clue.' Stroking. 'Babe, sorry, but could you stop?' She shuddered his hand from her back as she spoke.

'What? The stroking?' His eyes wide.

She nodded. 'It's like I can't handle anything. Any more sensation than I already have.' She grabbed at his hand and squeezed it. 'I'm sorry.'

He drew away. 'Shit. I had no idea.'

'I can handle the hug cos it's firm. And constant.' She moved into his arms again. 'It's the flickery stuff that's too much. And anything near my bum.'

'Okay.' He squeezed her gently. 'Maybe we should just relax like this.'

She could hear the sleep in his voice. Unbelievable. Like her body, her feelings tore her in opposite directions: cross he could relax while she hurt so much, relieved he had not thrown her from the bed, afraid he wouldn't be able to handle what she feared the future might hold.

Despite that worry, she must act. It was her body. How could she protect it? Safeguard herself?

She pictured the tired muscles with fiery nerves branching through them, the flaming membranes and irritated skin. Then she saw a line tracing a neon contour around her pelvis. A chastity belt. A barrier that Duncan must not cross – not until this thing was over.

His sighing breath was against her hair. Alice let her tears run again and settled into his arms. Hoped that the bleak comfort would carry her into a dreamless sleep.

*

Flames licking inside and out. Nails hammered here, and here, and here, and here – beaten harder, knocking the parts against each other, into each other –

And she was awake.

Sitting up in bed, then staggering to the door.

'Penny.'

'Jesus, Ali!'

She must look a sight.

'Oh, Pen. Sorry. Did we say? Did I –'

'No, no. I had a meeting down the road and I wondered if you were …'

'Oh, sorry, Pen. Come in, come in.'

Pen's heels tapped ahead of her to the kitchen. Alice filled the kettle and flicked it on, wiped her damp hands down her nightie. Looked at Penny's get-up: her smart trousers and button-down shirt.

'Could you grab the teabags, Pen?' she asked, then spoke over her shoulder as she stumbled, still only half-awake, down the hallway: 'I'll just pull on some clothes.'

In the bedroom she contemplated jeans for a moment, but opted for some comfort. Loose skirt and a t-shirt, that would do. Then she splashed her face with cold water, brushed her hair back. Frowned at her reflection.

She saw Pen's quizzical look as she walked into the kitchen.

'I'd ask how you are, but you look completely wiped.' Her friend's face was concerned. 'It must be bad.'

'Some days are better than others, but, yep, overall it's pretty crap.'

Alice sat herself down next to Penny and immediately needed to get up again.

'I've never known you in bed at this time, so …'

Alice swivelled. Eleven o'clock. Jesus.

'Sometimes I don't sleep well, so I end up nodding off again when Duncan leaves …' Her voice trailed away. She busied herself with emptying the draining rack. Plates, cups, knives, forks. Then grabbing milk from the fridge as the kettle boiled.

She jiggled the teabags. Put a teaspoon of sugar in Pen's cup and stirred the milk in. Leaned her body against the bench.

'No teaching today?' Penny asked.

'It's just the two units this semester, thank God,' Alice said. 'And I only have to be there for teaching and meetings – so just a couple of days a week. I can do most of the lecture prep and emailing here,' she patted the kitchen bench, 'and I can lie down when I need. So I'm lucky, I guess.'

She thought about how the weeks had been since this all began. Reading students' portfolios in bed. Refreshing her memory on the sofa with her notes for the next tutorial: writing a sonnet, creating voice in short fiction, 'wild writing' ... Distracting herself from Duncan, who wandered around her, unsure how to bring up the biography, now in its final stages. Five years of slog. At least he was gone all day Monday to Thursday and she could watch trash TV without his tacit disapproval. It was the first time she'd felt grateful for being untenured. For being a casual.

'And Duncan?'

But she didn't want to talk about her husband with her best friend. Not with the strange wariness that had always been between them and Duncan's jealous kind of ... guarding of her. So she didn't tell Penny that Duncan was solicitous, but that there were moments of irritation. Didn't say he was someone who couldn't tolerate problems without solutions. Not easily, anyway. Easier to brush it off – 'He's okay with it' – change the subject – 'I went to a gyno and had more tests, but everything's coming back negative. I reckon he has no idea what this is.'

'I can't believe it! Surely someone must have come across this before, especially when it's so painful.'

'Not so far. And it's frustrating, cos I feel like if I could treat this in the right way, it would go, but I just don't know what the right way is.'

'Do you want me to search a bit as well? See if we can find anyone better?'

'Oh, Pen, that would be great. Thank you.'

And then Alice was crying. And Pen came to her and held her sloppy, snotty face against her own pristine shirt. Patted her shoulder and soothed her with words that sounded unfamiliar coming from the mouth of her managerial friend.

'Look, I need to head off.' Alice made a show of glancing at her watch. 'How about sending me an email if you need a further extension? We already have the medical certificates, so it shouldn't be a problem.'

Alice had reached her sitting end point, which seemed to come more quickly each working day. She created fictional pressing engagements just like this one to deliver her from meetings. Slouched in chairs so the weight of her body rested on the base of her spine. Kneeled on the ground when typing emails, the door of the shared office locked so that she could leap up if she heard a key twist. And when teaching, paced about as if thrilled by words and language – everything's all good … everything's entirely normal. A bluff that worked, for the moment, even as she grew to dread standing in front of the roomful of students, to detest being split so definitively into two selves: the self who was passionate and creative, who wrote and laughed and loved, and this new, pained Alice, this pinched and pale Alice. This Alice who was not Alice at all.

'Thanks – that's so helpful.' Mia stood.

'Alright. I'll see you on Monday.'

'I'll be there. Bye, then.'

The student walked out of the sessional staff office. What was her surname again? Parsons? Levitt? There were two Mias in the unit and fifty-six students altogether. Details that generally found homes remained unanchored in Alice's mind, spiralling into forgetfulness.

How would it feel to be free of this role? To allow her own thorough, diligent, perfectionist self to sleep? Recover? No students to help feel better about themselves. No complicated departmental relationships to diplomatically settle. No more second-guessing her marking: was she being too kind? too severe? too accommodating? too inflexible? She did not know anymore. The pain had taken from her some vital sense of perspective with which she once navigated her life. It had become impossible to know her own horizon. Where she began and ended; what to make of herself, or others. And it was jealous too, the pain, crowding out thoughts and plans, leaving no room for her to consider her stories – all the writing of those five-odd years. No possibility of pursuing publication, even though her former supervisor continued to urge her on, saying she must follow up the success of the already published stories, make use of the momentum. *It won't last forever,* she'd said, *the interest in your writing.*

Alice walked to the window and looked out over the grassed quadrangle. Duncan had a large office almost opposite hers, but jacarandas blocked the line of sight. Soon they would be caped in blue-mauve, and then would come the summer break. What if the pain stayed the same? Surely it couldn't. But if it did. Could she last till then?

She sighed. Tugged at the side of her undies through her skirt, dragging them down. Pulled the skirt away from her buttocks. She avoided trousers now. They pressed against all the parts of her body she was trying to forget, shunting complaint into impossibility.

Soon she would have to drive home. The dreaded ordeal. Hemmed in by the boundaries of seat and door for twenty minutes and no way in which to twist her body away from itself. The current strategy: bracing her left leg so that her pelvis was lifted off the seat. Lucky the Toyota was an automatic.

Maybe she could grab a sandwich on her way to the car. She had to force herself to eat these days. But the café had –

Alice started at the shrill of her mobile. Penny.

'Hi there, Pen.'

'Hey, Ali. How are you doing today?'

'Oh, Pen.' The relief at her friend's voice. Who didn't question the reality of the symptoms, or their severity, even when Alice questioned them herself. Who had held her as she sobbed … She swallowed the tears this time – not here, not now. 'Fairly shit. But I'm heading home soon, so I'll get a chance to relax.' Before Duncan comes home, unspoken.

'Did you see that naturopath?' The efficient voice also concerned.

'Yep. She was really lovely but she said she'd never seen anyone with this level of pain in that spot. She was wondering about thrush. Because of the antibiotics.' Alice had purchased acidophilus on her recommendation, and other supplements, *To lift your immune system*, the naturopath said. She'd also basted herself in yoghurt after looking up thrush in Joan's handed-down copy of home remedies – a remnant of the 70s, its page corners worn by folding. The book also suggested vinegar douches, garlic pessaries and pawpaw ointment for various genital ailments. An ingredient list. But what was she cooking? Thrush? Dermatitis? A bacterial infection? A wound? 'I tried a couple of days of saltwater douching, as well, but it didn't seem to do anything.'

'Bugger. Would you like me to come over tomorrow?'

'That would be great.' She needed her capable friend right now.

'Good. I have an eleven o'clock, so I'll get there early.' It was a tactful warning. 'I've got some names and numbers that might be helpful. A couple of GPs and another gynaecologist – female, this time.'

They said goodbye and Alice gathered her belongings. She was tired of their every conversation being about her baffling disorder. Sick of life revolving around the centre-point of her pain. But the brief conversation had buoyed her too. Given her a sense of purpose. If the medicos who were meant to be able to help her couldn't, perhaps she could help herself. If this wasn't a UTI, what might it be?

She put down her bags and walked quickly to her uni computer, before the impulse faded. Tilted the screen upward so she could stand, leaning over, and still read. What to type? She started with *urinary tract infection* but found nothing she didn't already know: bacteria, causes, kidneys, bladder, urethra, symptoms, treatment … She thought for a moment. Why not try a descriptor? What about *genital pain*?

The pages that came up were diverse. Words stood out from their background as if highlighted: *dyspareunia, vestibulitis, genital warts, itching* – the words made her feel dirty, somehow. Diseased. She saw an entry with *endometriosis* in it. A word she knew; a less menacing word. She replaced *genital pain* with *endometriosis* and scrolled down the results. Saw a page in the list with *hysteria* in it, and *pain*. Replaced the search entry with *female hysteria*, following what interested her now, rather than what seemed most relevant, traces of the old Alice reasserting themselves.

The listed pages drew her in, and she found herself clicking back and forward between them, words jumping from the screen at her: *vibrators, water massages, Victorian-era England. Sigmund Freud*, of course. She moved to images. Countless shots of women with mouths open, their hands pulling at their hair, or clutching their cheeks, as if posed by an invisible man.

Click. Click. Click.

Click. What was this? An object that looked like some kind of clamp. Elegant yet utilitarian in appearance. But what was it used for? She clicked on *Visit page*. It was designed by a surgeon called Isaac Baker Brown and used with a cautery iron. Cautery? Burning? She began a fresh search with *cautery iron* and *Baker Brown*. Found herself needing her uni credentials for access to articles. *Baker Brown, ovariotomy*. Pages with *clitoridectomy, epilepsy, hysteria … masturbation …*

Ah, *cautery iron*, there, on the page of cramped Victorian font. *British Medical Journal*, 1867. The Obstetrical Society and some kind of medical meeting. She scanned to the highlighted phrase and read.

> *Two instruments were used; the pair of hooked forceps which Mr. Brown always uses in clitoridectomy, and a cautery iron such as he uses in dividing the pedicle in ovariotomy. This iron is made by Pratt; it is somewhat hatchet-shaped. The clitoris was seized by the forceps in the usual manner. The thin edge of the red-hot iron was then passed round its base until the origin was severed from its attachments, being partly cut or sawn, and partly torn away. After the clitoris was removed, the nymphæ –*

This couldn't be true. No, surely not. Alice swayed on her feet. Put her hand to the desk to steady herself. What were nymphae – the labia? She could feel the shearing. Smell scorching flesh. She clenched her legs. Would anything be left of this poor woman?

She returned, compelled, to the screen.

> *... on each side were severed in a similar way by a sawing motion of the hot iron. After the clitoris and nymphæ were got rid of, the operation was brought to a close by taking the back of the iron and sawing the surfaces of the labia and the other parts of the vulva [cries of 'Enough'] which had escaped the cautery, and the instrument was rubbed down backwards and forwards till the parts were more effectually destroyed than when Mr. Brown uses the scissors to effect the same result.*

The searing between her legs. The tears on her face. The nightmare she had entered.

Chapter 6

June 25th 1863

Dear Miss Rochdale,

Thank you for making me so welcome in your London home & for celebrating so generously both our engagement & Arthur's exciting promotion. I will do my best to answer the several warm & sincere questions in your letter in as unguarded a fashion, as I feel you have invited me to express my genuine feelings instead of merely clinging to the surface of things.

I hardly know how to respond to the request to think of you as a future sister, when you are like a mother to Arthur & Miss Cecilia Rochdale, & such a help to Sir George Rochdale in his political work. I feel as a child might next to you, although we are so close in age! Yet I have longed for an older sister all my life & cannot imagine a kinder, more certain presence than yours. I will look to you for help in how best to be a good sister & daughter to the family when that happy day arrives.

You ask me to forgive your father for those awkward early meetings, but I do understand why he might have been reluctant to embrace me as a daughter. Though my family has wealth & recent prominence, we lack the standing of your family, which has been on its estate for many years. I know, though, that my family's good fortune over the last several generations can only profit our marriage & contribute to Arthur's future, especially if he is to enter politics one day, as he dreams. Sir George has been most gracious in our most recent encounters, which makes both

Arthur & me very happy. I do so wish to live up to your family's worthy expectations.

As for our youth, it is true that Arthur & I have much to learn of the world & wish to marry when Arthur is younger than his father would have liked. But more than a year has passed now since we met & we have sustained our feelings through correspondence & occasional meetings over a long winter. This season has only confirmed our love for each other. We are determined, too, & both made stronger through the blows that life has dealt—brought closer through our shared grief over the loss of loved ones. Arthur thinks to build his position now he has been called to the bar & make connections that will secure our prospects & I will remain content with a year-long engagement while I plan for our future together. My mother & father are most happy with the match; their sole sadness is that they will lose their only remaining child when she marries.

We will meet again on Saturday at the Harrises', which Arthur tells me you are attending, & I also look forward to seeing your family at the Royal Regatta. Arthur says we must cheer from Henley Bridge for Tom Lawler, if he does well enough in the qualifying races!

With my warm best wishes,

Miss Emily Reid

July 14th 1863

Dear Miss Rochdale,

It was delightful to speak with you at the regatta & to meet Miss Cecilia Rochdale properly. How her beauty & animation will impress everyone when she is introduced to society! The memory of the day at Henley is now a perfect little gem that I will take from its cushion in years to come, polishing it carefully each time. The shouts of excitement as boats flew down the river, the tangy strawberries in their wee baskets, the sun lodging in the sky as if the day might refuse to end … What joy!

I was most pleased, too, that Sir George looked kindly on me. When you confided his great change with the loss of Lady Rochdale, I think he became real to me for the first time & I felt I could understand him more truly—not be quite so scared of him. I do not like to hear of the sorrows of others, but I do believe it makes me a better person to know that I am not the only one to have suffered in this way.

Are you happy at the prospect of returning to Herdley? Or is the thought of preparing the household for such journeys daunting? I know I would find it so!

With my warm best wishes,

Miss Emily Reid

August 10th 1863

Dear Miss Rochdale,

It was with great happiness that I received your most recent letter & heard of your preparations for the opening of the grouse season. The break from Parliament must be scarcely a holiday for you; I hardly know how you act as hostess for Sir George's country parties, or how you help organise his demanding life. I hope Arthur is carrying some of the burden for you while there, though from the mischief in his letters I suspect he is more hindrance than help!

I am so pleased that you would like to have Mother & I to stay with you when, as you say, "the hordes are gone". How often Arthur has spoken of Hierde House & how many times I have imagined myself there with him. My life is very fortunate, I know, but I do so miss the sweetness of country air & the true green of trees unblackened by London's dreadful smoke. It is a great pity that Arthur will again be busy in London by then, but he is already planning walks for us around Herdley & I rest in the knowledge you will be the best of companions.

With my warm best wishes,

Miss Emily Reid

September 10th 1863

Dear Beatrice,

I have spoken with Mother & we will be most grateful to stay with you early in November. Father is already wondering how he will manage without "my girls", as he calls us. No doubt Mrs Bolton will keep him nicely fed with her famous calf's head pie!

We anticipate confirming dates with you with great pleasure.

My warm best wishes,

Emily

October 20th 1863

Dear Beatrice,

Yes, November 3rd suits us perfectly! Thank you for corresponding with Mother about this. She tells me that everything is now arranged, with a carriage to meet us at the railway station & provision for Millie & Ann to stay in the servants' quarters. (How do you organise things so easily? Or is it just seeming ease? I do look forward to learning a little of such skills in your company.)

Father has settled on the Almsford estate that I mentioned, in Warwickshire. It has a house on it already & several hundred acres attached. Mother calls the house "a wee dear" & says it is quite adequate for their purposes as a retreat from the Great Wen, but Father has schemes for rebuilding—a "grand new mansion", he says—one day, when he is not quite so busy.

I am grateful for your continuing correspondence when your house is so full of activity. Your regular missives spark my intelligence & brighten my days, which are otherwise occupied with the tedium of needlework, drawing … Miss Roberts says I must polish my conversation & social graces for the wedding & marriage, which makes me impatient. And all Mam will say is, "You must listen to your governess!" At least Miss Roberts allows me to practise singing & piano—I harry her for the occasional dance around the schoolroom, which makes her grumpy, or for discussion on the affairs of the nation, which she ignores! Sometimes

Mam & I receive or make visits, but I do tend to dream of my fiancé in the midst of it all. Fortunately Arthur is often with us in the evenings. He says Morrison is keeping him very occupied at chambers & I see how all he must learn at court often weighs on him. How happy I will be to find employment as his wife in the years to come, to help ease his worries & create a calming haven to which he can return each day.

It will not be long now until Mother & I are in your haven. I am so very excited!

With kind regards,

Emily

November 22nd 1863

Dear Beatrice,

How to thank you for such a wonderful time at Hierde House! I was delighted to see the many places I had only previously imagined through Arthur's fond words: your dignified yet welcoming home; Hierde Farm, with the redoubtable Old Susan (how I loved her tales of naughty young Arthur); quaint Herdley & its busy market; the quiet comfort of Arthur's elm thicket. And then climbing to the wondrous Naze &, beyond, the top of the world—I think you will understand what I mean when I say how completely at peace I felt with grass below, sky above & you, dear Beatrice, next to me.

It was only your steadiness that kept me beside you with the arrival of such important guests on our final weekend. Otherwise, I might have hid with Cecilia in the schoolroom! How do you manage to stay so calm? I am sure I could not discuss housekeeping with your Mrs Malley with such equanimity. Can I look to you for guidance when I have my own house to run? I do hope so. (Did I tell you Mam insists I take Millie with me when Arthur & I are married? How comforting it will be to have the familiar presence of my dear maid as I make our new home.) Anyway, I feel a little more at ease with all these eminent people: it is hard to be overly discomfited when playing gaily at croquet on the lawn of Hierde House, or when guessing at a bumbling charade!

Again, the most sincere thanks from me & from Mam, who will also write to you—I could not wait. I will anticipate your return to London with great pleasure. Arthur is our frequent guest in Savile Row, of course, but we would also love to have you to dinner, & Sir George, if I am brave enough!

With love & best wishes,

Emily

December 18th 1863

Dearest Beatrice,

Thank you for your concern. We have been terribly worried about Mother, though I am relieved to write that she is now recovering. It is old troubles, I am afraid—the many misfortunes she suffered in mothering—Father too, of course. (I will tell this to you in confidence, as most of these losses were early & without her condition being guessed at by society.) Father is asking other physicians for their opinions, but he believes himself that the stress on her system at each past instance weakened her nerves then, & now bedrest is the best tonic. She is very sad at such times, as it reminds her of that most terrible of losses, & I do my best to cheer my brave Mam, though I am also reminded of our dear James. I know, too, that even though Mam has resigned herself to my future—is delighted with dear Arthur & fully supports my entry into the sanctity of marriage—she cannot but be saddened at the thought of her surviving fledgling flitting from the home nest.

Enough of such dreary talk! It is chilly but the sun is out, & Mother & I plan to take a short carriage ride this afternoon. It will not be too long before she is receiving visitors again with that sweet smile. As you will be in London within weeks, our very first visitor must be you. Pray agree!

With my love,

Emily

February 11th 1864

Dear Beatrice,

Yes, we will come to dinner! Mam is organising the carriage & we will be in Westminster very soon. How delightful it will be to have my Arthur & my Beatrice with me all at once!

Until tonight,

Emily

February 19th 1864

My dear Bea,

You would not recognise your happy sister in this sad countenance, yet I am grateful you could ease your long sorrow in my company, just as siblings ought, & I do wish to share my feelings with you, because it seems our families have a bond—an understanding that I felt almost immediately when Arthur & I began to speak beyond the usual niceties of social intercourse. I only hesitated to confide in you because it is hard to talk of loss & grief when others are nearby & to hide from company the agitation that rushes over me when I think of my beloved brother. But I know you will understand—you who have shown such sensitivity to matters of the heart—that if I write to you about dear James, it might help me to speak of him more naturally with you in the future, & for you to unburden yourself to me whenever you might need, as sisters do.

I was lost for years after James's death, dear Bea, as if in a dense mist that would not lift, even in my coming out, even in the excitement of my first London season. I was only fifteen when it happened, after all, & he was my only sibling. Though he was often away with his schooling, then his years at Oxford, there was always a great attachment between us, even with the difference in our ages.

Oh, how I loved his breaks! He would arrive home with pages of impressive words & meanings for me to memorise, & a reading list: Plato, Dante, Rousseau—so many books that I would muddle through! Then on his next visit, he would ask, "So, what do you think of Pascal then, Emmie?" & Mother would say, "Leave her alone, James—she has dear Miss Roberts," & he would tease Mother with, "Dear Miss Roberts does not educate her in philosophy, or Greek, or political economy …" & then Mother would interrupt with all the important skills the governess taught me, like French & the piano & dancing & how to converse in society. But whenever she would chide James & say, "The poor child should be concentrating on how to make a harmonious home for her future husband," he would laugh & say that my brain would grow as fat & sluggish as Toby, our old pug. And he would poke poor Tobes with his toe & then all three of us would laugh. I can hear us laughing even now.

How good James was for me! He was always my greatest support & my dearest friend, but he encouraged me to be strong & certain, just as you & Arthur do. I remember skating with him on our cousins' pond in Scotland—many, many happy memories of spinning & racing & falling, only to have his hand lift me to my feet again. Oh, & picking blackberries together for Mrs Bolton's tasty tarts; popping the juiciest berries into our mouths, & that burst of sweet-sour flavour like a hope, perhaps. A promise of all that is possible.

So when he was gone, I felt I was gone too—as if we were trapped together in some strange in-between world; as if he were a shade without awareness of anything beyond the repeating habits of our household & the terror of his own death. I was with James, but the closeness was a torment. It was like … How can I explain? I would imagine, Bea, imagine, imagine, until I was driven to distraction; until I hardly dare open my eyes or unstop my ears. When I ran down the stairs, his toes would be at my heels, his breath at my neck. When I reached for more cake at supper, his gentle hand would tap mine. When I turned the corridor corner, there his own dear self would be.

That I could stand. But the nights, dear Bea, the nights! In the dark solitude of my bed I would be claimed by my poor brother's last day on this earth: I would be with him on that sailing boat, a sunny holiday jaunt, a solo day-long voyage, the waves slapping salt against our faces, the deck boards jarring our knees. Together we saw the sky darken & heard the creaking complaint of the old timber; together we exulted, as we raced towards shore, at the climb to the crests of the waves, the plunge into their hollows. But then we heard that terrible thundering crack! & our hearts raced as we felt the boat undoing, as we slid over snapping, rending boards & clung to any that were not claimed by that devouring sea. And when, in the end, he was dragged from my grasp & into the grip of those cold waves, then finally, exhausted, bereft, I would succumb to sleep. But each night I would be woken by his shouts & his entreaty would come to me: "Emily. Emily! Please save me!" Each night I would hear his voice again, & each night I would lose him anew.

I have learned that there are all sorts of ghosts in this world. Brothers, mothers—babies without face or form; siblings who have never been. I have learned that those we loved fiercely haunt us the most. And here I write carefully, my dear Bea, knowing that what was lost to Arthur was lost to you also. Perhaps, then, you know the relief of sharing such despair & understand how Arthur came to me as a light through darkness. Why the ghost of James now gives me peace & why I can love him now, at last, without fear or consequence.

Poor Mam. We were no help to each other then, she & I. James was her last great loss, after the many silent, secret losses she & Father had already suffered. She had enough strength for herself alone. As for me: the nights I have spoken of enough, but the days were a trial of a different sort. All through that dreadful time I was plagued by terrible headaches & what Father said was anaemia & a "weak liver", & was made to drink ghastly tonics & rest in bed in daylight, where I would toss around in fits of boredom & loneliness. Was it the lack of the reading with which James used to stimulate me? Or the absence of our teasing debates? The want of occupation? The loss of all those activities from which the weaker sex is discouraged, but which James gladly encouraged? All of these, I suppose. What I do know is that my suffering lifted when I met Arthur, & when we sealed our future with a kiss a year later, it was like a union with someone dearly loved who I had forgotten & did not know that I would ever, ever see again.

Dear Beatrice, I hope I have not been too maudlin; Mother would scold me if she knew I had been indulging these old feelings. But I am sure from your own words & the tears you shared with me that you must understand a sadness that never leaves entirely. And now your willingness to hear this history has left me calm & newly grateful for my dearest sister.

With love,

Emily

February 24th 1864

My dear Beatrice,

Thank you for all your concern for our small family. For your caring questions & your messages of love & support when I showed you all of myself & worried what you might think of me—not only the merry, teasing Emily, but the Emily who fears & grieves, I find now, just as you do. When I met Arthur I not only gained my sweetheart—someone to whom I can devote myself as a helpmeet in the years to come—I also found a sister & friend, where I feared there might be a cool judge. I remember now as if it were another girl, how my heart hammered as I wrote that first letter to you. And how presumptuous I felt to suggest my family's wealth & Father's recent success might balance your family's prestige & its honourable ties to the soil of this nation. How inadequate my words seemed, unformed as my education has been, with gaps like holes in need of darning. It was only your warm manner that overcame my natural uncertainty—that terrible timidity that I believe is my bent.

Yes, I received the copy of Kingsley's Water Babies *& I agree. The story may be an enchanting escape from the worthy political tracts that you & Arthur recommend (best read away from Mam & Miss Roberts), but this "children's novel" is full of that prejudice against the poor & the Irish which Arthur & I both condemn. Will this ever change? we often wonder. It is hard to imagine, though Arthur thinks social attitudes can become more rational & kinder, & I would like to believe him …*

But enough! I wish to ask you something delightfully trivial, dear Bea: Will you be at the Wilsons' ball on Saturday? I do hope so! I will wear my dove-grey, if it is not too cold.

With loving wishes,

Emily

March 3rd 1864

Dear Bea,

Thank you for your willing ear yesterday. I am so glad I can speak freely with you about these difficult matters; Mam accuses me of coarseness if I try, & Father tells me not to trouble myself about such things as dowries

& marriage settlements—"That's for us men to worry about," he said to me last night. But I do need to understand how any independent income I receive will find its place within the marriage. How will we manage it in the running of a household & the pursuit of our goals? My darling Arthur is, of course, happy to explain it all, but sometimes we are a little awkward, mainly through my uncertainty &, also, his pride. He wishes to provide for us, & he assures me his income from the bar will hold us in good stead, but I would like my income to be available to the marriage without exception, so we can build connections in society & assure Arthur's future in politics, if that is the path he chooses. It does seem that property will be included in the dowry, so that will be kept protected as an inheritance … But I do not understand this fully, Bea, & Father will not properly explain. Surely it is important that I have some knowledge of affairs related to me & some ability to determine them, even if I am young & only a woman!

With fond wishes,

Emily

March 6th 1864

Dearest Beatrice,

You were right! Arthur & I spoke privately about the money question after dinner last night & the knot was gently untied.

How delightful it is to discover that such issues are readily solved through thoughtful conversation with my dear Arthur. I am finding that even small disagreements only occasion teasing & delight. When I observe other couples, & their little shafts of displeasure & discomfort, I see how well Arthur & I rub together & how carefully he takes into account my point of view.

Miss Emily Reid become Mrs Rochdale. How grand it sounds. I can hardly contain myself, but I must, until that happy day when I truly become a part of your family. Meanwhile, we have lots to plan—only five months now!

Your soon-to-be-sister,

Emily

Chapter 7

Perth, December 2007

Alice leaned against the wall of the reception area. She had been standing for twenty-five minutes now and her legs were tired. But she studiously looked at the Christmas decorations and the tasteful watercolours on the wall – away from the empty seats and the faces of other patients. She'd already knocked back the offer from that burly man with the whiskery sideburns.

Would you like a seat, dear?

No, thanks. I'm fine.

The back, is it? With a sympathetic and knowing nod.

Yes. A pained smile. Willing him to go away.

A screen above the counter cycled messages. *Ask our friendly staff about flu vaccinations. The play area is provided for your children. Please cover your mouth when coughing or sneezing.* One specific to this centre: *We specialise in women's health.* The demands and instructions were softened by whimsical cartoons of harassed-looking mothers, a friendly-faced needle, bawling kids and giant tissues.

'Alice Tennant?'

Dr Gibbs had a nimbus of fine brown hair and wore an Indian-style skirt that was friendlier than her face. She walked with a little tinkle. Alice followed her into a consulting room. There were posters of rainforests on the wall, with exhortations to *Believe in the truth of your body* and *Trust in inner health* arranged around waterfalls and creeper-entwined trees. She felt compelled to sit. The doctor looked at the writing that Alice had crammed between questions about the presenting complaint: the onset, the duration; what makes it better, what makes it worse. The diagnoses received: *a mystery STD, mechanical urethritis, herpes, possible vulvar cancer, a fungal infection* ... Alice had been diligent. She lifted one buzzing buttock off the cushioned surface of her seat and tried to pull reason from her macerated thoughts. *Stacey says she's really good.* A recommendation from one of Penny's colleagues. *Knowledgeable but thinks outside the box too.* Alice had stitched her hopes to this unknown Stacey's judgement.

'So I see you have ongoing genital problems, Alice.' The GP looked up from the notes. 'Could you tell me about how this began? And exactly where you experience the pain?'

'Okay.' She hesitated, but the fizzing and knifing precluded embarrassment. 'My vulva and vagina hurt. They've been like this since I got a UTI in September.' And because it seemed relevant, she added, 'After lots of sex.'

'So this was confirmed as an infection? Or do you just *think* this is what you had?'

'Oh, no. No. It was tested. From a urine sample.' Alice shifted onto her right buttock cheek, suspended the left. 'I went through a couple of lots of antibiotics but it stayed the same.'

'I see. So you have been like this for over three months.' Dr Gibbs looked over her glasses at Alice, her eyes a clear, cool blue. 'Could you describe the symptoms to me?'

'Well, at first I wanted to urinate all the time. And when I did, it hurt. That's when I thought I might have an infection, because I've had one before.' It was a stale story to Alice now. How many medicos had it been? Five? Six? How many 'alternative' health practitioners? 'So I went to a GP at the local centre. But after the antibiotics I felt the same. Worse really.' How could she describe it convincingly, woman to woman? 'It wasn't just the urinating that hurt. It hurt all the time, inside and outside.' Then, quickly: 'It isn't just in my head.' Had she imagined the aura of scepticism around the doctors she consulted? She'd heard 'psychosomatic' several times. Once from a male gynaecologist who said, *Try not to think about it too much.* And once from a psychologist who asked her questions about sex as she stood and cried.

Her back was trembling, right at its base. She shifted her weight to the left buttock cheek.

'Why are you doing that?' The GP looked at Alice's posture with a frown.

Alice felt the blush. 'Because it hurts to sit.'

'That's not right.'

Found wanting, Alice would abase herself if she could. Slide around on the ground and kiss the doctor's feet. Slit the throat of a lamb and splash it over an altar.

But Dr Gibbs had moved on. 'Let's have a look, shall we?' The part Alice dreaded. 'Just remove your bottom half.'

Alice went behind the curtain. Heard the rush of voices as the GP left the consulting room, then, silence. Off with her sandals. Down with the sensible undies, their crotch already loose and low. Off with the sloppy skirt. On, to the tissued napkin placed just so on the white sheets of the bench. Over, with the comfortingly clean sheet left discreetly at the end of the bench. It was a relief to have no undies against the rawness. She pictured it as swollen and red, but Duncan had looked there and said, *It's the same as always. Beautiful.* She didn't know whether to be relieved.

A click of the door and the doctor came around the edge of the curtain, pulling on one then the other latex glove. Alice let her knees flop out.

The GP had a cotton bud in her hand. This was new.

'Just tell me the pain you feel out of ten, with ten being the worst pain you can imagine.' Her hand disappeared below the sheet.

'Fuck!' Alice's body jumped away from the bench. The sharp stab pierced her genitals, whipped lightning-like upward and inward and echoed where she thought her bladder and uterus might be. 'Shit – sorry.' It became an ache that enveloped her belly and pelvis. 'That's a nine.'

Alice knew the pain could be worse. She had a ten when, feeling her way, she put that herbal ointment on her vulva. The ointment that the traditional Chinese doctor smilingly assured her, *Can't hurt. Can't hurt.* And after the antifungal cream that the local chemist said was *mild and effective*. The cream that burned for days and that rinsing over and over could not soothe. She knew that ten was a pain that crowded out all consciousness except the instinct to clutch the ledge of life from which she dangled.

'Alright. And what about this?'

Alice was rigid in preparation. The pain was the same, but this time she managed to lie still, to hold the expletives behind thinned lips. A tear slipped along the side of her face and into her hair. 'Nine.'

'And this?'

'Seven.' The pokes seemed less ferocious. 'Six.' Again. 'Six.' Dr Gibbs looked at her expectantly. Alice realised she could no longer distinguish the individual bursts of flame from the fire that now consumed her genitals, pelvis, inner thighs and buttocks. 'Five,' she guessed. The rest of her body had shut itself away. Even her mind seemed numbed. As if she had no volition; as if she would do anything this woman told her. 'I'm not sure … five?'

'Okay. Let's get dressed now.'

Again Alice was alone, though she could hear tapping behind the curtain. She lifted her hand and blew gently on the palm, then placed it so her fingers curved around the outside of her genitals. She wanted ice or some kind of soothing poultice. She wanted to nurse the ache or attack somebody or beg for forgiveness. She did not know what to want.

Her feet slid sideways and she found herself standing. Then her skirt was eased up over her hips and gently zipped at the back. Her undies stuffed to the bottom of her bag and her sandals pushed hard onto her feet. The curtain drawn back.

Dr Gibbs's fingers were flying at the keyboard, then moving to a chart on a piece of paper. The little elephants on her skirt gazed at Alice, who realised she must sit again. She eased onto the side of one buttock, letting the other hang off the edge of the chair, and braced herself with a tensed leg. Her own skirt settled around her awkward pose.

The GP was putting numbers on the diagram. With a little shock, Alice recognised the upside-down view. She realised that the numbers referred to her vulva.

'You are lucky you didn't get this ten years ago.' Dr Gibbs put her glasses next to the keyboard and turned.

'What is it?' Alice rose slightly, shifted to the other side of the chair and the other buttock cheek. She would have to stand soon.

'Vulvar vestibulitis.' The words sounded familiar. Maybe she'd seen them on the internet, before the image of the cautery iron, and the account that drove her from her trawling. She'd not had the courage to resume her online search since.

'Ten years ago it would have taken much longer for you to be diagnosed.' The doctor's voice was wry. 'Twenty years and you may not have received a diagnosis at all.' She turned the chart and pointed to the numbers. 'You see here?' Alice leaned forward. The posture relieved the pressure on her genitals and bottom; she placed her weight on her elbows and exhaled shakily. 'These numbers are where I was pressing in the vestibule.'

'In the what?'

'The vestibule. The entrance to the vagina. The inflammation is typically focused at these points.'

'It's worse at one end.' Alice saw that the nines were placed towards the front of the vulva, near to what she thought might be the urethra. No wonder weeing hurt so much.

'Yes. That's unusual,' the doctor said. 'Generally the pain is worse at the back of the vestibule, near the Bartholin's glands. Maybe your pain is more widespread and that's why you're having trouble sitting.' Her tone was musing, its surface unruffled. 'Though most women have pain primarily with intercourse, not all the time ...' She smiled abruptly, briefly, and, just as suddenly, Alice realised that the GP relished this twist on the typical. 'But I think that yours is simply a more severe case. There's no reason why you shouldn't respond to treatment.'

'So, how do you treat it?' Alice felt her heart thump.

'Ah, that's something I've had a lot of success with.' Satisfaction lifted one corner of the doctor's mouth. 'I've found that the anti-candida diet eliminates any candida in the vulva that might be causing inflammation and lets the area settle down.'

Success. Who with? But Alice's mind skipped quickly over the idea of other women with this pain – of an inescapably real, established, long-suffering population out there, somewhere – to land on the possibility of treatment. She'd been on the anti-candida diet once, years ago – why, she couldn't recall. A momentary illness? A youthful fad? She did remember feeling healthy and virtuous.

'How long does it take?'

'I've had a ninety-five percent success rate in women who stick with it for three months.'

Could this be true? Alice did not know whether to feel relieved or deflated. Three months. She was hoping for a miracle cure. A series of toxic tablets or a nasty injection. It seemed impossible that food could defuse this relentless pain. But what if it could? She felt herself expanding around the new information. Plans began to form in her mind: a visit to the health food shop, whole foods and supplements, meditation.

Shuffling broke into her thoughts. The GP was tidying her papers. Preparing to move on to the next person.

'What about sex?' Questions were returning to her now, too late. She felt panicky. 'We haven't been able to have sex for a couple of months.' She didn't really want an answer; even the question wasn't hers.

But Dr Gibbs paused with her tidying and looked straight at Alice. 'Well, you could try an anaesthetic cream. So that you don't feel the pain.' Alice thought about Duncan and how pleased he would be. If she told him. 'But have you thought about why you might have this disorder?' The question was at odds with the GP's impersonal manner, but not with the posters and the clothing and the dietary advice. Alice felt a little give in her tense body. Impressions flitted through her mind: communes and rainbows and organic food. The dawning of the Age of Aquarius. Then the doctor spoke again: 'What do you think your body is trying to tell you?'

Alice settled on the day bed in a sideways, semi-reclining pose, buttressed by cushions. Bees were buzzing at the orangey-red grevillea flowers. She closed her eyes. Tried to recapture the floating heaviness of sleep. The bees' hum blended with the touch of the sun, which, for now, was soft.

What do you think your body is trying to tell you? She had no idea. Not because she couldn't hear it – her genitals now screamed and yelled at her in a ceaseless assault from which she had to block her ears – but because it was a language she could not translate. The only words she could separate from the formless babble were, it hurts. It hurts. It hurts! And the response: oh God, take it away. Make it stop. Oh please, God. She did not know who was doing the screaming, who the begging.

Her mother, when she rang from Melbourne, reminded her of the words of the mediaeval mystic Julian of Norwich: *'All shall be well and all shall be well and all manner of thing shall be well.'* And when Alice sobbed and moaned, beyond vanity, beyond restraint, *This suffering will make you very strong,* her mother said. Alice had wanted to demand, 'What's more strength when I'm already as hard as stone? as heavy as lead?' But she kept that anger, almost as great as the pain, sealed inside her body, acting out the violence only in her imagination. Her mother's head wrenched sideways, cheek flaming. 'I'll give you sainthood.' Her own stinging, satisfied hand.

She opened her eyes, slipped on her sunglasses. In a week or so, even this early-morning sun would be too much for her. And too much for the garden. She scanned the flowerbeds. Saw the remnants of spring flowers, bowing low at summer's entry. The person she once was would have spread mulch on the beds by now. Kept the little patch of lawn a pristine green. Instead, it was a holey rug patched and threaded by winter grass, and weeds that nodded their tough little seed heads at her, emboldened by her lack of action.

Last night's dream returned. The house and the dry, flat, barren block of land that, it seemed, was her home. The bed of sand that she combed for the minute seeds of weeds. Dream-Alice picked them out, one by one.

Then she uncovered a cocoon. It had a brown creature inside it, so she put the cocoon in a plastic bag for protection, tying the opening closed. But the creature in the cocoon heaved, its movements faster and faster, its hole of a mouth pressed tight against the clear skin that separated it from the world. And suddenly it came to her: because she had tied the bag, the creature couldn't breathe. She punched a hole and it emerged, gasping for air. She saw it was like a little bat. She dropped the bundle of life in surprise and woke, the tears still wet on her cheeks.

A wattlebird flew industriously in and out of the powder puffs of melaleuca blossom. Snow-in-summer – was that its name? The melaleuca tree that she and Duncan planted to mark her moving into his house. Their home. Over seven years ago now. She sipped her tea and wondered when he would wake. Unusual for him to sleep so late, even over the Christmas break.

Her vulva felt heavy. It dragged against itself, like the lagging anchor of a boat adrift in a storm. She knew that, were she to move right now, it would flare again. Even the outward bulge of her belly as she inhaled seemed to stir it. These days, her chest rose in small, shallow breaths as if she were in the midst of an emergency.

Thank God she'd knocked back next year's units; deferred the sessional lecturing and tutoring built up over the last few years. She understood, though, that she was saying no to far more than teaching. She was sacrificing acknowledgement and respect, forgoing work with colleagues who sparked passion and ideas, suspending the honorary fellow position bestowed after what was considered a highly successful PhD. She was saying no to this role she had created – with Duncan's support, of course – saying no to a goal only partially achieved.

Even harder to bear was that other loss: more critical writing on family and fiction, attempts to edit stories already written – to find publication for her collection of families, languishing now for months. This was where her joy rested: in the shaping of ideas, of characters and worlds; in being herself shaped by what she learned. But her imagination was as arid as their garden, her strength and confidence drained by the battle with pain. It was impossible to generate anything new, or to improve anything already written. And so she must release that joy, although loosening her grasp on it was like another death.

But, she reminded herself, it was the end of the year. Recovery was more important; she couldn't do anything until then. She could take as long as she needed – all of 2008, if necessary – to free herself from the pain she had nursed over long months, holding it like a sickly baby against her belly, feeling her shoulders and head slowly curling down and around it.

She looked at the garden through a mist and wondered, who was this Alice who could do nothing but cry? Who was, now, nothing? Nothing without her husband, who must support her, emotionally, morally. Financially.

'Hello, there.' A hand on her shoulder. Duncan leaning over from behind. 'How are you doing?'

'Oh, the same.' Alice quickly wiped at her face. She was growing to hate the recurring question and its implicit demand. She wanted to be able to say, 'Oh, it's so much better!' and was angry at herself and, unreasonably, Duncan that she couldn't. She reminded herself that he was being caring and understanding, and she forced herself to smile at him.

'Do you want to try a drive today?' Duncan rounded the day bed and squatted next to her. He was already dressed in shorts and a sports shirt and looked vital and healthy. Years younger than his forty-two years. At that moment, she was older than him. A hag; a crone.

'No. I just want to lie still.' That wasn't quite right. 'I mean, I would love to go for a drive somewhere. But it would make things worse, so I can't.' There was something about saying no all the time that wore away at you. 'I'll stay here and read.'

'Okay.' A small frown. He walked behind her again, squeezed her shoulders with his hands.

The wattlebird perched on the gutter and leaned over, its head jerking and swivelling. Searching for the juicy spiders that had been colonising the eaves. It swooped suddenly through the net of webs. A fleeting glimpse of black at its beak, then the bird was gone.

'I might see if Brian is up for some tennis,' Duncan said.

'That sounds like a good idea.' She wanted to be left alone. No, she wanted to be held, nestled into an embrace that asked nothing of her.

He leaned over her shoulder again, rested his cheek on hers. 'I want to be able to help you,' he whispered, 'but I don't know how.'

Chapter 8

London, December 1864

He skips down the front steps—freshly scrubbed and whitened; good girl, Mary—and sets off for Lincoln's Inn with Emily's pure, clear voice still sounding in his ear. And though it is bleak on the street—a heavy, chill winter with the night's rain in the day's puddles and the usual dirty, yellowish fog choking the air—and though other noises nudge the edges of his thought—the shriek of the servant girl trotting across Portland Place as water spills from a pail over her boot; the distant strains of a brass band overlaid by the pealing bells of All Saints; high-pitched giggles and a clatter of hooves left hanging in the wake of a cab—and though this brisk walk is but a prelude to a hectic day with disconsolate clients and papered stacks of unsolvable cases, still, even with all this, "All Things Bright and Beautiful" sings to him in his wife's voice—his wife, his!—and his feet beat a rhythm to the tune. He knows that if he were to bump into someone—his old Rugby School friend Thomas Lawler, say, freshly qualified as a physician and stepping from cab to kerb, a respectable top hat taming his pale curls—a fond smile would be there, just as it has been on every single morning of their newly minted marriage.

She delights him. Emily. His Emmie. Singing morning songs of praise and thanksgiving, voice and feet tripping, childlike, up and down the stairs. Listening to stories of his clients at breakfast, head tilted, grey eyes narrowing in concentration. Commanding him, mock-imperious, to dinner, where they touch toes under the table. Challenging his serious-minded politics while she sews by the fire in the evening, plump mouth twitching. Calling him to bed, hair undone and swaying like a promise down her back. He wants to make love to her; he wishes to protect her; he would like to shout his unbelieving, unbelievable bliss to the world. Instead, he holds it close, a luscious secret: the world of her and him, into which no-one else can intrude.

When had it been, that moment, that piercing sense of recognition? The knowledge that she was for him and no-one else? Not at the first sight of her, just another amongst the flurry of girls "coming out" like butterflies after their demure presentation at court; he'd not even properly heard that lilting voice. Maybe he'd not been ready. It was the following year, 1862 … May—he'd just come down from Oxford, was reeling in the unfamiliar expectations of Lincoln's Inn and the befuddled intricacies of the courts—yes, it was May when he first really saw her. The tartan sash bordering her ball dress—Ah, Scottish, then, he'd thought—the heavy mass of red-gold hair coiled at the back of her head; the slanted eyes and lips like an invitation; the soft, white, intimate hollows beneath the jet beads at her neck and shoulders. He'd had to look away for a moment to compose himself. And then when she spoke he'd felt a shock within him, a sensation like something shifting in his chest. That she felt it too was in the darkening of her eyes, the hand to her mouth.

Why, Arthur, Bea had exclaimed the following morning, *someone has put a spring in your step!* And he'd blushed and laughed and held his tongue, not ready to trust the sense of revelation, even to his teasing sister.

He pauses for a passing cab at the corner of Weymouth Street, sees a maid shaking a small rug out of a second-storey window, another emptying a bucket into the gutter of the street. A phantom shape in the fog becomes an upright matron shepherding two young women in gay walking dresses and bonnets—one brilliant red, the other a bold blue. A little terrier trots next to them and sniffs eagerly at Arthur's boots as the group passes behind him, then round the corner. Off for a walk in Regent's Park, perhaps.

They'd had to abide by convention, he and Emmie, follow the forms of society. So giddy dancing at balls, then, and urging on horses at Ascot, and partaking in those interminable dinners where ambitious men form alliances and ambitious women plot for their daughters. The evenings only given light and promise when she and he drew together in corners or on terraces, her mother always just a glance away, and shared moments of their lives: losses mourned, futures hoped. That desire for her taking shape, becoming a parching need only eased by little sips that were never quite enough: fluttering touches, quick whispers on staircases. Then, later, when he could dare to believe in her, sightings in Hyde Park, she with her mother—always, always with her mother!—and sometimes a friend, taking the air, and he—why, he was there to accidentally bump into her, of course. On every occasion he sensed her lithe body under the layers of clothing and corsetry, felt it being pulled towards his. The fever for her kept him awake at night but he did not regret the loss of sleep, though it made him bleary-eyed in chambers and short-tempered with the clerks. The memory of the charge that sprang between them was a careering energy that carried him through his training in the bar.

And now, two years later, he is a barrister, and she is his. His new wife in their new terraced home, where the gracious spaces match their happiness and willingly give room for it to grow. Their home on Portland Place, a wide street in which, by day, the trundling cabs, men on business—their wives on visits, their servants on errands—seem to move smoothly and with contentment. *Rose-coloured glasses*, laughs Beatrice when he speaks of the harmony that haloes their home. But she is happy for him, he can tell. And *he* is happy that the two women he loves best have become, already, the closest of friends.

The road shrugs to the left. He follows its twist onto Regent Street, skirts a lurching mud cart and leaps a sludgy puddle as he crosses to the eastern footway. The city's hum becomes a clamour: important-looking men hailing each other at a distance; women clucking at store windows, crinolines ballooning their skirts; a cad inviting a spindle-shanked old gentleman onto an omnibus with the shouted, *Plenty o' room for you, sir!* Hard to believe that just a short cab ride—ten minutes with a fast horse—separates him from the sedate Westminster home in which he spent his summers growing up; that he is but a hop, skip and jump from Savile Row and the quiet home of Emmie's parents. Quiet now, at least.

It's a knotted relationship he has with her parents—Edith, he's been invited to call her mother, and Charles, her father, though the familiar addresses come only with effort and leave his mouth sounding strangely formal. Charles and Edith like him, that much is clear, and are grateful for Emily's happiness, so obviously the result of love, but they also silently resent him, he feels: he has claimed their daughter, their only surviving child, taken her from them, and their house now rings with her absence.

Then there's the matter of money. It is Charles's money from his ironmonger grandfather, parlayed into enormous wealth by his father, that enabled the son to train as a physician and to enter a strata of society otherwise beyond the Reid family, which, in turn, permitted the presentation of his daughter to court and her welcome into society. More recently, it has financed the wedding and set-up of home so she can be secure. Arthur is under no illusions: the money is not so much for them; it is for Emily's future.

But they don't speak of such awkward matters. Charles is a no-nonsense man; a man who respects actions rather than words; a self-made man who admires other self-made men—like William Gladstone, for instance, a politician on whom the families see eye to eye. Though Charles had the wealth of his industrialist forebears to start him off, it was he who decided on the family's move from Edinburgh, where he'd trained, to a fresh start in London; Charles who built his fashionable practice from nothing and moulded the small, raw, "new money" family into a sophisticated urban presence; Charles who now holidays at their country estate and complains about *those messy tailors invading Savile Row*.

Yes, funnily enough, Arthur has discovered, the man is a greater snob than many of the Belgravia set. *My wife, Edith, God bless her, had some rather radical notions when we first married*, his father-in-law declared when the men removed to the smoking room after their most recent dinner together. The Scot had dismissed, with a flicking hand, his wife's early attempts to befriend their servants. *What rot!* he'd blustered through great puffs of smoke, and held forth about not confusing the lower classes. About how knowing your place keeps you satisfied. Content. It was advice, that much was clear, and not just on how to treat servants. *It didn't take her long, y'know, to see sense*, Charles had said with an air of finality, then slapped decisive hands to thighs and risen abruptly to his feet. He is a man who announces opinions as indisputable truths; on this occasion, Arthur had thought it wise to keep Emily's kind friendliness with all their own servants to himself.

Margaret Street. He pauses on the kerb, looks down the road they take to church each Sunday: to All Saints, where he surrenders himself to voices made resonant by devotion, and where the rays of pallid light pick out the gold of Emmie's hair like nothing other than a special form of holiness.

Thank goodness Emily inherited her mother's disposition; she did not need money to sweeten her appeal, although—and they admit this only between themselves, he and Emmie—it's a pleasant addition to their married life. It has reduced the strain on Father's face, too, the worries over the low income from their rather small estate and the cost of being a politician—ridiculous that such important work is unpaid—while all the time making certain his children do not go without. It's hard to tell how low the family coffers dipped, but several conversations were had about staying in London the year round and renting out Hierde House. Bea had given a cry at the suggestion and he'd had to contain his own emotion. *Airton says we can stay on his estate whenever we like*, Father had tried to console them; he'd kept close ties with his old Rugby friend. *He assures me we can treat it as our own.* Then there had been the relief: a risky business investment paying off; Arthur's own marriage to someone without great status, but with seemingly unlimited money. His father could not, at first, hide his warring feelings. But he'd come around; Emmie is hard to naysay with her curiosity and her clear and honest gaze. And there's no need to hide worldly concerns from her either; she may be young and lacking a fully rounded education, but she is subtle and pragmatic, he finds, and understands that if his family has benefitted from the marriage, so has hers. How many new and titled patients are now calling for her physician father might only be guessed. Certainly his carriage is becoming seedy with hard use, his horses always fagged. So there is a balance of sorts between the families, a fair—

He jars to a halt at the edge of the footway and Regent Circus North rushes towards him, as it does every time and yet is always new, teeming with life: a mother and three daughters in their elegant barouche, each with the same doughy face stretched by excitement; the *Hoy!* of a cad leaning counter-ways from the back step of a tilting, top-heavy omnibus as if to save it from crashing to the ground; the tang of steamy droppings mingling with the smell of hot pastry, lilac flower, pea soup and the wafting Thames; a chattering, rattling, clanking and ringing of innumerable wheels and hooves and boots and voices. And amongst all this, men and boys with tatty brooms and clothes circle cabs, 'buses and vans, scooping up dung and throwing it in a brimming cart, even as more is dropped by trudging and trotting horses—those thousands upon thousands of doughty beasts without which London would seize up like an unoiled machine. And the din! Costers—men and women trundling their barrows laden with whatever they can scrounge the pennies to buy, whatever they can hazard a guess might sell—hawking their wares with throats made scratchy by the city air: *Eels, pickled eels, best price in town! A nosegay for your lovely lady, sir? Pease porridge, fresh and hot! Here, buy a muffin for the little one, isn't she a treat?* … And this kaleidoscope of sight and sound and smell and taste; all this weaving and plunging and bumping of bodies whirls through his own body and is mirrored, muddily, in the windows of the stores at the intersection of Regent and Oxford in a riot of motion and colour. The Circus is London in miniature, a huge beast on mismatched legs, vast and lumbering, colossal and ungainly, yet it is a city to be admired, even celebrated, for its verve and the staunch adaptability of its people. The energy of the place fills him, gives him a sense of possibilities as broad as the long thoroughfare of Oxford Street.

He can't see the far side of the road through the haze, but he takes it on faith: lunges into a gap in the melee, side-stepping a pile of fresh manure, dodging a speeding cab with its clatter of wheels and hooves, skirting the inevitable puddles and barrows and sweepers, racing in front of a looming 'bus, knocking shoulders with a fellow crossing against him, finally making the footway. Then it's east along Oxford at a clapping pace, stumbling here and there at wads of straw thrown to soak up the putrid muck at shopfronts.

Away from the Circus, Oxford Street quiets a little and he can take in the surroundings, laugh mildly at his muddied boots, glad for the dry replacements waiting in chambers. The city streets are like a wave of filth in winter, and in summer a choking pall lies over them, but he still squeezes in this dash to chambers several times each week. He misses the long walks he's been used to his whole life: the streets of Oxford, calmer by far than London's, and the paths alongside the River Cherwell; the clutch and stretch of Herdley's hills; the blossomed air of Rugby in the spring. In their absence he must settle for the rhythm of his stride and the way it jogs his loose, tumbling thoughts into unconsidered combinations, nudges them into more comfortable homes.

Like his life before Emily. Lately he's been thinking about it at odd quiet moments. His parents, the particular details of his upbringing. A taking stock of what they had, before it was sliced through by the guillotine of Mother's death.

It's only recently he's understood that his were unusual parents: they did not observe the distance from their children common to aristocrats; they allowed them physical and intellectual freedom; they encouraged them to treat the servants with respect and as if they had equal rights, though they didn't, of course. "Before" held assumptions that he and Beatrice—maybe Cissy too, although she was so young then—did not realise until they were snatched away: trust in the myriad possibilities of their lives; the belief both parents would always be there to watch their futures unfurl.

An arc of tea-coloured slurry. It's a rumbling, tipping omnibus, the fault of that nasty hole near the corner of Poland Street—will it ever be filled? Arthur skips sideways; sees it splash up and under the raised skirts of two women looking for a gap in the crisscross traffic, instantly soaking their boots; hears their dismayed cries; strides on.

But Mother was taken from them, and in her place came deep, dark, aching loneliness and the sense that he himself had suddenly to become a man—surrender the softness of his youth, hide the tearing in his heart; the growing understanding that he must turn from intimacy with the remaining women in the family and join a club determined by his sex, that he must assume responsibilities beyond his years and fulfil, now, only Father's expectations. *You must be at Christ Church*, Father had exclaimed many times. Then, *You must join Lincoln's Inn*. And, yes, he knew why this was so important: William Gladstone had been at Christ Church College in Oxford and was then admitted to Lincoln's Inn. So he too must find his place in these communities of men: the monastic Christ Church, with chapel every morning, the tolling of Great Tom every evening, its cathedral and canonries, its debating and pranking; and Morrison's chambers in the Inn, the senior barrister's rooms fuggy with coal smoke and the sweat of young men competing for places at the bar, striving to become one of the wigged and cloaked.

It has its own joy, this world of men, its own rewards for challenges met and overcome, its own hearty back-slapping bonhomie. Even so, the call of his early years remains: the still-barely-there sensation of being held and cherished, of being listened to with an open mind, an open heart. It was Mother, of course—his father always busy in Parliament, or shut away behind a definite door—it must have been Mother. She is just a shade now, though the scent of lavender or the unexpected glimpse of his own eyes—the gentle dip at their outer corners—can raise her with a sharpness that makes him gasp, and a rook's harsh caw can return him to the moment he was told. And how she died? He's unsure when he found out about the stillbirth, but he does remember Bea telling him, years after that time of numbing fog, that it had been another son and that Mother had lingered with childbed fever for many days. He remembers that he understood his father's grief better after this, and that he drew closer to the man again after years of blame and distance. This past year has continued in the same vein: brought them mutual appreciation, a greater ease. Perhaps his new life as a husband has allowed a window to open on the view of his parents, previously lit—he sees it now—by the idealistic glow of childhood, then warped by the exacting righteousness of youth. Perhaps his marriage has permitted a new reckoning. Perhaps it is the workings of love.

A smiling man strides towards him as he crosses Dean Street. He reaches the other side, stomps his icy feet in their stiff boots, rubs and beats his gloved hands; sees the man do the same, his smile widening. Arthur laughs along with his glass counterpart and the warmth runs through his tingling body.

His father is a good man, he knows this now. A man who is warmly welcoming his new daughter to their Hierde House Christmas, a season he usually guards fiercely, as if to protect his reduced family from further catastrophe. A man committed to the nation, to finding solutions to all the problems this rush to the cities has brought—this dizzying propagation of machines, this animated trading with a larger, multitudinous world. And Gladstone has been his father's man, from his lowly beginning and all through the inordinate length of time it took his star to rise. *Finally, finally*, Father had sighed at the birth of the Liberal Party five years ago, and they'd clasped hands and downed ales and brushed tears from their eyes, father and son.

Yet there has been a change since then, a cooling that is only now finding voice. Why is Father suddenly pulling away from his idol? Does he not wish to be in Gladstone's cabinet when—one day, surely!—the man ascends to power? Where has his old enthusiasm for the game of politics gone?

New Oxford Street. Another ten minutes or so and he'll be there. The shops on either side of the road throng with women and men peering through plate-glass windows, exclaiming at boldly coloured trousers and the sparkle of gaslit dresses, milling in and out of store fronts, balancing parcels onto 'buses or into cabs. Father says this was a dangerous place, once upon a time, a rookery crammed with petty thieves, a maze of fetid courts and alleys to be avoided at night, or when alone. He says the new road changed all that, pushed the slums south and north. It's hard to imagine how it used to be, and sometimes it seems to Arthur, sitting in the drawing room with his wife in the evening, that there is little to separate them, London's rich and poor. They all drink the same water, after all, from cesspool to sink via the smelly Thames; they all suck in the same smoky air, feel it choke their bodies and their minds.

And in important Westminster, it seems a hardening traditionalism is now choking his father's mind, overcoming that early liberalism, the concern for those less fortunate, the emphasis on social equality that was so important to him and his wife.

His wife. Maybe that was when it had begun, that movement towards a newly tough yet brittle attitude towards the powerless and the poor. Maybe that was when Father had begun to shut down, as if the plucking away of joy had left him fearful of life. He'd lost, it seemed, his ability to believe in the possibilities of change, to trust in the fundamental goodness of things.

And now, even as Gladstone seems on the verge of supporting the gift of voice to the lower classes—a right to vote, perhaps, at last—Father draws further away from that original goal, provisos and qualifications hedging his comments about his old hero and his old hero's choices. And when he himself talks with Father, optimistic about the possibilities of further electoral reform, passionate about improved pay for the lower classes, laughing at the new and unfamiliar adulation of Gladstone in the provinces, then his father replies with a grunt, or the cryptic, *We'll see, shall we?*, his tone filled with presentiments of failure and doom.

How strange the way it has worked out!

Bloomsbury Street is a black soup of soot, powdered granite and horse muck, but the pavers are a dryish path over the road and the boy Tommy is here, as always, sweeping filth from the crossing, growling at challengers to his turf. Sometimes an even smaller version also wields a ragged broom. *Our Peter*, Tommy introduced him one day, and Peter bobbed, *Sir*, and bounced on bare feet. Sometimes a girl approaches with a wooden tray of oranges, a rope digging into the back of her neck. *Annie*, he's heard Tommy call her. All three have the same squat, industrious body and bowed legs, the same dark brown eyes, the same voice with an Irish cast. Now, as he strides across, Tommy approaches with the usual practised wink and outstretched hand—"Flip us a brown then, sir?"—and he gives the usual reply, dropping a penny into the urchin's grey fist: "For dinner then, Tommy." The lad always sports a scampish grin, but he is skinny and pale under the sticky grime coating his skin.

What tragedies has this boy had to endure? Does a whole family wait for the day's pennies? And so Arthur is reminded: no, we are not the same; I am one of the fortunate. The fog *is* browner here in St Giles, and even thicker down the side streets pointing to the river, the air more clogged with cinder and ash, the mud from rain and horses and chimneys more densely cluttered with broken glass, old newspapers, mouldering hats and shoes, and, sometimes, other ill-formed sludgy brown shapes he'd rather not guess at. His boots give a squelch as he gains the black-pasted footway, and he toes the torn glove that hangs at its edge—hard to imagine it ever protected the hand of any woman, let alone a lady.

But he must move on, even if his mind, unlike his feet, will not be turned from the slums and rookeries. They have not chosen to live in this muck, the beggars and vagrants, the poor and homeless. Though some of them are rogues and vagabonds, it is true, their lives filled with colourful dodges and thieves' cant, surely this would change if they were given opportunity, or if their children were born into a better world. A kinder world. *The people have turned against begging,* Father said at dinner last week. *Once they tolerated it, even looked with sympathy on those children trotted out to pull the coins from their purses—now, no more.* But Arthur himself is not convinced that public self-righteousness is the right approach, or that treating homeless people with cruelty will benefit anyone. They have not chosen to be without a home, after all.

What was it Mother said to him, all those years ago? *We must fend for those who are not able to fend for themselves.* Yes, that's it. Kindness and fairness are things it seems he could not leave behind. It's what first drew him to Gladstone: the politician's work with prostitutes; the support of his wife's charitable work—aid to orphans, to the victims of the cotton famine in Lancashire, to the homeless who slink in the shadows at day, only one step ahead of the bobbies. It's what continues to draw him to Tom: his passion for bettering the lives of the sick and impoverished, especially children.

He knows what Charles Reid would say to all this: "You hold yourself separate from that riffraff, my lad." And of the walks that skirt poverty, flirt with danger: "Why mix with those dirty ne'er-do-wells when you can take a cab, y'know. Waste of time!" Arthur would like to respond, "We need to guard against the desire to blame those who are different from us for their misfortune," but the words are like glue in his mouth. So he does not speak to Charles of his walks and has noticed how Emily, too, holds silent on the matter in her parents' presence.

But things are changing. He and Emmie have marked with relief the plans that are afoot—measures that will keep London at the heart of the civilised world, where it belongs. Like improving sanitation. He's read the papers' reports on the vast network of sewers mazing under the city; seen with his own eyes the preparation for a new embankment on the Thames, stonemasons consulting with engineers, pointing this way and that; spoken with Father about the drainage that will take the city's waste beyond its own reach. Progress, all progress. And the poor and unfortunate have not been forgotten: Tom speaks fervently about the refuge that gives supper to homeless boys in Drury Lane, just a stone's throw from this path he is making through London's hectic streets. *It's one of many*, his physician friend has assured him. *Shelters that give food, a roof in winter.*

A blur of movement through the fog as Arthur turns down Little Queen Street. An official-looking fellow running with cane aloft and, beyond, men jumping and laughing in flashes of blue and gold—acrobats, from the looks. Are they trying to outrun the beadle? Heading for Lincoln's Inn Fields to entertain holiday-makers? He'll do well to catch up with them! The beadle's coat flaps as he runs, then swells as he stops and collapses at the waist. Up close Arthur hears the *puff puff*, like busy bellows, and sees the drops of sweat, despite the cold, on the beadle's forehead. He should stop, commiserate or offer help, but the mischief suits his mood. And he must keep on, make chambers by nine, read through his lists and reacquaint himself with papers whose contents have been shunted to the back of his mind, all before racing to the courts. He'll be cutting it fine.

It's two and a half years now since he joined Lincoln's Inn and began his final training with Morrison. Eighteen months since being called to the bar, though it feels just weeks ago: the celebrations with his father and sisters, and with Emily, his then-fiancée, both of them overflowing with ideas and dreams. But being a barrister is no longer new to him. His heart no longer thuds a fierce tattoo as he approaches the courts, nor does he spend long nights worrying about troublesome cases. Morrison has him on Common Pleas settling civil disputes, reassuring or disappointing clients, pacing the stretched in-between hours up and down, up and down underneath the angels in Westminster Hall. Recently, the old barrister has threatened to move him to Chancery. *You have a fine brain, Rochdale*, he'd rumbled through his lavish beard. *Let's see if we can't have you sorting out some of the tangles.* The idea of being caught in Chancery, though, appals him. The serpentine coils of decades-long disputes, the stacks of papers curling with age, the stale court air that insists on sleep.

Lincoln's Inn Fields. The acrobats are quickly swallowed by the thick, yellow fog; top hats float on the pea soup, attaching themselves to heads only as he approaches; the beadle's pattered steps fade behind him. On dry days the grass of the field is inviting, but there are boggy patches in winter and he knows better than to test them. Instead, he skirts the top edge.

What he really wants is to make some kind of difference … And here his thoughts become oft-repeated imaginings: a gleaming future in Parliament; electoral reform to give those without voice the vote; legislation to enact better work and pay conditions for the poorest in the realm, so many of them right here, in the streets around him; electioneering in rural pockets—in his own candidacy, wherever that might fall in Derbyshire … perhaps Warwickshire—representing their interests in Parliament …

Sometimes he has to remind himself, order himself, slow down! Say to himself, you are only twenty-three, Emmie barely twenty. You have years ahead of you—years of happiness and unconsidered possibilities; years in which to create a life for yourselves, though Emily is impatient, for the imagined family, at least. And it is important to him, a matter of pride that he should provide for his family, even as his wife protests. *All in good time*, Father says. *All in good time*. So, learning the ropes at law, then building up capital through his work as a barrister and investing in industry under Charles's canny guidance. The rest, all in good time.

The gatehouse emerges from the murk, Old Samuel's cheery face an invitation. It's a home of sorts for now, Lincoln's Inn, its thrust and parry the complement to his homespun happiness with Emmie. He raises a hand and the white-haired keeper waves him in with a raspy, "Hoy, young Rochdale."

Soon he will welcome his eager colleagues. Soon he will gather the bundles of papers tied with red tape. Soon he will make his way, with all the other scurrying barristers and clerks, along Chancery Lane, powdered wig itching, black robe billowing like the wings of a rook that tests the wind and takes flight, trusting the air to hold it aloft.

Chapter 9

Perth, March 2008

Bars of light sneaking through the blinds. Creeping across an arm, silver threads of hair hypnotic. Morning talk shows, snowy teeth. Sips of water. Not too much now.

Standing, legs apart. Tipped forward, cheeks held open. A quick stream into the toilet bowl. The hissing brand. Skin bubbling and stripping. Oh, no.

Speckles of sun on floorboards. Midday movies and American doctors. Women stalked by men they trusted, problems sorted in an hour.

Warm stripes sidling over her back. Coarse rug against her legs. Detective novels. Red herrings and ingenious solutions. A burst of needles. The fresh knife up and in. Twisting. No. Please, no.

White slashes dissecting the bookshelves. News theme music trumpeting. Look busy in the kitchen.

Pulled from sleep. The consuming ache inside – outside? Her body? Her mind? Slinking to the lounge room, closing doors.

Eaten away. Sinews, tendons. 'Who am I?' Raw. Gore. 'Where have I gone?'

Throwing her body about. 'Fuck. Fuck.' Beating at the floor. 'God … oh, someone.' Pulling at her hair and face. Beseeching the night, 'Please, please.' Howling at the darkness, 'Fucking, fucking, take it away!'

The days. The lounge room. The doona and pillows. The litter of tonics and pills. The novels. The television.

The evenings. The dinner prepared in shifts. The plates of food on the coffee table. The conversation. The collapse on the sofa. The sound of dishes. The television.

The nights. The lonely pain. The crying. The retreat. The television.

The seconds. Minutes. Hours. Days. Weeks. Months.

I can't do this anymore. Her thoughts calm and collected. Reasonable.

The diagnosis was inadequate, the treatment ineffectual. Her ceaseless symptoms were more severe than the symptoms listed under 'vulvar vestibulitis' on the net. The constant suffering of a different order to the women whose words she had read: the women who despaired solely about pain with intercourse. If only.

I can't do this anymore.

Maybe it would be a relief for Duncan. Maybe he would – secretly, guiltily – be glad to be rid of her. He had never bargained for this: no sex and endless crying, all the unspoken appeals for help. The inadequacy of his response.

Why not, then?

Freedom from the sensations that invaded and colonised her thoughts. Release from the images in black and red: a bloody piece of meat, that gaping maw beneath, a mouth biting and shredding. Escape from that voice inside: you are useless; you are pathetic; no-one can help you – no-one wants to. An end to her violent nights: a city stormed; a woman with a cloven head fucking incessantly, unproductively; animals murdered, then raped.

No more horror on waking: it is me. *I* am the dreamer.

The smoke coiled around her, exotic and sultry. She closed her eyes and inhaled. Recreated the dream, its sensations and atmosphere. Dark, but the awareness of walls on every side. A temple. Claustrophobia. *I am alone and terrified. I take a step, arms outstretched, and touch a cold surface. Trace its intricate carvings upward and feel them slant in, towards me. I breathe in, but there is no air. I shout, but there is no sound. I remember: I have brought this on myself. I am buried; I will die here. Oh, what have I done?*

What had she done? Shudders rippled up her body, settling in a knot around her neck. Wait. She needed to have the suffering brimming at the edge of her mind, but she also wanted to sound strong. She held the sobs in her throat. Lowered the flimsy barricade of her will and allowed the pain to consume her until she became the scream at its core. Little left of Alice but the knowledge that she must appeal to a force in the face of which she was nothing.

Now. Do it now.

She opened her eyes and intoned.

> *'O goddess of men, O goddess of women, thou whose counsel none may learn!*
> *Look upon me, O my Lady, and accept my supplication,*
> *Truly pity me, and hearken unto my prayer!*
> *Cry unto me "It is enough!" and let thy spirit be appeased!'*

Her own cry rose to her mouth. Sh. Quiet now.

> *'How long shall my body lament, which is full of restlessness and confusion?*
> *How long shall my heart be afflicted, which is full of sorrow and sighing?*
> *Unto thee therefore do I pray, dissolve my ban!*
> *Dissolve my sin, my iniquity, my transgression, and my offence!'*

There was more, but it was all she could manage. She let her body fall back into the pillows and wrapped the doona around her. Pulled it over her head. Released the sobs lodged in her throat. Allowed her tears to soak the cotton till it moulded to her face, wet and salty. The raw complaint between her legs the same.

'What did you expect?' she demanded, her voice harsh in the small room. 'A goddess descending in a moon boat? A revelation? A frigging miracle?'

'Alice?' Shuffled footsteps. 'Alice!'

Ena's voice came through the door. Alice kept her eyes trained: the serial killer was about to strike.

'Alice.' The voice insistent. 'Are you there?'

Pen, now Ena. Why couldn't they leave her alone?

'Alice!'

She hit the off button. Drew her feet under her, wincing at the stretch and stab, then pushed herself up. Breathless. She was so weak these days.

Ena took her in as she opened the door. 'Alice. My dear.' The long t-shirt and leggings. No bra. Hair unbrushed, unwashed. Alice knew what her face looked like: pale and worn, eyes dark-ringed, lips chapped. 'My poor love.' Ena's arms came around her and Alice breathed in the familiar scent of butter and sugared spice. Before she was aware that she would even begin, she was crying. 'Come on now. Let's go inside.'

'I'm sorry, Ena.' The words broken.

'You've nothing to apologise for.' Ena walked her to the sofa. 'Now, what's most comfortable for you?' She sat herself down. 'Why don't you lean on me?' Alice slid into her sideways pose, crying harder and falling against the older woman's shoulder. Slid down further so her head was in Ena's lap. Ena stroked her hair. 'My poor dear. It's no better, is it?'

'It's never better.' She had to say it. 'Oh, Ena, I don't know how long I can keep going.'

'What do you mean?'

'I can't deal with this pain anymore. I can't.' The sobs harder. 'It's like a hole that's sucking me in. Until there's nothing left of me.'

'What else, my dear?'

She was a baby in her mother's arms. 'I need it to stop hurting, but everything makes it worse. Everything. And I'm so tired.' Ena rocked her gently. 'I can't go on anymore. I can't.' She stopped talking. Let herself cry and wail and moan while Ena rocked her. The minutes passed until there was nothing left but the pain, and Ena.

'You know the scariest thing?' Her voice calmer now.

'Tell me.'

'It's that …' She hesitated for a moment. How could she say it? 'When I think about doing something to myself, it's the most logical thing in the world. It's only now, when I'm telling you, that I can see how close I come' – the words in a rush – 'and that terrifies me more than anything else.'

'It *is* awful, Alice.' Ena's voice was sympathetic. 'The loss of all that you feel is yourself. The impossibility of continuing.'

'You sound like you know what I mean.'

'Well, I know what it is to live with pain.'

'Oh, Ena, I forgot.' Alice looked up at her face. The white hair that was, when Alice met her, still auburn. 'You know about the kind of pain that never goes away.' She considered all the years she had known Duncan's mother. Her support – which had only grown stronger since Joan's move to the other side of the country, how many years ago? Six? Seven? – her steadiness and constancy. 'It's hard when you're in agony but it's invisible.'

'Maybe it's a blessing.' Ena's voice was thoughtful. 'Imagine how it would be for other people to be conscious of your pain all the time. Their helplessness. And your own guilt at being the cause of their suffering.' Then, 'I know that Michael felt helpless around me.'

Ena did not talk about her dead husband often. The heart attack when she was herself still dealing with a torn and broken body, and trying to meet the demands of a small child.

'You never complain, though. You're so brave,' said Alice. 'Maybe I exaggerate it.'

'No, Alice.' Ena's voice was certain. 'I know you and I know pain. You are not exaggerating. You have probably been underplaying it, if anything.' Alice felt lighter at the words. 'Have you considered that you might be just as brave as me, but that your pain is simply more severe?'

'I don't know.' Another thing she could not understand: how do you measure pain? 'It's impossible for me to gauge. The whole thing is so peculiar – why I am even in pain at all – that I feel like something must have gone haywire inside me. As if it's not me living my life.' I sound crazy, she thought, but Ena nodded.

'Yes, I know that feeling. I remember having to get used to this body that no longer worked properly. Sometimes I felt I was possessed. Or that I was an imposter.'

'I didn't think anyone would understand.' Alice sighed. 'It's so good to talk to you.'

'I'm glad. But I'm also sorry I haven't been as available as I might. I didn't realise it was this bad. And I wanted to give you and Duncan space while things were so difficult.' Alice still did not understand the way Ena tiptoed around her son. Or Duncan's subtle distance from his mother, who was always so warm and sweet.

The familiar pressured ache brought her back to her body. She rolled sideways and out of Ena's lap. 'I must go to the loo.'

'Why don't I get us a drink while you do that? A cup of tea, that always helps.'

Alice watched Ena as she walked to the kitchen doorway, the awkward lurch at each step. She wondered when she had stopped noticing.

When she came back, the room was washed with light and the cups were already on the coffee table. Ena had realised she couldn't sit on the kitchen chairs. The little kindness brought fresh tears to her eyes.

'Can you tell me what the pain is like?' Ena placed herself at one end of the long sofa, leaving the remainder free.

Alice sipped at the tea. Held its astringent comfort, for a moment, in her mouth. 'It's hard to put it into words. Sometimes it's burning – but it's not the usual kind of burning. It's like ...' It was so hard to find words for the sensations. 'You know how you go each year to have sun damage treated?' Ena's skin was littered with freckles and with other markings, some browner, some paler than the surrounding skin.

'Yes.'

'And you know how he freezes the spots?' Alice had a plantar wart treated once, the cotton bud, loaded with liquid ice, drilling a deep ache into her foot. Years ago, when she had never imagined a pain so intense could last longer than those little minutes. 'Well, that's how it feels. A freezing that's on the edge of burning. When you can't tell the difference, you know? Only it's worse because it's spread all over.'

'And how often is it like that?'

'It can be for hours at a time.' The horror spilling from her mouth now, now that she was released. 'But that's just one kind of pain. There are other ones too.' How to tell Ena of the relentless grinding at her body and her spirit. 'I never have a moment without pain. It's day and night. It's endless.' The small sob was involuntary. 'Oh, Ena. It's as if this guillotine came down on my life and chopped it into two parts. I don't know who I am. And I want to go back to who I was. But I don't know who that is anymore.'

'You were a lovely, intelligent woman and you are still a lovely, intelligent woman.' Ena reached across and gripped her hand. Squeezed it tightly.

'Really?' Bitterly. Sadly. 'It doesn't feel that way to me. I feel useless. I *am* useless.'

'Is Duncan being supportive?' Ena's voice tighter.

'As much as he can be.' Alice felt the heat in her cheeks; the reluctance to confide too much. 'It's hard for him, you know. Hard to empathise when he hasn't had pain that never goes away.'

'Yes.' Ena's smile was wry. 'He's not so good with weakness – or what he perceives as weakness, anyway. But he is a good man, I think, fundamentally.'

Alice looked at the cover of the book. *Woman's Mysteries*. M. Esther Harding. One of the handful given to her by Joan during the first flush of her mother's passion for all things Jungian. *These are old, but good. Let me know what you think!* Back when Joan wanted to share her discovery with her daughter. Before she got the message that Alice was distinctly uninterested. The book had rested for years in a cardboard box holding the other mouldering tomes: Jungian texts on symbols, archetypes and dreams – even feminism. A copy of *I Ching* had been stuffed in there too, an unsuccessful birthday present. And a pack of tarot cards. The only item Alice had ever looked at was the cards, years ago. Their images drew her into another world and she hid them away in case she couldn't return to her own.

Duncan's judgement when he carried the box into her new home: *A lot of mumbo jumbo*. And, in reference to the books: *Isn't Jung a little passé?*

Not to Mum. But she bit the words back, before they could escape. Watched him push the box into the alcove and shut the doors on it.

She had been thinking of her mother more. Imagining her embrace. Because, reduced by suffering, she was a child again? Her mother messaged her daily and rang her every few days. Offering comfort rather than analysis. Finally. But she was so far away.

Strange that in her extremity Alice had been drawn to this past. That she had found the old box and dragged it from the alcove, its seams splitting with age. The book had sat on the top, an invitation that she accepted. She had flicked through its pages and stopped at the invocation – the hymn to Ishtar – its words speaking to her. For her.

Maybe the books held other rewards. Maybe the dreams she now recorded each morning held clues. Where else could she find knowledge or understanding when it was absent in medicos and their textbooks? When the internet only gave her forbidding words that offered no easy answers, like 'vulvodynia' and 'non-bacterial cystitis', only drew her into the suffering of other women, who repeated her own questions: *Does anyone know a reliable treatment? Why does nothing work?* She could not afford to be proud or dismissive. She would search wherever she could to find some way to crack the code of her mysterious disorder, some way to understand herself.

Was she so different from her mother, after all?

Lying on her stomach, books and paper the spokes of a wheel, herself its hub. Vulvar vestibulitis ... vulvar vestibulitis ... vulvar vestibulitis ... the words spinning the wheel of her mind into giddiness. Vulva: the site of her pain; vestibule: … vestibule, what? Vestibule … vestibule … dictionary anchoring … wheel slowing … ve … slowing … vesti … slowing and …

Stopped. *Vestibule: an antechamber … lobby* … A transitional space? And *porch of a church* … Entry to a holy place?

Scanning words that come after … *vestment* … *vestry* … and back, skimming pages, to *venerate* – was this connected? Flipping the pages … *reverend* … *revere* … Were these?

Returning to *vestibule*. Now, *a chamber or channel communicating with others*. The mouth; the inner ear, and that labyrinth at its core; the opening to the vagina. All these passageways between inside and outside. All these vulnerable, in-between places. Mind snagging: entry points to a holy place? Meeting point of humans and gods?

Eyes caught by *vesta*, higher on the page. Returned, again, to the primary-school class. Myths of ancient Rome. Gods and goddesses. Sun through the skylight illuminating the word on the board. *Vesta*.

The pad at her hand, the here and now: notes jotted just yesterday, drawn from that drowsy memory.

> *Vesta, virgin goddess:*
>
> - *Not represented in art as human (as were other gods and goddesses).*
>
> - *Present in flame kept burning at centre of homes and cities and in temples devoted to her.*

Turning to the dictionary: *Vesta, Roman goddess of the hearth and household*. Then *vestal … chaste, pure … vestal virgin* … Reaching for the book that came to mind. There … Plutarch. Taken as young girls from their families, made vestal virgins. Her hand flicking to the half-remembered words.

> *That they should vow to keep a Lease of their Virginity, or remain in a chast and unspotted Condition, for the space of thirty Years.*

Thirty years tending the sacred flame and whipped if it died. Buried alive if they broke the vow.

Chastity. Did they choose to take it?

A lithe young body dragged from a weeping mother. Smaller sisters and brothers grasping at bare legs. Was their sister lost to them? Was it an honour for the family?

The vestal virgin the gateway to holiness? The hearth its threshold?

Virgin ... that other meaning. That challenge to its modern understanding. The anthropology stack. Where? Holding the pile firm from the top. Sliding out *The Mothers* and the book beneath. *The Golden Bough*. Skimming the tabbed pages. Scribbling in her pad.

> *James George Frazer & Robert Briffault: correct translation of Greek word* parthenos *(e.g. applied to Artemis) not 'virgin' but 'unmarried woman' or 'unwed' – not woman without sexual experience, but one who was independent.*

Her pen scoring the page: *independent*. Fixing it in her mind.

This changed things. Permitted paradox. Vesta, the patroness of virginity; Vesta, known as 'Mother'; Vesta, inspiration for a cult with phallic emblems. And Artemis, chaste yet fruitful, goddess of childbirth. The other one ... Virgin goddess Ishtar, 'the Prostitute'.

A link between virginity and holiness? Where did it come from, centuries before Christ?

Christ.

The dream that had made even less sense than dreams usually do. Stretching for her journal. Scanning ... scanning ...

Here.

> *I am a prostitute. Though I can't have intercourse I am in high demand because I am so sexy. I have a boyfriend & I have a little lamb that I saved from slaughter. It follows me everywhere.*

The rush of meaning quick. *Mary had a little lamb, Its fleece was white as snow* ... Virgin Mary and Jesus, the Lamb of God.

She, herself. Virgin *and* prostitute? Sexual priestess – vessel for the divine?

What on earth did any of these whirling, spinning, weaving thoughts have to do with *this* pain? *This* suffering?

Slow down. And breathe. Finish them off, the thoughts. Let them settle where they need.

So. A portal. Where did it lead? An entrance. How could it be crossed?

Scanning the wheel of papers and pages. Dragging the bits and pieces towards each other. Images, ideas, memories, thoughts all swirling together. Letting them coalesce. Feeling them point, like an arrow, to that book – *Woman's Mysteries* – that tab – that quote. Philo of Alexandria:

> *For the congress of men for the procreation of children makes virgins women. But when God begins to associate with the soul, he brings to pass that she who was formerly woman becomes virgin again.*

Ah, of course…

Visited by gods. Made virgin, once again.

Chapter 10

January 6th 1865

Dear Bea,

Yes, we are home—though I feel we have left home too, so pleasant was it to be with my new family for Christmas at Herdley. Portland Place may be smaller than Hierde House, but it feels larger, just now: an echoing cavern in which I am nervous even to ring the bell for my Millie! But I must re-assume the mantle of housekeeper after our little holiday—after all, we had barely time for me to assert my authority as mistress of our London home between the honeymoon & Christmas, & now I must decide on further servants. I have dear Millie, of course, & we have Mary downstairs & Mrs Fennell, our wonderful cook, as well as the new tweeny, Gladys, & the yard-boy I told you about. Upstairs there's Johnson, & Nancy is doing a fine job as parlourmaid. What do you think? A coachman is probably most pressing ... I am dreading the idea of more interviews & decisions, especially with Arthur returned to work from Monday.

Will this ever come easily to me? Will I ever stop wondering why all these people should run around for us? It is something Arthur & I discuss often, this accident of birth, this set of circumstances that privileges us above others, & how awkward it feels to support better conditions for others less fortunate, while relying on them in our daily lives. We usually reassure ourselves that we treat our own staff with as much courtesy & respect as we can—&, of course, we look to the future & the possibility of Arthur having influence upon such matters as equality & suffrage in the political sphere ... Time will tell, as Mam says!

I am so pleased & relieved you plan to return to London before our soirée. You know how nervous I am at the thought of the important people who will be here. The Dowager Duchess preached Liberal politics at me on our only meeting & I did not know enough about Peel & his influence to answer her sensibly—I could benefit from further instruction if you have time? Lord Hargrave alarms me very much, but Arthur says I will find him a perfect darling once we talk. I cannot imagine it; I am sure they will all see through the veneer I have carefully painted over this trembling form. Yet I am excited at the same time, & keen to show society how well the young Rochdale couple conducts itself.

I have been "counselled" by the good Mrs Beeton & have decided to pull ideas from all her suggested menus for our party of twelve. Mam swears by her own white soup recipe, so I might add that, if Mary can find veal knuckles near the time … & Mam also suggests Scotch bread along with the other desserts, to bring in our heritage & remind them of the link to Gladstone. Will that be elegant enough, do you think? Please hurry to London, precious guide!

Your sister,

Emmie

January 30th 1865

Dearest Bea,

Is it my imagination or was the evening a success? How smoothly everything ran! None of the misfortunes I imagined came to pass: no burned turkey, no dropped platters, no servants in a pother … How strangely satisfying it is to host a successful evening & to have intelligent conversation to which I feel I can contribute. It has given me confidence to have more—& I am glad of this, as I know how important these connections are for our future. Which of the politicians should we approach next? Do you think a ball would be too much for me to organise? I know the season has barely begun & Cissy is yet to come out, but I have a certain gentleman in mind for her already … Can you guess who I mean?

We can put our heads together at dinner on Wednesday!

My love to you, dear sister,

Emmie

February 4th 1865

My dear Bea,

How well you know me already & the way in which I run ahead, scaring myself half to death! Yes, I would find arranging a ball dreadfully frightening; you are right to advise me, "slowly, slowly". A debutante ball at your Westminster home will be a wonderful way to show off our beautiful Cissy & an opportunity for us to plan together, while you bear the burden of responsibility. Thank you for your thoughtfulness. I have noted April 22nd in my diary; in the meantime, I can practise here with smaller dinners & "evenings".

I am so glad you agree with me about the Earl of Whatley: he is rather earnest, & older than Cissy might like, but he is kind, I think, & might settle Cissy's youthful giddiness. We will see in April … I do hope she enjoys coming out more than I did. It is rather discomfiting to wear an expression of happy unconcern on your face as you wait for a young beau to ask you to dance!

Arthur & I are about to take advantage of this cold snap: we plan to skate in Hyde Park this evening. Arthur insists he is terribly balanced on the ice & I insist he can be taught!

Love Emmie

February 12th 1865

Dear Bea,

I do apologise for my absence yesterday & am grateful for your concern. Don't worry, it is only a slight indisposition, I'm sure, & a niggling discomfort that is settling already. Will you be free to ride on Wednesday instead?

Emmie

February 22nd 1865

Dear Bea,

You understand your brother well. There is something worrying him: a client who might lose his living, if the findings are against him. Such cases upset him terribly. Though you say Sir George is grown "tougher" with age, I see a likeness between father & son, especially in their diligent sense of duty, & I am glad we can be of service to the male members of our family—to provide quiet advice & to ease their worries.

Arthur & I have decided that we will take on a housekeeper after all, & the other staff you suggest, even if it makes both Arthur & I uncomfortable. It is something we can manage by drawing on my money & it affords us a respectability that I'm sure will benefit our future. It would be helpful to have a housekeeper in place, too, before children come along & I am less able to manage a larger household. (I might sound as if I am all practicality here, but you know how often Arthur & I imagine our family-to-be!) In all seriousness, I must confess to fear when I think on it all too much—how could I not when I consider dear Mother's trials? That you & Arthur share my concerns, & that such concerns prey upon you, too, when you recall your own dearest mother, helps me to bear the anxiety & to trouble Arthur with it as little as I must.

Beatrice, I hesitate before asking you about marriage & children, because you say how content you are acting as a help to your father—both secretary & housekeeper in one industrious package, it seems to me—& how it satisfies your mind's calling. But I wonder, is there any small part of you that dreams about love & a family? And, if so, are these dreams locked away through fear of a perilous confinement? Pray forgive me if I presume too much in asking you these questions, but you are still young, after all, & it would be terrible to put such needs aside & miss opportunities that present themselves.

Your loving sister,

Emmie

February 27th 1865

My dear Bea,

Thank you for answering my questions, when I feared you might find them too presumptuous. I see now that we are different: while your independence is valuable to you—critical you say—I wish to devote myself above all to the domestic life & the sanctity of marriage. My goal is to be the best wife & mother it is possible to be, by understanding my husband's work & discussing what is important to us both, while yours is to constantly develop your intellect & to use your knowledge of social & political matters to question what is established—even to challenge this. But I am glad you have not discounted love entirely; you have many years ahead to change your mind, as you say. I can vouch for the contentment of married life & can confirm that, while I am not as free to make choices as you, or to carry them out, Arthur considers me in every important decision. It is a blessing to imagine our future years together & to continually discover that we are happily suited in all things.

Are you bored with me yet? Has my constant eulogising of your brother & our happiness wearied you? I will not apologise!

Oh, Bea. How contented I feel to be part of the Rochdale family. I cannot imagine greater happiness than this.

Your Em

March 8th 1865

Dear Bea,

How are you faring in Westminster? Spring is still hiding, but she has sent her messengers to us in Portland Place: the cherry blossom has <u>*burst*</u> *open, & I'm almost sure I heard a friendly cuckoo call this morning, but maybe that is wishful thinking! Still, I feel full of vim without winter's chill in my bones & quite ready to plan cleaning our stale home from top to bottom. I must ring for Nancy & Mary; I believe it is fine enough for us to launder* <u>*a whole houseful*</u> *of bed linen.*

I will see you tomorrow at our usual time. Hyde Park will be <u>*hectic*</u>*, with society's most fashionable enjoying this early taste of spring. I hope the horses aren't too skittish!*

Till then,

Emmie

March 10th 1865

Dear Bea,

No, it is the same problem I had some weeks ago: pain without obvious rhyme or reason. Maybe I should avoid unnecessary activity, for the moment, & see if it settles. And, yes, I would love you to visit me. I feel that I can be utterly myself with you—my muddled, nervous, unguarded self—in the same way I can with Arthur & Mam.

Your Emmie

March 14th 1865

Dearest Bea,

Better apart from a lingering niggle, thank you. But I am trying to ignore it & to get on as usual.

Do you remember our tweeny, Gladys? I am having all sorts of trouble with her. She picks fights with Millie & Nancy, & seems to generally sow discontent amongst the staff. Millie tells me Gladys is also a terrible gossip downstairs & chats too easily with tradespeople, so when she is not making little Mary cry, she is setting her a bad example. I am terribly afraid I will have to dismiss her, but I do want a harmonious household. What do you think? (Between us, I am hoping I can swap her for a nursemaid before very much longer. How happy Arthur & I will be, & how our little sons & daughters will love their aunty.)

Mam is hectic in preparation for their move to Harley Street. The house is perfect for them: there is space for Father's surgery on the ground floor &, upstairs, room for a commodious family home, so we will all be able to visit them regularly! Mam is very pleased to be moving closer to me & it will be lovely to have her "around the corner".

Love Emmie

March 20th 1865

Bea,

Thank you for recommending Mrs Wilson for housekeeper. I have several others to interview, but I feel I have already settled on her. She is altogether efficient, mature & courteous—the perfect combination.

Really, I do not know why I write so many letters to you, when you are only streets away. What will I do when you move to Herdley for summer?

Love Em

March 22nd 1865

Dear Bea,

We are planning an expedition to Swan & Edgar on Saturday. Mam wishes to look at some velvet for curtains & I have heard they have some new bolts of very jolly cloth. I know shopping is not your favourite pastime, but would you like to come with us? We can fetch you in the "growler" & after purchasing we might have luncheon in Regent Street … Say yes, dear sister!

Emmie

April 3rd 1865

Dear Bea,

If you wish to discuss supper details for the ball, I can be there straight after luncheon—I do agree that it must not become vulgarly lavish.

I am glad we have already secured musicians & settled on the dances. I think polkas will successfully weary all but the hardiest of the young, slow waltzes will allow for some intimacy without matrons having to become too outraged, & even we mature women will be able to enjoy our favourite quadrilles. I know which dance will be Cissy's favourite: how perfectly delightful it will be to watch her satin whirls about the hall!

Love Emmie

April 18th 1865

Bea,

Yes, it's the same trouble, I'm afraid, but the niggling has become sharp & burning. Arthur is worried & I am in such pain I hardly know where to put myself. It is a mystery I cannot account for.

I do not wish to be a nuisance, when you have so much to do before Saturday, but could you visit, do you think?

Em

April 20th 1865

My dearest Beatrice,

You are such a comfort to me. Your advice is practical & has settled my panicked thoughts—& you are right: it is a malaise difficult to discuss with Father, but he will know who might help.

As to your other advice: I cannot imagine not being there for my youngest sister at her introduction to society. I know you are concerned for my health & spirits, but I feel that I must be there, no matter what.

Oh, Bea, I wish I could feel myself again!

Emmie

Chapter 11

Perth, June 2008

This morning it was the bite that assailed her. Since reading about the *vagina dentata,* she pictured the gnawing sensation as a rapacious woman, all teeth and devouring intent, and sometimes woke with arms flailing against the jagged points of a mouth. *I press myself against the battlement of an unforgiving castle. Lean backward, away from the crazed woman. Grey sky looms. Her hair coils around me as I fall.*

In one *vagina dentata* myth, she recalled, the hero broke the teeth out of the vagina of a maiden and made her a woman. So many heroes in these myths … What would the maiden say if she could talk? Did she want to have those teeth cracked out?

She reached groggily for her journal and pen. Turned the pad around so she could scribble on the back of a page of dreams. Her brain stirred, drawing together fragments of thought.

> *Is the breaking of teeth a way of enabling the union of mature man and woman? A patriarchal fantasy of female subordination? E.g. a means of taming a woman and corralling her sexuality?*

A mumbled exhalation, then a cry. Duncan was asleep but protesting his own dreamscape. His long face was candid, childlike, the bristles and hairy shoulders incongruous. Once she would have been able to comfort him. Once she would have wanted to.

There, the bite again. She held herself rigid until it eased. Her disordered body was becoming more familiar: she recognised the way increased pain made it react – the tight throat and drumming heart, the lemon on her tongue and looseness at the base of her belly – and named it panic. She willed her taut thighs and buttocks to relax and reminded herself: long, deep breaths.

Sometimes she woke to the bite, sometimes to the needle or the clamp. The needling made her think of the pink satin of her old nanna's sewing cushion, its bulges riddled with pinheads. Then the flushed swelling and cruel pins became all that she was – she was nothing but that torn and tearing place between her legs – and anxiety rushed upon her in a wave. The clamp? Her father's array of tools one of the few childhood memories of him that remained, along with his words: *That's not a clamp, you dill. It's a Stillson.* Duncan had one, too, though she'd never seen him use it. *HEAVY DUTY* on one side of its handle and *DROP FORGED JAWS* on the other. The tool rusty with age. Who tightened that jaw so mercilessly? Who pushed pins into her softness?

Perhaps the worst was the iron: that 'hatchet-shaped' cautery tool. When Alice first saw the terrible words on her screen and tried to imagine the barbaric procedure, the searing of that iron branded her thoughts. Now, when the burn started up, or when she woke with it, she saw antiquated surgical implements and the men wielding them, and shrank away from herself.

So there was the bite and the needle and the clamp and the iron. There was never nothing. She was starting to forget how nothing felt and berated herself for not giving thanks when she had it. What she would give for the bliss of nothing, in this place of too much.

She slipped from the bed, wrapped her dressing gown around her and lifted the journal and pen from her bedside table. Closed the bedroom door softly behind her and stepped carefully to the kitchen, legs slightly parted. Poured water from the filtering jug into the kettle and took the whistle off. Lit the gas.

A cup of tea, that always helps.

Was it her imagination, or had the pain eased? She thought about the unbearable tumult of those sensations for which she could not find words. Was the amitriptyline starting to work? Or was it simply that the clamour was now so familiar she could name its separate voices? She must not allow this state to become normal. If she struggled against it with all that she was, it must leave – as suddenly and bizarrely, perhaps, as it had begun. She could overcome it. Surely.

The sun edged over the windowsill, bringing the bowl on the kitchen table to life, the oranges heaped within it glowing into and through its glass. The bowl's heavy solidity had been ugly to her at first, and she'd had to pretend a little when they unwrapped it after the wedding, so Joan wouldn't guess. But the gift had become reassuring over the years, with its dense, clear glass, more satisfying somehow. And the thought reminded her: she must return her mother's call. Pick up their conversation where they'd left off – that idea of psychological virginity, woman as one-in-herself. The sharing of insights still new and surprising, but something she had begun to welcome.

Crimson smudges of light grew on the kitchen wall and the sink gathered sharp glints. Alice shifted her weight. It was only morning, but already her body slumped wearily against the bench. She felt insubstantial. Wraith-like. She loosened the tie of her gown and lifted her t-shirt. Her belly was flat, her ribs jutted. Pain had destroyed her appetite and the anti-candida diet had further pared away her flesh. Now she couldn't retrieve the ability to nurture herself – not the woman she'd become, anyway. She, who was skin and bone and suffering.

Images came to her in glimpses: uniforms and a regimented holiday camp. She opened her journal and wrote quickly, before her dream was lost in the morning's post-medication fog.

> *Travelling in a bus with a group of women. Arriving at a 'camp' & realising a betrayal. Foreign women, buxom and strong, harvest meat from the newly arrived women – from us – in efficient cleaver swoops to the shoulder. Arms are thrown in vats as we move in line, wearied. Acquiescent ...*

The rest of the dream came in a nauseating rush.

> *... I manoeuvre myself to the end of the line, hoping they will have enough meat by the time they reach me. I try to reason with them but they are unmoved & I have no alternative but to have my arm chopped off.*

Water was bubbling and hissing at the kettle's spout, the kitchen window misting. She swallowed her queasiness, lifted her floral mug from its hook and poured boiling water over a teabag. Inhaled deeply and then breathed out, swirling the rising steam.

Six months on the anti-candida diet. Did Gibbs include patients who had not returned in her *ninety-five percent success rate*? Maybe the doctor assumed that no repeat visit indicated success. Alice recalled the GP's certainty and saw it now as smugness, felt a spike of anger. She would bloody well send a letter to Gibbs and all the other practitioners she'd seen, now she knew more. Include information downloaded from the International Society for the Study of Vulvovaginal Disease website, print it in large font, underline current terminology, highlight possible treatments in bold. So the next woman in line might be received with some knowledge; so the next woman might be responded to with some fucking compassion. Alice sucked in air. Felt a shudder of fury through her body.

Into the lounge. Cup and journal on the table. Gas heater on: *click, click, click* and hold. The tearing between her legs as she opened the door. Slowly. Across the verandah and down the red concrete steps. Reach for the Sunday paper, its plastic wrapping wet and gritty with sand. Gently now. A residual nip within the raw ache and a wince on the turn.

She took in the boxy shape of their home. The verandah pillars and the angel finial on the roof. Recalled her tactless words when Duncan first proudly presented his house: *It's a mausoleum!* But he had laughed and squeezed her shoulders as they stood together, right here, and it had become a joke. When they believed their love could trump any portent, when they thought it would survive disaster or ruin.

Alice sighed. She seemed to sigh so much now. Like an old person. Another as she climbed the steps, short-breathed. Another as she lowered herself onto the sofa, using her thigh and outer hip to take the weight as she slid into that reclining sideways pose. Like a bloody nineteenth-century hysteric, prostrate on a chaise longue, or whatever it was they used then.

She picked up the CD remote and pressed the repeat and play buttons. Music swelled against the walls and she pressed the volume-down button quickly.

She knew the Bach cantata so well now; she listened to nothing else when she was alone. It seemed to match her mood yet also to hold her, reassure her. The instrumental themes that repeated and grew, the calm voices in counterpoint. She had looked it up on the internet and laughed when she saw the subject of the 1599 hymn on which the cantata was based: the parable of the ten virgins in the Gospel of Matthew. Was this what Joan would call synchronicity?

Alice closed her eyes and sank into the cradle of music. Allowed the recurring question to form: *What do you think your body is trying to tell you?*

At least she might have a more complete diagnosis from the GP she first saw in April. Who said to call her Susan, not Dr Sutherland. Who admitted, *We don't know much about this condition*, yet had known more than all the physicians and gynaecologists before her. She'd listened to Alice intently, waiting till her words and sobs ran dry, had taken samples gently, giving reasons and explaining each action, did not press Alice when she baulked at the sight of a cotton bud and asked, *Could we do that Q-tip thing another time?*

Susan had run some tests and given Alice words she'd already seen, but turned away from: *vulvodynia. Generalised unprovoked vulvodynia*. Then she'd given her a new, it would seem more recent, word: *vestibulodynia*. Alice had protested that these important-sounding terms gave her nothing, really – *But vulvodynia just means chronic vulvar pain, doesn't it?* – and the doctor looked sympathetic, suggested she thought of all these words as a description rather than a diagnosis.

Alice sat up and sipped her tea. Cool already. She shifted the cushions to the other end of the sofa, her body onto its other side.

Medication, Susan had suggested. *Amitriptyline. An old-style tricyclic antidepressant*, she'd said ... *could sometimes reduce neurological pain ... the difficulty of diagnosis ... the need to be patient ...* Then, she'd outlined strategies to help reduce the symptoms: an oral antifungal, and oestrogen cream to thicken the vulvar tissue ... abdominal breathing, other relaxation techniques. Again, patience. Because pain caused stress and tension that fed into the pain. *A downward spiral*, Susan called it. A downward spiral: yes, that's exactly how it felt to Alice. As if she had been sucked into a vortex that had spun her around and down and into that great, dark maw. *We might look at physiotherapy down the track. I think you're too sensitive just now.*

Alice had tried the oestrogen cream, thinking caring thoughts as she smoothed it on, but after a couple of weeks it had begun to burn and she had to stop, well before the suggested three months. She had no idea if the oral antifungal did anything. The amitriptyline, though, was unambiguous. A tiny tablet that levelled her each evening, arriving so suddenly she didn't even have time to feel sleepy; Duncan had to shake her awake when he went to bed. But, oh, the blissful sleeps! The brief window of painlessness between consciousness and unconsciousness. Waking up in the morning dazed, but rested. Weekends only distinguished by Duncan's presence, who went to uni each day of the working week now, who no longer excused himself from work functions simply to be with her.

She swallowed her tea, testing residual nausea. Thought about the submission of the women in her dream, lining up to have an arm chopped off. Her own resistance. Still fighting against that invisible enemy who would strip everything from her, leaving only a torso, or bones, or a screaming vulva.

Was there another way? Recently, she'd sensed something in herself. An impression – like the pillow seam ridging her face on sleep-logged mornings. Where was that dream? She searched through her journal till the remembered words caught her eye.

> *Ugly, primitive cone-shaped creature with shell-like structure & teeth at the mouth. I/the girl know/knows what must be done with it. She lies during the night on a log resting in brackish water with the creature & most of her body submerged. And in the morning, miraculously, the creature has transformed into a little being, like a little pink girl – pink-skinned, large-eyed, with a dot/mark/its name on its forehead.*

The pink girl brought an image to mind: cherubic infants in a watery world. She clambered to her feet and scanned the bookshelves. Ah, *The Water Babies* – there it was.

Placing the book and her journal on the rug near the heater, she lowered herself to the ground, rested her weight on her elbows and was immediately absorbed in the colour plates. The chimneysweep made clean and new. The frilly gills around Tom's neck and, here, Ellie's. The two of them embracing underwater. Marked as between worlds. Or initiated into an unfamiliar world and able to survive. Even thrive.

Was that possible? She read the dream again, thinking about the teeth at the mouth of the creature that became this miraculous girl. Was this some form of toothed vagina? She picked up her pen and wrote below her early-morning questions,

> *The Freudian model: girl-woman abandons clitoris as inferior penis and embraces vagina as primary site of sexual pleasure. Is my cone-creature dream a recommendation to remove the teeth from my vagina? Am I stuck at an early stage of sexual development, my passage to being a 'real' woman delayed?*

But her written curves were marred by blots and angles, and she wondered at her own reluctance. Something more subtle and interesting was meant, she was sure of it. She considered the dream again, recreating the atmosphere within it and remembering her feelings when she woke. Her excitement at the girl, and the breath of hope.

> *Is the discovery of these primitive teeth a necessary prelude? My illness the trigger for transformation into a new being? An initiation? Are 'teeth' necessary – to protect, to discern, to 'digest'? And how does this relate to the psychological virgin – whole, self-possessed and the property of no man or woman, independent, yet with the ability to give freely –*

A heavy tread reverberating through her belly. Duncan. He walked over to the heater, twisted the knob. Yes, she realised, it was hot and stuffy now.

Alice saw the room through his eyes: the books, the doona, the incense set and ready to burn. Heard the Bach cantata through his ears. *The dirge*, he'd pronounced when she first discovered the piece of music that sounded, to her, like a story. Strange that two people could hear the same composition in such different ways. 'Sleepers Awake': the union of Christ and the wise virgin a cause for joy, surely. Though he hadn't stuck around for the final movements. She pressed pause and registered the heavy silence, saw that he was dressed already. It felt like an accusation.

Duncan lowered himself into the armchair facing her. Passed a weary hand over his face. A talk, she realised. He is readying himself for a talk.

'Look. I know how hard this is for you,' he began without preamble, and stopped. Looked at the ceiling, gathering his thoughts. Did he? she wondered. Could anyone who had not felt this pain comprehend? 'But sometimes I wonder if you encourage it, indulge it a little with all this, this ... self-absorption.'

She dampened the quick rush of anger. It seemed impossible to explain, when his understanding had so many gaps. But she must try.

'I don't have any choice about going into this – about going deep. The pain takes me there. The only choice I have is what I do while I'm here.' She pulled at her tracksuit pants, loosened their clawing at her buttocks. 'I've tried escaping, but the pain is too much.'

'Can't you fight it?'

'Sometimes it hurts so much it's all I can do to just survive.' It was an appeal, the first time she'd hinted at the possibility. 'But, you know, I do fight. I fight against it with all that's left of me. And I tell myself I will not be this person in pain.' He was listening attentively. 'But it's not getting me anywhere and nobody seems to know enough to help. So then I just feel like shit.' Could she share the remainder? 'If I can't get away from it or fight it, then maybe all I can do is listen. So that's what I'm trying to do. Through what my body tells me. Through dreams and myths and symbols. And I know that makes me look weird and not like the person you know. But, Duncan, I don't have any other choice.'

'Alice, I don't see that.' He rested his hands on his knees. 'Look. I love you – I do. And it hurts me that you hurt. But what *I* see is this beautiful, smart woman going down a path that just makes her sadder. And I wonder if that's necessary.' He leaned towards her. 'Isn't it possible that the symptoms are nothing to do with needing to change yourself – that this is just a physical problem that needs to be sorted? That before long you will come across someone or something that helps?' His voice was clear and sure. So unlike her faltering defence. 'I don't want you to look back and think, "What on earth was I doing all that time?"'

'Duncan, it's just –' How to explain. 'It feels right, you know? Like when you started the biography. Remember?' She could hear the appeal in her own voice. Its supplication.

'But think about all your work to build up the teaching. Do you imagine they'll hold those units for when you're finally able to return?' His questions had the bite hers lacked. 'And think about this research position. I know you're not being paid for it, but it's important. It's a relationship with the university that needs to be nurtured. That will help you in the future.'

So. These thoughts had been circling within him, pent up, waiting for the gate to be opened. But she couldn't say this, just as she couldn't tell him that leaving uni also gave her space. From other people, but also from him. How could she possibly say this?

'If you're going to stay at home for months on end,' he continued, 'why don't you use the time to submit more stories from your PhD? Or put some energy into getting the collection published?'

'Because it's not who I am anymore.' Duncan's eyes widened. Even she hadn't known this till she said it. 'Or not the *only* thing, anyway.' She paused for a moment. Gathered her courage. 'Maybe I can go sideways,' she said. 'Aim to write, but make it about this disorder. Start with some research. About the history behind it. About what it does to women. About the process, the arduous process you're forced to endure with this relentless, never-ending pain.'

She didn't tell him that she had already begun: jotting down research topics, propping herself on rolled-up towels when she drove to pick up books from the uni library.

Duncan shook his head. Walked to the window. Placed the flats of his hands against his lower back and leaned into them, flexing his body, easing an ache. He turned to face her again. Spat it out: 'You sound like your mother.'

The strength of her anger was a surprise. For a moment she felt invigorated, then the energy ran out of her like sand.

Where was she? Wandering where the certain light of his opinion was swallowed by darkness. Alone in an underworld he could not visit. Trapped in a realm for which he had no token.

They watched the program together, hands intertwined. A softness admitted, a peace of sorts brokered.

In the light thrown by the TV, Duncan's face was unlined – years younger than the man who had challenged her that morning. When she saw her husband like this, it was easier for Alice to believe the best of him. To think again about how her illness must affect him, this man with his sharp, directed thoughts, his ability to shape creative solutions from complex problems. But worrying about his place in this – about how he would love to be the cause of improvement, or how she might soothe his hurt feelings – only made her feel guilty. Reduced. And there was so little of her left, she couldn't grow smaller. Could she?

On the screen, buffalo forged a river somewhere in Africa. The narrator described the action in a hushed voice: 'There – predators wait hungrily.' Opportunistic snouts and eyes poked from the surface of the water. 'The young and the sick are especially vulnerable.' Alice did not enjoy these nature docos as Duncan did, especially now. The battles and blood. The fight for survival.

If they could only have sex. *Proper* sex. Not these fraught encounters in which more and more parts of her body felt off limits, unsafe.

How could she tell him that she could hardly bear his touch? How could he believe in their love while she rejected him? How could she reassure him of her own desire, when, if she moved to touch him, the rawness stabbed, as if she were caught on barbed wire? Her mind, too, was unequal to the task. What she needed was an embrace without demand. This new Alice could no longer meet Duncan's demand, and she realised – with a start, with a sense of desolation – that he was powerless to help her.

Duncan was absorbed. Alice refocused on the TV. Had the buffalo survived?

It was raptors now. Monkeys screeched and flung themselves from tree to tree and the two birds circled above. 'They are watching and waiting,' said the voice-over.

Was the rift between them solely because of her illness? The new, pained Alice questioned all that had gone before. Suggested there was a flaw in the foundation of their relationship. Wondered if the baby she had imagined, it seemed like years ago, would have been a mistake, anyway. But could she trust the thoughts and feelings of the new Alice? Was she a superior version of herself – more insightful, more mature – or a hag who no longer saw the good in her husband? Who now saw the world itself through a glass, darkly? What did she make of herself? Of their marriage? Obscure doubts that had hidden within the folds of her pain, only to emerge now, as she tried to translate the language of her suffering.

'But the raptors have a strategy.' The narrator's voice again. 'While the monkeys, from their swaying seat in the tree canopy, watch the male disappear, his mate flies in behind unnoticed. Ready to swoop.'

Alice closed her eyes.

From the moment of meeting, Duncan had provided an answer to her world. And she had always believed that he looked to her as some kind of compass. That life made more sense for both of them in each other's company. For what other reason had they married? She remembered their early melding and nights when he'd recounted his childhood troubles: his mother's many hospital absences as her body was remade; the loss of his father just as Ena was returned to them, fixed, after a fashion. Alice had held him as he cried, felt his need for her in those boyish tears.

But when she looked back through the eyes of her new self, she read a different story. A young woman in the grip of an older, seemingly smarter, man. A woman who had bent herself into the form defined by his interests – his beliefs. Her thoughts and hopes fenced. The compromises made to bring him pleasure a slow whittling away at herself.

She allowed it to return: the end of that terrible phone conversation with her mother, years ago; the words she had tried to keep at arm's length ever since. Recalled the phone in the corridor of the share house and the old stained-glass front door through which afternoon sun had poured. Her body bathed in colour and youthful ire.

You understand what I mean, Alice. Duncan took advantage … Nineteen! Why didn't he go after someone his own age?

Why should he?

Alice looked back at her younger self. Realised that Joan's dismay only fused her more closely to Duncan. Understood that all of Joan's misgivings about Duncan – why he was drawn to someone impressionable, naive … why she herself responded – only drove mother and daughter further apart.

She remembered her own righteous anger that day. Her digs at Joan acting the analyst, and then, broaching the news. *Anyway, he's asked me to move in.*

There'd been a hush. A pause when she'd wondered what her mother was thinking. Heartbeats when she'd hoped this new status might change things.

But – and her mother's words had come in a rush – *Oh, Alice, I'm worried about his hold over you.* She'd gone on, Joan, said something about Duncan himself and who he was in the world, about *what* he was, *grandiosity* and *needing admiration* and *excessively demanding* flowing like something viscous through the phone line. And then, *then*, that quiet sentence, *Sometimes I look at him and think …*

Alice had made her voice weary, she remembered. Ironic. *What do you think, Mum?* The tears that hid behind.

I wonder whether he is a narcissist – the personality disorder, I mean.

There, they were out. The horrible words a diagnosis. A judgement. And, just as momentously, her decision had been made: she would say yes. She would move in, make Duncan her family. Maybe Joan would come around, she'd reassured herself. But they never had that make-up conversation. And Alice didn't know if that was because Joan felt too embarrassed, or because she had not come around. Would never come around.

Was it a betrayal to recall the words now? To admit their possibility?

Narcissist. Her bloody know-it-all mother.

Personality disorder. The words that rankled and rumbled, growing more potent with each unspoken year.

Despite their new warmth, she wanted to ring Joan and accuse her, force her to carry some blame. Tell her mother that she could no longer wholly believe in her own husband. That she doubted their ability to recreate that space in which they had affirmed their love and desire. That she might never again trust the embrace that initiated this horror.

Her face was wet. She blotted the tears with her sweater and opened her eyes to a burst of motion.

'Look!' The raptor had grasped a small monkey from the treetops. 'There is no escape now.' The bird flew with her prey to an outcrop of rocks, then thrust large talons into the belly. Her wings were outstretched; she raised her proud head and scanned the sky.

'Isn't she beautiful?' Duncan's voice was resonant with awe. She loved that about him: his eager curiosity about the world.

She loved him.

What if this disorder were to disappear tomorrow? Would the crippling doubt in that love reveal itself as a chimera? An effect of pain? Of despair? Surely she could – no, *should* – work harder to safeguard their marriage. To hold onto the remnants of what had been between them. She called back the memories. The week away last year that had shown her something different: their love and the thought of a living proof of that bond. When she recovered, they would return to that point – even plan that future. They would see the softness in each other and laugh together again.

It had been good. She must remember.

The raptor's cape-like wings shielded the dead monkey from the view of other predators. 'Mantling,' the narrator pronounced. Alice could see the monkey's milky underside. The scattered splotches of brilliant red. Her skin prickled, top to toe. She could feel the pecks to her belly, the tearing at her innards. Glistening membranes ripping.

She moved closer to Duncan and he put his arm around her. She leaned into his long body. Became heavy and slack. Ah, here it came: that tiny, sedating pill; that nightly bulldozer. Her eyelids dropped. A glowing afterimage: the monkey's white belly and the raptor's pale eye, the round absence at its core. Then the heavy surge rolled over her body and she fell into that black hole … going, going …

'Alice.' Her shoulder gripped. Shaken. 'Alice, come on. Time for bed.'

She lifted her eyelids. Saw a shadow hovering over her, its wings darker than the night-filled room. Mantling. Was it shielding her? Preparing to eat her?

She couldn't move her arms or legs. Couldn't fight the shadow, or the heaviness. The blackness came again and carried her away.

Chapter 12

London, June–September 1865

She is not a topic of conversation. Despite her beauty, despite that elusive quality that pleases the eye and fosters the affection of both men and women, despite the care with which she listens to them, gently drawing from them their apprehensions and attending to their joys, rendering these fashionable people deeper and more true, despite all of this, she is no longer discussed. It is as if she has been forgotten by society, has never even existed, after being absent for—what, how long? Nine weeks. Only nine weeks.

Is it diffidence on society's part? Concern for her, for him? Or simply a determination to build an unbreachable wall against something that has not been explained—that can never be explained? Do they sense disorder and pull away from its contagion?

Emily isn't a topic of conversation; nevertheless, when he is not with her, she is all he can see or hear, and he must struggle to banish her beloved form from his mind, wrestle with the urge to leap to his feet and summon his carriage so he can race home to her. Even at this instant, on this fussy society evening, when he looks at the people who surround him, it is not them he sees, but Emmie in all her guises: it is her intelligent forehead he finds in the Duchess of Aldington's arch brow, her confident bearing that straightens General Leyton's stoop, her pliant willingness that softens Lady Darch's intimidating bosom, her musical laugh that overlays de Courtenay's pompous posturing. Even in her absence, Emmie obscures them all.

She has turned away from society—withdrew at first reluctantly and with tears of disappointment, then deliberately, with an air of quiet stubbornness. The debutante ball in April, the celebration of Cissy's coming out: that was her last public appearance. There she sat in one of the nests of chairs edging the ballroom, battling her body, her face drained with effort. Only he and Beatrice, whose worried eyes met his, really knew with what pain she must be dealing to be unable to respond with her usual kindness, her winning interest in those around her. She rose, tried to speak with other scattered guests, her weary shoulders curling; she hovered in the corner of the hall, face wan. Then Cissy's plump body whipped past his own chair, was whirled about the dance floor, her face shining out at her admirers, and when he turned to look again, Emily had vanished.

It was in the chill air of the balcony that he had finally found her, leaning over the balustrade—her shoulders shaking, her hot breath clouding the air—and he'd gathered her to him, smoothed the lines of pain that scored her forehead and bracketed her mouth, and whispered words of comfort while she whimpered like a small animal, holding the worst of her distress inside, for Cissy's sake.

Come, he'd said. *Let's take you home.*

And now? Now he must attend these society dinners and balls and daytime jaunts alone, at Emmie's insistence, even as they mean nothing to him without her. For she is concerned with their place in society, she says, and he knows this to be true, but still he wonders what she does when he is not home with her, wonders how it is to be free of his presence and the weight it seems to place on her. And so they continue the illusion that hers is a passing indisposition, even as it drags on week after week, even as she disregards elegant carriages outside their front door and the calling cards that are left with bewildered servants, Millie wringing her apron in uncertainty and dismay.

And when he rushes home from these interminable gatherings, eager to see his Emmie again? Then he finds the stranger who, it seems, has taken her place.

The horse's hooves might be rattling, the reins flapping, London's streets whizzing by in a blur as they race along the Strand, but he himself feels like a wheel grinding a stationary, ever-deepening rut. It's been two years now on Common Pleas and suddenly he feels fed up. Heartily sick of it all. The legal institution has become too familiar, with its tangle of corruption and conservatism, each day bogged down in endless, pointless ceremonies, while he winces at the lack of respect for jury members amongst his fellows, the bullying of clients and witnesses—the badgering that twists their words and traps them in contradictions, until they stutter into silence, twisting their hands in confusion. It's a game, he sees now, a never-ending, ham-fisted game, and sometimes he wants to throw his own hands in the air at the inefficiency, at the sheer waste of it all, even as he learns the rules and plays to win.

Would the Queen's Bench be any better? More purposeful, more ... productive? He's visited the Old Bailey, seen the goings-on: the charges of larceny, rape, murder and so on—more interesting, by far, than disputes about property and tussles over debt, as well as graver in effect. But the passage of justice is no less flawed in the criminal courts, surely, if sometimes defence counsel is not even permitted, if in serious crimes the accused cannot defend themselves, or question their sentence?

The cab wobbles, slows, then pulls to a near halt. Dust swirls over the doors and into the cab, billowing against him, and he pulls the kerchief from his breast pocket to shield his face, knowing that by tonight his hair will be full of the grit and grime of the city, the creamy linen at his wrists filthy with it. Once, he would have anticipated cleaning up properly at the courts, but he knows too well now how unlikely that is: towels, combs, even water, are scarce in the robing room and the place stinks like an overflowing cesspool.

The cab driver wheezes behind him and clears his throat with a hacking cough. Wellington Street: that's why they've slowed. It's humming, as always, clouds of dirt rolling from beneath the feet, hooves and wheels destined for Waterloo Bridge, that stream of traffic flowing against his, 'buses jamming up behind and around their cab. But they are still moving at least, and there is the reason for the delay: a 'bus horse upended in the middle of the crossing, legs flailing and the driver taking to it with a whip, the whistle and crack arriving moments after the downward sweep of the man's arm. Arthur winces at the casual cruelty—the pointless attack on a helpless beast—but then he hardens himself. What difference could his concern possibly make, anyway?

Lately it seems to him that London is full of them: helpless beings he is unable to help. Look at the poor, those downtrodden by the classes above them; what justice is in the criminal courts for those with no money to pay, no access to some kind of public defence? Does punishment benefit anyone turned criminal through poverty and circumstance? Those narrow, dark cells in Newgate Gaol have stayed with him, along with the yard in which the prisoners must take exercise. Exercise! The sunken enclosure is like a long chimney and the men trudge at its shadowed base as if they are turning the workings of Hell. He's witnessed a hanging, too, heard the crowd in the street roar and bay like animals as the skinny man jangled and twitched into death. Afterwards, Arthur walked away as quickly as he could, as if he could leave the image behind.

Maybe it's time to reassess. As a barrister he can do little to help these unfortunate wretches, but as a politician he might have some decisive effect, influence the will of Parliament and push for legislation that might aid London's sorry, heaving mass of humanity. He will speak with Father again, see if he has suggestions about a seat—though Father has grown stiffer still over the last year, his ideas calcifying … Anyway, there will be time for talk once Emmie is at Herdley and he going to and fro, balancing his different, disparate worlds. Only two more weeks and, pray God, the sweet air and Bea's ministrations might alleviate the pitiful torment of his wife.

The air is full of the Thames's stench; it is only their passage along the Strand that whisks into the cab a semblance of freshness at which he sucks, cursing the heat and stink of London in the summer. Why, even the trees look miserable, their leaves blackened; even the feathers of the birds perched on the statue of Charles I seem to droop despondently. And he knows his cynicism, even despair—the way he sees his work, the city and the plight of its people—is coloured by the helplessness he feels every time he thinks of Emily. But this makes no difference to his mood, to his sense that everything is hopeless. Sullied. And it seems to him, as they rattle their slower way down Parliament Street towards Westminster Hall, that something vital has withdrawn from him over the last months. Faith in the legal system. Perhaps faith altogether. The worship at All Saints seems a dream to him now, his gratitude for his fortunate life and, most of all, for the miracle of his wife, premature, some kind of punishment. God's joke on him, his pleasure, his celebratory pride.

The cab is slowing, pulling up at the water trough in New Palace Yard, and he must remove himself, busy himself with clients, carrying Emmie's pain about with him like a weight he cannot put aside. *Will* not put aside.

Oh, if only he could help her!

*

It will be late by the time he gets to chambers, but there are no clients until the afternoon and he must speak with Mrs Wilson, still new to the job, see how she is coping with a mistress effectively absent, ask how she is managing the preparations for his wife's journey to Hierde House, all this before Emily and her mother return from the consultation—yet another physician specialising in "women's complaints", yet more pills and potions. Thank goodness the housekeeper was engaged before Emmie became so ill and that she has taken it upon herself to make sensible decisions without troubling them. Without troubling his wife.

He hears the roar as he leaves the library, another as he trudges up the stairs. When the wind is in the right direction, they can hear them from Regent's Zoo, those exotic lions; picture them pacing behind their bars, demanding meat, their claws and teeth sharp and keen.

He goes through the bedroom, quietly enters the dark chamber beyond, now claimed as hers; eyes the narrow bed that has replaced, for her, their cosy nest with its tousled bedclothes and his ready embrace. *I must be alone*, she'd said. *I have hardly the strength to be in my own body*. And when he'd entered this chamber one day without knocking, thinking to ease her loneliness, her hands had made fluttering movements like birds trying to take flight, and she'd blurted out that she couldn't tolerate the presence of another person, their unspoken expectations … and he knew that she meant *him*. That *he* was another person. She cried and apologised, over and over, as he made to approach her, as he backed out quickly without a word.

It is damp here, the coals cold in their hearth. The new couch is naked save for a pair of lady's drawers strewn over it, legs without feet. Emily retreats to this so-called spinal couch regularly now, clutching at herself, and he can't help but resent the object for the time she shares with it, the tears she weeps on it that should be shed in his presence. Was purchasing the couch a sound decision? How much of the back pain that has now joined the list of her other, private, pains is a true part of that complaint and how much simply a result of the way she must sit now—when she *has* to sit, for convention's sake—her hips forward and posture slumped? Does it benefit her to closet herself away from the natural light, the busyness of the everyday?

He sniffs and turns, draws in the unfamiliar scent, finds it most pungent at the cabinet next to the bed: musky, like newly turned earth; bitter, but swaddled in cloying sweetness. Laudanum, perhaps, prescribed by her father, who does not seem to know what else to do, apart from recommending physicians and throwing out words that mean precisely nothing for all the good they do. *Unmoored*, he says. *Nerves.*

But the outlandish words do fit this stranger, somehow, this new wife who is at turns excitable and despondent, restless and inert, buoyant and despairing; whose steps he hears in the night, boards creaking under her sleepless feet; whose muffled sobs and wails reach him even in the stillness of his study; whose joyful, tuneful voice has surrendered to a querulous and fretful tone he tries not to dislike.

The bed is as yet unmade by Millie and the disarray reminds him of something, the tatters of clothing and bedding return a memory: the ragged feathers of a rook in their yard yesterday, its torn and crimson-flecked wings spread as if in flight; Ginger standing over the blue-black corpse yowling proudly, waiting for praise, his own striped and gnarly body smaller than his prey's; the old tom fighting ferociously for his prize as the yard-boy tried to reach the bird's body, do away with the mess.

In these times everything seems to remind him of violence, and to bring back childhood feelings he'd thought left long behind: resentment at being so needed, helplessness in the face of an appeal, guilt at his own incapacity. If only there were an enemy, if only it would show itself, then he would fight it. Be her champion. Why, it was only short months ago that he felt—no, *knew*—his love could overcome this obstacle. For Emily had turned to him trustingly when the pains first began, and he'd soothed her when she cried *It burns*, held her when she returned from the water closet, clutching her belly, walking in a strange, halting motion so unlike her usual grace. And when, in the quiet night, she sobbed her dismay—*I hate to disappoint you, Arthur, but it stabs and I cannot, I cannot*—he assured her that his own needs could be put aside, that his love for her was not dependent on love-making, that he would always care for her, no matter the complaint. He'd felt protective, strong enough to carry her through this ordeal, even when it had no name, even when finding the words to describe it made them both blush, even when it struck at the very heart of their marriage.

But he has not been able to help her and now something is changing between them, has already changed. It seems to him that she cannot forgive him for his inability to solve this terrible mystery—or does he imagine the accusation in her eyes? He does not imagine his own guilt; the relief as she turns inward and away from him.

The journal sits by her bed. It travels with her around the house as she moves from place to place, unable to find comfort or ease. She scribbles in it at her little portable desk, reads it avidly, treats it as her closest companion, confesses to it, perhaps, and no longer writes her almost daily letters to Beatrice. And so, it seems, she is turning away from his sister too.

Now his fingers itch to open the journal and he thrusts them in his pockets, swings his body around the chamber, thinks to conjure something precious, leave a part of himself here, in this, her refuge. Something to reach her, remind her, bring the old Emmie back to him. For she can't have gone far, can she? His Emmie, her face alight, her gaze always running ahead to a precious something she might catch if she were to run or skip or laugh with joy. His Emmie, understanding his own childhood loss, knowing the way that grief can break time down, make each tiny moment a pocket of existence that swells and becomes forever. His Emmie, singing her trust in life's goodness, lifting her praise to the heavens. His Emmie, who if you were both starving and had only one morsel of bread, would give it to you without thought. His Emmie, whose shade comes to him at night as he hovers between sleep and wakefulness, pulling him into her with a ragged exhalation, groaning in pleasure, cradling his head against her breasts.

That roar again. He feels it roll through his body and reverberate through his mind, trespassing on all he thought to keep safe, threatening its very existence.

They cross Devonshire Street and continue towards Regent's Park, their feet finding a matching stride, just as they used to all those years ago at Rugby School. Arthur feels his body shifting as he walks—tense shoulders dropping, taut face releasing—and in the thick, grey silence he is almost able to think himself into someone other than a man with a tormented wife; is glad now for Tom's insistence: a walk through the breaking day, just as they used to in that last spell at Rugby, the masters less strict as their charges became men. And now, when he senses Tom smiling beside him, he is again a carefree school fellow, off to make some mischief with his friend.

The homes of Portland Place are still shut against the night, the only signs of life a servant girl emptying slops and a sweep tucked into a doorstep waiting for the household to rise. Under a streetlamp at the corner of Park Square, a bobby sags wearily inside his uniform, lifting himself to attention to return their greetings, pretending only now to notice a vagrant rousing himself for another hopeless day and shooing him along. A black cat slips shadow-like over the road, its rakish glance at Arthur conspiratorial, as if recognising him for another creature of the night.

They pause for the market cart laden with fruit baskets, then cross the Outer Circle and make their way onto the Broad Walk. The park is monochrome in the dawn, its pathways empty. Several blackbirds sing from the small trees.

Arthur draws his coat more tightly against the nip of autumn. It should take them thirty minutes, he calculates, walking slowly and with conversation. Primrose Hill in time to see the sun rise. He must do as he planned while they walk, as he and Tom planned together: speak about Emily and what ails her. Despite his reluctance, he knows he must.

It's not that he lacks faith in his friend. He trusts the bond forged years ago, when Lawler stood to support him in that terrible fight with Rattlin. For even with separations along the way—himself at Oxford, Tom training in medicine at the University of London—that trust is still there, along with the memories and all the things understood from a shared history, where nothing needs to be explained. And it's this he clings onto for a moment, to justify his hesitation, his resistance to surrendering their companionable silence, the momentary ease, to dark feelings and hard thoughts. Aren't some things best left unspoken between men? But he must confide in someone, when all is a terrible mystery, he tells himself, and he cannot think of anyone better than Tom, with his knowledge and his calm common sense. He studies his friend's level gaze, the startling white hair more a golden-blonde these days and always kept cropped and tucked away under a hat. When he'd teased Tom about the frequent visits to a barber shop, before the bad times had begun, his friend demanded, *Well, would* you *trust a physician in curls?* They'd laughed then, and punched each other's shoulders.

Flowers are waking in the Avenue Gardens, brightening into day-colour, purples in fine green skirts. Are they asters? Some kind of autumn daisy? Emily would know, he thinks. And then, when a dusky magenta peeps from the bottom layer of the next bed, he is reminded of her favourite petticoat, and could cry.

"Do you miss her?" Tom is the first to break their silence.

"It's been only five days."

"Still, Arthur."

"Yes," he admits. "Yes, I do."

Would it be a betrayal to tell Tom he also feels a sense of respite at his wife's absence? That he misses her, but not who she has become? He strikes at the grass with his walking stick.

"You say the issue is with congress?"

The directness is a relief. "Yes. But it is more than this, far more." He considers, searching for the words. "She has severe pain."

What more can he say?

Can he speak of how, at the beginning of it all, her body would clench when he reached for her? How she winces now when he touches her? How her frightened eyes shift from his? How she no longer tells him that she loves him?

Impossible.

They circle the Griffin Tazza, the winged lions muscular, their gaze blank and foreign.

"Is the pain always in that area?"

"Yes. And beyond."

He feels the familiar stab of guilt: how his wife must bear this alone. How she *chooses* to bear it alone, says a voice in his mind.

They brush through shrubs busy with tiny flitting birds and return to the avenue of plane trees. Here and there, grimy-looking boys now trot along the Broad Walk, and suited and hatted men make their brisk way southward. A party of eager young women cluster at one of the lampposts, pointing out the George IV cipher to each other. Are they from the country? Spending a day in the "Big Smoke", just because they can?

"It isn't my field of expertise," Tom says. "But I know enough of disorder that has no easy answer to tell you how readily such nervous malady can be made worse." He scratches his chin thoughtfully. "You say that Charles is monitoring her health? Suggesting specialists?"

"Yes."

A pungent, earthy scent fills the dawn air. What part of it is elephant or hippopotamus dung? What part lion? They walk through the cries and rumbles that drift over the hedge of the zoo and Arthur tries to say the words, but they skip away from him like flat stones across murky waters: Emmie at Herdley … not ideal—Bea busy, Father confused … going to Hierde House when work will spare me … And, what should I do, Tom? What *can* I do?

The paths are filling with people of all sorts, strides purposeful and busy. At the bridge their own boots ring hollow; below, the canal is fathomless, its water dense and green. Then it is over Albert Road, noisy now with clattering carts and the hoof-fall of smart cab horses, and up the path towards Primrose Hill, where young lads, up early, trundle their hoops down the grass, shouting and laughing.

"I'm loath to confuse the issue," Tom continues tentatively. "Charles is a very knowledgeable physician."

"Yes, yes, of course, but even Charles seems lost … And I'm worried, Tom. All I can think is that she must be somewhere nourishing. We're hoping that—"

A loud honking interrupts, drawing their eyes to the dark V in the lightening sky. Some kind of goose, Arthur thinks. A flock making its way to warmer climes.

"So we're hoping that Hierde House might give some comfort, some healing, where the city can't," he finishes clumsily.

Tom gives him a reassuring smile. "It is a sound decision, I think, Arthur. Really, I do. The situation can be deliberated anew when she returns to London—if the symptoms persist. These mysterious ailments can pass equally mysteriously. Don't lose hope."

Tom's clasp of his shoulder is comforting and he feels his heart lift. It has been such a short span of time, really. She may yet recover, with Bea's help, in the sweet air of Herdley. If not now, then soon. Very soon, perhaps.

So they walk on, he and Tom, speaking more easily, the matter having been broached, the worst said. They round the Shakespeare Oak, flatten the damp grass with their boots as they climb, note the first signs of russet and amber in the plane trees and chestnuts, mark the lean of the hardy little hawthorns near the summit, join the small clutch of early walkers and sightseers at the top of Primrose Hill.

A bruised mist hangs over the city. In the distance, church towers are indefinite battlements. The horizon spills orange and the air fills with bird calls, the *tap-tap-tap* of stick on hoop, awed whispers, and there is a clarion call in his mind, through his body—he feels his very soul vibrate with a demand. Fingers of light uncurl through the dusty city air and up the grass, a great hand reaching for him.

Chapter 13

Perth, October–December 2008

Alice leaned against the back of the seat and tilted her hips forward. Something sturdier was needed, something … specific. Particular. A high-sitting horseshoe shape, perhaps; a 'special' cushion. She imagined the looks, the speculation. Pushed hard with her left foot so her bum was suspended and hoped she was close. She glanced at her mud map: a left at Ennis Ave, then right onto Braid and she'd be there.

It would be a relief to stand again. The tiny nightly pills had softened those neon spikes but the pain was still relentless, still swung back and forth between buzzing, aching and burning. What could account for it? Her mind refused to form definite thoughts, let alone convincing words. The only approach to understanding seemed to be through recent phone conversations with Joan and the relief of sharing those terrible dreams – the tearing mouth, herself consumed. Still, she felt able to survive now, when for months that had seemed impossible.

Who else could she appeal to? She thought of Pen with her rushed visits, her phone calls in between, the suggestions that led … nowhere, really. She thought of her old, stone home with its sturdy columns and shadowed verandah, the beds of natives where hairy grevillea and callistemon flowers jostled for attention. The house that was closed to her, these days. And the man. The man who no longer raced home from work with that old eagerness, his face tenderly true, his smile opening to hers.

Where else could she turn? She'd resisted joining the online groups Dr Sutherland – Susan – had told her about months ago. The idea of talking with disembodied strangers made her cringe. But she wanted to continue her research, look more into the history of vulvar pain and see how modern medical understanding compared, dig into Freud's collected works. Further contemplate writing fiction based on all of this. And she'd made other steps into the unknown, seeing a physio – Sasha of the warm hands – for weekly sessions.

Today was the next step.

There, Braid Terrace. Halfway along, a scattering of cars, and neat beds of succulents lining the verge, the pinkish ones like flaps of flesh.

The house was a modern statement, one of those stern designs without eaves, and with windows like dark eyes that wouldn't let you look in, that assessed her blankly as she walked towards them.

She knocked and heard the tapping of heels, then the door opened to a tall woman with wild, blonde-grey hair. It must be Sally. The woman she'd spoken to on the phone, the organiser. The one who'd told her, *I'm a psychologist – in my other life!*

'Hello! You must be Alice. I'm so pleased you came.'

The voice at least was familiar, certain and with that residue of New Zealand in the vowels.

'Thanks. It's a bit strange. You know …' She wasn't sure how to continue.

But the older woman's smile was sympathetic. 'I sure do.' She stepped back, into the hallway – 'Come on, you'll be fine' – and touched Alice's arm in a way that felt like reassurance.

Alice followed her along the corridor and then out, into an expansive living area with a vaulted ceiling. A couple of women chatted near the entrance and two more lounged on white beanbags in the far corner. Only four strangers then. What would they make of her? Sally's words rose in her mind – the phone call made when Duncan was out, when she'd felt composed, had begun calmly, but ended up in tears – *It's okay*, Sally had said. *I know.* Then she'd gone on to tell Alice that she was not alone and how this group, started by her some years ago, was to support women just like Alice, how they were *a friendly bunch*.

She swivelled, taking in the room. Irises burst like peacock feathers from a vase on a blonde-wood table; spring light washed the clean, straight angles of the room and its understated – but expensive, Alice guessed – works of art on walls and plinths. She looked out of the wall of glass that separated the living room from the backyard, though 'backyard' was a little hick for this classy garden. A cream birdbath presided from its centre, a neat flowering ash bobbed sedately and the prim lawn forbade leaves. It was a home of air and money. New money, not like her and Duncan's old-money home. She suddenly felt reduced, a negative lifted from the developer bath too early and hung to dry, an image lacking clarity and strength.

'Alice?' Sally's voice pulling her back into the here and now. 'This is Simone … and Atikah.'

The women greeted her and she tried to mentally link their features to their names, to lodge them in her memory. Simone, with a protective hand on her small bump; Atikah, in a blue hijab that sheened in the bright room.

'Come and meet Denise and Maria.'

Sally had talked about Denise on the phone, how she'd joined the group at the right time – *when I'd just about run out of puff* – and now helped organise it, spreading the word to GPs and gynos. Sally had told her of Denise's ability to *call a spade a spade*, too, and about the cluster of ailments she battled with. Then Sally had stopped herself. *I'd best let her tell you all about that,* she'd said.

Alice slipped onto another beanbag, wondering if the seating was providential, or a thoughtful alternative to the usual right-angled chair.

'Hi Alice –'

'Hi Alice –'

The woman with a fierce face and the girl with black hair and a flurry of piercings laughed together at their overlapped greeting.

'I'm Denise.' It was the woman who looked ready for a fight. 'It's great to have you here.' She laughed again, this time with an edge. 'Well, not great for you, I guess.'

'Thanks.' Once more Alice's words refused to flow.

She wondered if anyone had ever walked out of their first meeting with these women. Wondered how talking with other … sufferers could possibly help. How anything that didn't involve lifting the weight of pain she hefted around could do anything at all. But then Sally and Denise and the other girl, Maria, started chatting like old friends, and just listening to them speaking about all sorts of things – work, relationships, sport – with the thread of pain weaving its way through the conversation and holding it together, made her feel she could stay, after all. So that when, finally, after she'd added a few words here and there and then was asked for the first time about her own particular suffering, she could answer.

'Stabbing, aching … burning, sometimes. And this clamping sensation around my bum,' she told them.

'And when is that? With tight clothes, like jeans? Or with sex?' Sally knew the answers to these questions already. She smiled encouragingly and Alice realised this was for the benefit of the others.

'It's there all the time,' she said, 'but it's worse with sitting.'

'Oh, Alice.' It was Denise. 'That's crap.'

'I used to have it like that too, back in my thirties,' Sally said. 'But these days it's manageable. Sometimes just a dull ache. Maybe a little burning.'

It was terrifying to think of someone having this pain for decades. Distressing to imagine the fabric of your life snagging on this burr, over and over. Was it possible that it could change? That being with it – *living* with it – might become a smooth hub around which spokes of meaning whirred, equidistant and gleaming? No, surely not.

'I guess I just think of that as normal, these days,' Sally continued.

'I don't think there's anything normal about this,' said Denise, her voice clipped, as if cutting off the terrible stories Alice could sense lay beneath.

Alice felt the questions bubbling up in her own mind. Was Denise's anger like her own, a mix of fury, bitterness and grief? Of disbelief? How on earth did Simone get pregnant, and was she scared about the approaching birth? What did they all do in the world, this Maria, Atikah, Simone, this Denise, and exactly how old were they? The questions spun and roiled, demanding she know more about these women, telling her she should stay, reassuring her she could be with them, at least for today.

Outside, a willie wagtail swooped to the birdbath and flicked its compact, sprightly body about in the water. The world, framed like a picture, glowed greenly.

It only made sense if there were two bodies, both equally valid. One body seen through the gaze of an early caregiver – 'mother' was probably best avoided in the essay – and the other body formed through sensation.

Alice leaned back from the laptop and shifted her bottom so it fell more neatly into the kneeling gap formed by her lower legs. Thought about her patchy, nonsensical body and its unbridgeable distance from her visible body. One, a symmetrical image reflected in the mirror and the sight of other bodies, whole and cohesive. The other, a figure in fragments, its bits and pieces scattered through the brain.

If you accepted the reality of the bits-and-pieces body-in-the-brain, then it became believable that pain could be felt in undamaged nerves and muscles. That it might seem to lodge deeply and stubbornly in a newly assigned anatomical home, or roam at whim, greedy for unclaimed territory, only answerable to a nervous system that has forgotten how to command it, or keep it in check.

How best to express these complex ideas? Some context first, perhaps: Freud's idea of the bodily ego – a theory that did not raise her hackles as did his insistence on female sexuality as a warped version of the male model, a theory that normalised pain, made it somehow approachable.

Alice bent over the coffee table again and typed.

> *Freud argued that the ego is initially forged through bodily sensation. He also suggested that the way in which we gain knowledge of an organ through pain, as an adult, might reproduce how we arrive at the first sensation-driven idea of the body.*

The rasping cry of a crow lumbering past the lounge-room window returned Alice to the complaint of her legs, cramped under the low table. She stood and stretched her hamstrings and calf muscles, swung her body in semicircles at the waist, felt looseness return. If only such measures would ease the ever-present throb and sting. They returned to her, the words spoken last week by the gynaecologist at the pain clinic: *Do you think you might be dragging this on a bit?* Tears prickled, and then the anger came again, weighted by that feeling of hopelessness.

How could she make people understand this kind of pain? What made it so different? So bits-and-pieces and arbitrary? Was it possible to relate it somehow to what medicine accepted? What people already understood?

She thought about the women in the support group with their abiding yet illogical conditions. What if this fragmented, 'sensation-driven' kind of body was the one active in other seemingly senseless disorders: pain in limbs already ripped away in shocking accidents, frantic itching in unblemished skin, the 'shell shock' of World War I or modern PTSD, disabling whiplash without anatomical damage ... maybe fibromyalgia? Who could tell a person with any of these weird symptoms that their physical suffering was any less than that experienced through a torn Achilles, or acute appendicitis? And what if she were to argue for the validity of this pain?

Should she resurrect and champion hysteria?

She disconnected the open laptop and carried it through to the kitchen bench. Bent forward at the hips to type again. A sentence for later in her essay.

Hysteria makes sense as a signal of disorder, not necessarily at the site of pain, but at the level of fragmented body parts and their central nervous system complementarities.

Too cerebral. Too abstract. How might she bring it to life?

What about all those miserable patients in Jean-Martin Charcot's case notes? The photographic images from the 1860s – men and women with their bodies in strange, dramatic poses. And those described in the neurologist's lecture-demonstrations at the Salpêtrière hospital in the 1870s and 80s, displayed like, like ... objects, really: men shouting without sound; hypnotised women becoming, at command, unparalysed, paralysed; the famous – or infamous – epileptic-like convulsions of *la grande hystérie*, with its dramatic *arc de cercle*. She could feel it herself, a backbend of suffering grounded by flexed feet and neck, agony wrenching the mouth open.

A flash through the kitchen window. Ah, the wattlebird, a fat black spider in its beak, swooping to clear the eaves, shooting above the garden, arrow-like, disappearing into the snowy blossom. The melaleuca eight now, its snow-in-summer blossom heavier each year. How old would the wattlebird be? Was it the same one that had been so busy last summer, feasting on spiders, cleaning their eaves?

Alice walked to the window. Kangaroo paws leaned towards her from the new bed of natives, planted by Duncan in the cooler months, their orange heads swaying on elegant necks. The tiny pink flowers of a native pea bounced cheerily in the breeze. Then the skimming wattlebird cut the blue bowl of the sky again. She heard some maggies warbling, noticed a cluster of winging twenty-eights in the distance.

Quarter to five. Duncan would be home from work soon.

She'd made the mistake of showing him those photos from the Salpêtrière, thinking he might understand images if not words, wanting to share her fascination. He'd raised his eyebrows and said, *Are you up to the end-of-year staff bash?* Carried on about how she still needed to be seen – when she wasn't. Not really.

She turned back to her laptop and notes.

Maybe she could describe some of Charcot's cases in detail, represent some of the lives from his published lectures. Like Ler—, whose contorted arms and legs crisscrossed each other compulsively as she screamed the cumulative distress of years: *villains! robbers! brigands! fire! fire! O, the dogs! I'm bitten!* Or the paralysed Le Log—, another of Charcot's hysterics, who, though he had no lasting damage to his legs, remained frozen in that moment when a heavy laundryman's van, pulled by horses at high speed, bore down on him and his loaded handbarrow.

How else might she legitimise her idea of the 'sensation-driven' body? She scribbled on her notepad as ideas coalesced.

- *Nineteenth-century understanding of different diseases: functional/dynamic versus organic (tie in with own idea of 'two bodies'?).*

- *Scene at the Salpêtrière. Recreate a hysterical attack?*

No, don't get too lost in that world. Find a way to link then and now.

- ~~*Scene at the Salpêtrière. Recreate a hysterical attack?*~~

- *Compare 'hysterical' symptoms at Salpêtrière with e.g. modern-day whiplash – case from each (both 'sensation-driven'?).*

People needed to know how Charcot took his patients seriously. How the neurologist saw in the bizarre contractures and strange shifting anaesthesias of his patients something that made sense. *These motor paralyses of psychical origin are as objectively real as those depending on an organic lesion*, he declared.

So,

- *Hysteria as real and legit outcome of Charcot's 'dynamic lesion' in nervous system.*

What about Charcot's post-trauma regime? She scrolled back to an earlier spot in her essay –

> *Dealing with two patients with hysterical (traumatic) paralysis, Charcot recognised the value of specific physical exercises, not to build muscle strength, but to 'revive' the 'motor representation' in the brain; a necessary precursor to voluntary movement. He notes the way in which, through repetition, this movement strengthens.*

– and jotted more ideas to be included:

- *Charcot's modernity, despite spectacle and showmanship.*
- *Parallels past and present:*
  Charcot's findings along with recent research and practice with stroke victims (retrieval of motor programs in nervous –

This time it was her tight neck that brought her back.

She straightened, rotated her head on its base and checked the kitchen clock. Five pm. Time to think about dinner. Finish the scribbled sentence, save the document, close the laptop. Later she would return to it, this writing – historical culture uncovered and examined through a modern lens, current medical knowledge understood differently through it in turn.

Already, though, she could sense something else, something different from academic enquiry ... something beneath, or just out of her line of sight – so hard to know how to think of it! – that sensation of density, of urgency, so familiar to her from years of writing fiction. And she knew ... yes, she remembered what she must do: hold it there, just hold it, until she was ready. Until *it* was ready.

Three things Alice liked about these sessions: Sasha always remembered that she couldn't sit, always asked first, always warmed her hands. That attentiveness told Alice she might trust the physiotherapist, even when this session, and what was done to her here, was always an invasion, no matter the liking.

'And how have you been going at home?' Sasha's pen at the ready.

'I still have that day or so of more stabbing and aching after each session, but I don't think it's as bad lately,' Alice said. She wasn't entirely sure whether this was true, or whether she simply hoped it was. 'But I leave the pelvic floor exercises until it's settled down.'

'That's a good idea,' said Sasha, jotting a note. 'And what about the TENS unit?'

'I reckon it's helping with my bladder – I don't feel like I have to go quite as much? It doesn't seem to be making any difference to the vulvodynia though.'

It was a new sensation, that low hum through the electrodes near the base of her back, the muted buzz momentarily overriding other sensations. But her vulva always bit back again when she turned the little machine off.

'Well, it's early days, so let's keep trying – if you're fine with that?'

'Sure,' Alice said.

'And the massaging? Have you tried that? Or asked Duncan to?'

'He's done it a little.' She didn't want to tell Sasha that Duncan's hands were awkward when it came to relieving pain rather than creating pleasure, or how she herself felt uncomfortable directing her husband, correcting his clumsy efforts. 'It's easier if I do it alone, even if I have to be a contortionist!'

Sasha laughed.

It had taken weeks for Alice to feel brave enough to venture inside her own body. There she'd found rigid bands and sore walls, not the welcoming and erotic space she remembered.

'And what about today? Are you okay to work?'

There it was: her permission requested.

'Yes.'

'Okay, then.' Sasha stood. 'You're doing really well, Alice.'

This she liked too: that Sasha simply left the room with a smile lately, trusting that Alice knew the order of things. It gave Alice a little glow, the familiarity. Perhaps it helped with what had to come next too.

Alice pulled the curtain across, took off her skirt and undies and climbed onto the bench, pulling the crisp sheet over her torso. Let her knees relax outwards and tried to forget the other people with whom she'd opened herself this way – the cold metal implements and even colder fingertips. She breathed deeply into her abdomen, into her pelvis, trying to send kind thoughts there, but her mind skittered and her heart still drummed its warning.

She heard the snick of the door as Sasha returned, the whoosh of the billowing curtain.

'Okay, so I'm going to begin with seeing how the vestibule is doing.'

Alice put her head back on the pillow, closed her eyes and waited for the first sensation: the cotton bud like a pin.

'How's that?'

'A three.' Not too bad. 'Five ... Four ... Five ...' Alice tried to place each discrete sensation on the map in her mind. 'Seven – is that nearer the urethra?'

'Yes, one of the glands close to the urethral opening. What about this?'

'Seven again, I think.'

The needling slipped down the pain scale again.

'So, a little better overall,' Sasha commented.

'Still worse at the front than the back.'

'Yes, the pain's always been more focused there for you, hasn't it?' Alice heard the sound of the bin closing, and water running down the drain. 'Non-latex gloves, Alice. And warm water to help.' Sasha always remembered this too: how reactive her skin had proven, even though it was just latex, just gel. With a stab of grief, she recalled sex with Duncan in the early days: ribbed condoms – *for her pleasure*, announced the box – and raiding the fridge, foods outside and in. The laughing, sweaty joy. The utter abandonment to pleasure.

Sasha's hand brought her back, lodging her in her body with stretching and pulling, then pressure.

'Okay, so I'm inside the vagina now and I'm palpating the muscles around the vaginal wall. Can you feel that?'

'It's sore, but it feels okay. It's like it needs to be stretched.'

'Good. Yes, there's some tightness, but not as much as you had, perhaps.'

The pressure was reaching into her body now, and swivelling.

'Is that the obturator internus?'

'Yes, that's right,' said Sasha.

In her mind's eye, Alice recreated the tracings she'd made from the anatomy atlas. Muscles and ligaments and tendons; busily interweaving nerves; and blood vessels, blues and reds tidy and contained. The journeys taken by all these unfathomable structures around and between jutting bones, this intricate web that somehow held the pelvis together in a beauty of form and function. And the rhythm of the words she'd copied from the atlas, whispering them to herself like poetry: *ischiococcygeus*, *puborectalis*, *ischial tuberosity* …

Was Sasha visualising all this as she pressed and massaged? Making sense of threads, knots and bumps by placing them in the anatomical bowl she carried in her mind? Alice tried to hold it, too, that picture of her pelvis, rotate it into depth and life; strained to marry what she could now feel with what she'd seen: neat, discrete anatomical parts. But it was as if the two things were entirely different. Completely unconnected. Two bodies, she reminded herself. And two senses: sight and an unfamiliar kind of … It was hard to know what to call the other. Inner sensation? Kinaesthesia? In any case, less precise than the kind of touch she was used to and almost as if she were underwater, or immersed in some kind of viscous flux where she was the feeler and the felt, the prober and the probed, and inside, the spongy muscular warm wet around her – gooey, mucousy, ropey, gluggy and straining aching needling and everything muddled and messy in a passageway, a cone, a cylinder, a vortex … nerves wetly sparking a body a mind a brain? Something is wrong, and swimming through it, the wrongness, dissolving in it or dissolved by it, boundaries gone and just the feeling there. Right there.

'Could you try a contraction now?'

'What?' She swam back to the room. To Sasha. Opened her eyes to the light above and the charts of body parts on the walls.

'A contraction. Just like you've been doing at home.'

'Oh. Okay.'

Alice returned her mind to the imprint of Sasha's hand, breathed in and out, then pulled that part of herself up and into her body.

'Yes,' said Sasha, 'and ... let go.'

She tried to relax, felt the sore judder as her muscles loosened, then jammed.

'So, the contraction looks good, but we're still going to have to work a little on the release.'

It had been measured, the contraction and release, in earlier sessions. A small probe slipped inside by Sasha had told them the muscles were always slightly tense, her body perpetually on alert, stuck in some kind of faulty loop.

'I still don't get why there's pain in my vulva if it's the muscles inside that are the problem.'

'Well, we don't really know yet if it is just the muscles. It's probably nerves and muscles feeding into the problem together.' Sasha pressed and stretched, a little frown between her eyebrows. 'It's like a tension headache. The pain is referred to the head from the muscles in the neck and shoulders in just the same way.' Her hand shifted inside. 'Try it again, if you can, focusing on the release.'

This time Alice breathed out as she let go, imagining everything dropping away from her.

'That's better!'

'I love that feeling of release when I can get it properly – like a flower opening.'

'Exactly. Well done, you.'

Her dark core throbbed and she knew she would suffer even more by the evening, but for that brief, solitary moment Alice was warmed by the praise – by getting one single thing right.

Chapter 14

November 2nd 1865

Dearest Beatrice,

You have charged me with continuing to confide in you as well as my journal while I am in London, just as I have done over the last several months at Hierde House, & I'm sure you are right, that it does me good to share my suffering, so I will try, even though it is hard to order the jumble of words & sensations that often spill onto pages no-one will ever see. Pain is a terrible thing, Bea, a devil that twists my thoughts & tosses my feelings about till I no longer know who I am. I only hope you, Arthur & Mam can continue to remind me.

We managed to book with Normand next week—he is very busy, so I think Father must have pulled some strings—& Mam will come with me, as Arthur is busy then. Arthur did come with me today, though, to the appointment with Middleton. Nothing new, I'm afraid, just advice we've received before: the need for rest, avoidance of excitement, a resumption of marital intimacy, et cetera. You know the details about all that this pain keeps me from, so I don't have to explain to you what I would like these men to understand: "resumption of marital intimacy" is what I want, what Arthur & I both want, but it is impossible, upsetting to even contemplate, when this terrible pain affects every area of my life. Of Arthur's life too now.

It is difficult to carry the burden of this illness, let alone to be the cause of suffering in another person & having to bear that extra weight—the weight of guilt. I know you've noticed that I shut myself away from Arthur in all ways, but I cannot do better just now. And you are right: I am very nervous when I attend these appointments & most anxious at the thought of the consultations ahead, especially as I can no longer lean on Arthur as I otherwise might. But I suppose I must consult these physicians & apothecaries & nerve doctors & do exactly as they suggest.

Love Emmie

November 7th 1865

Oh Bea,

Normand was awful. He applied some caustic—told me it would reduce the nerve irritation—& neither Mam nor I felt equal to questioning his decision. The burning continues now & I must lie down, take laudanum, take anything to numb me to this dreadful pain. It is so hard to know what to do next, when nothing helps!

Em

November 10th 1865

Beatrice,

You say I must assert my rights—that it is my body—& that may be true, but I am not you, ~~nor should I~~ you who are so certain in your thoughts & feelings, you who have the confidence to act on ideas in many spheres, & I cannot tolerate ~~being told what~~ bossiness when I am on the verge of breaking, of snapping like a dry, old stick. Do you not understand how exhausted I am through simply marshalling the vitality necessary to write this letter?

Emily

November 14th 1865

Dear Bea,

I feel dreadful. Your generous-hearted letter makes me ashamed for being angry at one of the very few in this world who understands me truly. Forgive me, dear sister, &, if you can, continue to make allowances for my irritation & topsy-turvy feelings. For myself, I will fight the torment that tries to snatch away all that is best in me.

Yes, the worst of the burning has subsided & I am back to where I was several weeks ago: just able to tolerate my suffering body. I had Millie prepare the spinal couch & a darkened room so I could have some days with absolutely no movement or stimulation in order to regather my spirits, & that seemed to help. Father will visit again tomorrow, Mam says, but this does not give me ease, for he does not seem to hear me properly, even with all his knowledge.

I'm not sure what will be advised next in these attempts to determine what ails me, but I must relay to you something that the horrible Normand told me: there are other women suffering in just the way I do. It gives me strength somehow, to know that I am not the only one in the world like this.

Yours gratefully,

Emmie

November 17th 1865

What am I to say? I cannot do that which God designed me to do. I cannot fulfil my God-given duty. I am more of a failure than my own mother, who tried over & over, more than your mother (forgive me), whose longing to bear children brought about the ultimate sacrifice. I am a failure in all I should be: a dutiful wife who tends her busy husband; a mother who births & raises children. What use am I to anyone?

Maybe Father is right & this complaint has its roots in the past. Maybe something went wrong in me when James died. Maybe it has overcome me now, this black pall, so that I am hidden from all who love me.

Is the fault with me or with my God?

I must confess something to you & pray you forgive me. The only good thing I can think to do with my life now is to protect Arthur by releasing him from his vows. It is not enough to pull the tendrils of my being from his heart; to pull his from mine, terrible as that is. No, all that might solve this is to remove myself from him, to leave him free to find someone who can do for him what I cannot. And because he is an honourable man—because I can see that he does still love me, though I am useless—it would be best if I were to make the decision for him & remove myself from life altogether. Surely that would be best for us all?

Oh Bea, what can save me from these dark thoughts?

November 21st 1865

Dear sister,

I will try, though I cannot see what good I am to anyone like this, & I don't know what to do with love that insists on me trying, when I would rather give up & find peace. I am so weary, Bea, bone-weary. So utterly worn with having to sit whenever I must leave the house, with being bumped & jerked about in the carriage, with taking off & putting on layer after layer of clothing, with having strange men examine me whilst I pretend I am elsewhere, all the while having to tolerate the intolerable: the breeze on my skin, the chafe & rub of clothing, the pressure of seats & chairs, the intrusion of cold fingers in that most private part—that part that is hardly private any more.

Do you know what is most wearying, Bea? The never-ending battle with the burning & stinging & aching that has made its home in my body. I'm beginning to believe this devil will never be ousted; that all the efforts I make—that Arthur & I make—only seem to provide food for it, keeping it strong, while I fade away. I have lost count of the tinctures I have swallowed, the poultices dear Millie has applied, the instances of advice I have received, the aspersions that have been cast—softly, softly, but I still see them in the eyes of the men it seems I must consult.

If I cannot find the hope you say I must, you must hope for me, for I am worn to the nub.

Emmie

London, November 1865

The men walk to the smoking room—the Reids' *new* smoking room in their new and fancier home, in this newly fashionable street. *Harley Street*, Emily's father told him when they were looking to move from Savile Row. And the desired location, *As close to Cavendish Square as we can get.* One thing about Charles, he has never hidden his ambition, or his social aspirations. Well, he got what he wanted: with this and his flourishing practice, the country estate, his daughter's successful marriage, he has surely secured a permanent place in society.

Now, Charles shrugs on his smoking jacket and allows the butler to light his cigar with the flickering candle. Their forms on the wall leap and dwindle.

Successful. Their successful marriage. But how do you count success?

"Has Emily told you of her early troubles?" Another characteristic of his father-in-law: the abrupt beginnings; the taking charge.

"You mean the family loss?" Arthur sinks into the armchair.

"I mean the symptoms she had. Her menses commenced at the same time as the loss, y'know."

It's uncomfortable to hear these intimate details from Emily's father. Arthur has to remind himself that Charles is a physician and such words are his stock-in-trade. Still, he feels their intrusion.

Charles fills the pause, counting off items on his definite, pink fingers. "Headaches, anxiety, fatigue, palpitations, a weak liver. A loose kidney, perhaps. Globus hystericus."

Arthur does not know the meaning of globus hystericus, but the sound of the last word alerts him to the direction his father-in-law is taking.

"She was not simply suffering with a terrible grief? Or, perhaps, experiencing the difficult but normal changes of a girl becoming a woman?" He knows he is out of his depth, yet Charles's words feel wrong to him; when Emily told him of those terrible years, all the elements of her suffering made sense. But, he reminds himself, he is no expert.

"That's what I determined at the time, but now I'm not so sure." Charles puffs out his smoke. "Such nervous problems can indicate a certain moral … instability. They can resurface, y'know, and often in a more pronounced form. More dangerous."

"Instability?"

It is a strong word, an ugly word, with implications beyond his mind's compass.

"There is a man who deals with such problems," Charles says. "A surgeon."

"What possible reason can there be for surgery?"

Charles looks uncomfortable for the first time.

"He believes that moral education is not enough in some instances ..." Then, in his usual resounding voice: "He is impressive—audacious, and very skilful, so I'm told."

Education? In what? And, audacious: Arthur can hardly imagine what that might mean.

"But what does the treatment involve?"

"Ah, here he was not clear. Gentlewomen were present at the meeting I attended." Charles taps the side of his nose. "Must protect their delicate sensibility."

"It seems odd to talk about cures while offering such little information."

"Well, yes, but he has an impressive list of supporters, y'know. Tiptop people." It is the kind of thing that wins over his father-in-law, the approval of society. "He's a pioneer in ovariotomy—uses methods that others have avoided, in risky operations—and now he's President of the Medical Society of London. As for these experiments in this new procedure? He's been publishing on this for some years now."

"Experiments?" The word is hardly reassuring.

"You must understand how we use such words." Charles speaks with satisfaction through a plume of smoke. "All surgery involves risk. And he has extended an open invitation, y'know. To physicians, surgeons. So I can observe this operation. Be properly informed. Some positive action: that's the ticket!"

He hates the way the words roll so glibly from Charles's tongue. As if such terrible suffering might be removed in an instant. And the implied criticism: as if Emily is not wanting to be better. As if he and she are not doing all they possibly can.

And he thinks of Tom, who has warned against ill-considered action. *Maybe we should continue to wait and see*, Tom said when he confided that Emily's symptoms remained unchanged. *It is important to avoid precipitous or ill-considered action.*

The different impulses jostle in him: Tom does not have to live with this suffering, be helpless in response, fail the person he loves most in the world; Charles does not have to watch his daughter suffer after calamitous treatments. As for him, no-one knows how much he longs for certainty, to urge Emily to try harder, to ignore her pain. How he dreads falling back into the, the … weakness of his boyhood. But no-one knows, either, how her cries of pain tear at his heart. And yet … But still …

"Maybe we should wait," he says. "Try further rest at Herdley." He holds his father-in-law's eye. "I will be able to be there for some weeks. I will know if she does not improve and if more action is necessary."

"Think on it, Arthur. I would urge this treatment before the condition becomes ingrained."

November 26th 1865

Dear Bea,

So Arthur has written to you of this Isaac Baker Brown. No, I do not know the details of the "operation", do not understand what logic it is based in. Arthur himself is not clear. Like me, he cannot understand how surgery could cure such a stubborn & widespread malaise, though we are too uncomfortable to share our concerns in the way we once did—too estranged from each other altogether, though I will not say more, knowing how, even though you understand our dilemma, this distresses you. My father seems to know a good deal, but pulls back when I ask him & says, "Arthur should make an appointment & then you will know."

It all makes me terribly uncertain & uneasy. What I do know is that it would be folly for me to make decisions, affected as I am by pain & confusion, folly to resist the advice of those who surely know better than me. I have no choice but to place my trust in my father & my husband, & this I have resolved to do.

Emmie

November 28th 1865

Dearest Beatrice,

We have decided not to see Mr Baker Brown, for the moment, & to find what several more months at Herdley can achieve. If there is no improvement by the end of January, we will make an appointment then. It is a great relief, I must say, if for no other reason than to have a break from examinations, & treatments that seem to harm more than heal.

Arthur is organising the transport & I am speaking with the domestics—we will leave skeleton staff in Portland Place & bring our usual. Arthur will write to Father Rochdale, but you can expect us on the morrow.

My loving Bea, thank you for your forbearance. It will be good to be with you, to be home.

Emmie

Chapter 15

Perth, January–March 2009

They were still difficult, these support group meetings. Each month an unfamiliar house, another woman's home. Claremont and Sally's, then Maria's student share house in Freo, and now long sweeps up the 'scenic route' to Simone's home in the hills, the flashing toy blocks of the city in the distance, the Swan River a sparkling filament threaded through the city and its lazy summer suburbs.

Yes, it was still frightening, this entry into a different kind of space. But Alice remembered the last few meetings and the women who had drawn her out of her dark, repeating thoughts and into their conversations. Into their lives. Sally, the go-to psychologist, her life seemingly organised around this illness. Simone, her attention turning inwards now as she readied herself for the birth. Volatile, potty-mouthed Denise. Atikah, quiet and thoughtful, her words carrying authority. And Maria, urban and edgy and into jewellery design, with metal wrapped around her arms and through her skin. Hearing these women, listening to them, having to take them into account, it lifted a weight from her. So it was early days and, yes, still difficult, but she was beginning to feel … What did she feel? That she could, perhaps, trust these women who shared her pain?

Alice zigzagged the Toyota up the escarpment, thinking about the words she'd known in her old life. Dysmenorrhoea from her mother, when she'd been troubled by painful periods as a teenager. Endometriosis as some kind of gradually dawning common knowledge. Words she'd been made to learn since. Vulvodynia. Vestibulodynia. And words she'd heard for the first time with these women. New diagnoses. Speculative causes. How insignificant she felt each time the clinical-sounding terms were voiced. Interstitial cystitis, like a UTI that never left; a tiny, pressed and painful space, the rock and the hard place scraping on each side. Lichen sclerosus? A term that, horribly, conjured multiple sclerosis and growths that flourished in moist darkness, but really described a skin condition. Atrophic vaginitis: a thinning, shrinking vagina that was atypical. Like her. No longer typical. No longer normal.

Were these hard, exotic words the language they must learn? Or might their bodies teach them a kinder language? One that might lift them, hold them, carry them home?

Near the crest of the hill now, time to focus. She followed the directions Simone had given her, along hilly twists, to the timber house on stilts. Cars were lined up on the narrow verge, but the driveway was empty. Maybe Simone's partner had left for the afternoon, as seemed to be the unwritten convention. Would Duncan hang around when these women came to their house, or would he escape to the tennis courts? Not that he looked for an excuse these days. Not that she wanted to bring these women into that cool space either.

Simone came at the knock, nut-brown and heavy with baby, and led her into the lounge room before easing her own pregnant bulk onto a chair with a sigh. Alice glimpsed whimsical watercolours and wall-hangings and guitars, before her attention was caught by Denise's avid gaze at Simone's belly. She wasn't surprised when, after all the greetings had been exchanged – Sally, Maria, Atikah already kneeling or sitting around the chunky coffee table – Denise raised the subject: 'How long now?'

'A couple of weeks.' The movement of hand to belly and small, proud smile were involuntary. But Simone looked anxious too. She was still opting for a vaginal delivery, but worried that it would increase her pain. *How will I handle a newborn if it does?* she'd said at the last meeting. No-one could offer a definitive answer; not one of them felt able to adequately reassure her.

It was a delicate subject all round. Alice had learned that Denise wanted a child – had wanted one for years. But life had not cooperated, and now she was thirty-eight and single. The men drawn to her spiky independence were unprepared for her demanding disorders, her pressing hopes: a loving partner, a family.

Even worse for Denise must be Simone's seemingly miraculous pregnancy. *God knows how it happened*, Simone had already confided. *Sandpaper between two razor blades*, were the words she'd used for sex.

Yet she'd fallen pregnant and Denise had remained her friend, in and out of the group. And what about Sally? She'd said that surrendering to the fear that swamped her at the thought of a baby, and the belief that barely tolerable pain might become intolerable as a result, was her biggest regret. Alice had contemplated repeating this to Duncan, but she wasn't even ready for that conversation herself. The feel of the floating embryo further away now. In another life; really.

And what about the others, the occasional participants in the group, teenage Ashleigh – tottering on giraffe legs and impossible shoes – and Eileen, in her eighties? How utterly disabling to be elderly and unable to sit or stand. How tragic to be young and unable to have sex. *It's driving Ryan crazy*, Ashleigh had said. And of course it was understandable, the craziness – a young bloke with hormones zipping around his body and a gorgeous girlfriend who flinched when he touched her.

Alice sighed and tuned back into the conversation, which had segued from pregnancy to topical treatments and the most recent chemist-compounded concoction – to soothe, to numb, to desensitise – tried and discarded by Denise as ineffectual, tried and adopted by Maria as helpful.

'That's one of the problems,' said Sally. 'This thing's a chameleon. Can't be pinned down, won't be properly understood by doctors, or by anyone, really. Not yet, at any rate.'

A sober silence.

'Who's up for a cuppa?' Simone, hostessing.

'Good idea.' Sally stood. 'Alice, let's help.'

Different kinds of tea waited on the jarrah benchtop: herbal, green, English Breakfast, Earl Grey. A coffee machine made willing noises. A pity she'd cut out caffeine a couple of months ago on a naturopath's suggestion. *It might be a good idea to let your nervous system calm down*. What else couldn't she have? The wicked-looking sponge might have been her choice a year ago. But it seemed that Simone had also baked a gluten-free option; the aroma of the inevitable orange and almond cake filled the kitchen as Sally sliced it into portions.

Sometimes Alice woke to the fading dream-smells of pungent coffee and sugary pastry and almost cried at all she was denied. At all she denied herself. It seemed every woman here refused small pleasures as they made valiant stabs at wellness. Who knew if all that self-restraint made a difference? Though Atikah said she only had occasional tickles of discomfort now and swore it was the effect of the low-oxalate diet. And Fleur, who no longer came to the meetings but who held mythic status, was said to have completely recovered, though diet appeared to have little to do with it. *She doesn't know!* Denise had exclaimed when Alice had asked what treatment worked the miracle. Fleur had tried different meds and changed the contraceptive pill she was on and one day she had no pain.

Alice tried not to hate her.

'Tea or coffee, you two?' Simone was pouring boiling water.

'I'd love an Earl Grey,' said Sally.

Alice selected peppermint, wanting the coffee. Then Denise bustled in, and she and Simone carried mugs and cake out to the lounge room, leaving the other two alone. It was something Alice had noticed about this group, the way the women picked up on each other's need for one-on-one conversations.

The tea was scalding. Alice blew at it, looked out the kitchen window and into the bleached summer sky and thought about the question she'd been too scared to ask – not wanting to hear that complete recovery might take many years, or might *never* happen, not wanting to believe that might be the case for her.

But she must be brave, just like these women.

'What did you do to improve?'

Sally sipped thoughtfully from her mug. 'I guess I gradually worked out what made it worse and what to avoid. And one day I noticed it wasn't as bad. But I had to think of how it was the year before, or the year before that – even the decade. It was no help to think about improving over weeks or even months.'

'But the pain was still bad, right?' Alice wanted to get the rest out quickly. 'How did you handle having it all the time you waited, and without knowing that you *would* improve? I'm not as bad as I was a year ago, but it's still so hard! My fanny and … that whole area keeps telling me that I'm full. Like a cup that's overflowing before you pour anything into it. Some kind of weird nausea, a horrible too-muchness. Does that make sense?'

'Sure, I know what you mean. I suppose … I just had to find a way to live with it.' Sally leaned next to her at the bench and they gazed out at the view, towards the distant city. Cars throbbed in the distance. Parrots argued in a treetop beyond the window. 'I was listening to someone talking about tinnitus on the radio and it sounded similar. The trick was about making the sound of the tinnitus – ringing, high-pitched whine or whatever – a background to your life. Accepting it made it bearable. Fighting made it worse.'

Alice questioned, just for a moment, whether it was her own daily battle that had made the aching and sizzling and knifing so vast that she was blind and deaf to the world. Whether fighting the pain had signposted it so stridently that she might as well have taken to it with her bright pink highlighter.

But, no, as reasonable as Sally sounded, there was a point to be made: 'I reckon there's a level of pain that's impossible to make normal. And that's not a personal failure. No-one can live with pure torture.'

'I guess I need to be reminded just how bad it can be.' Sally paused for a moment. Then, 'You're right, you know. I do remember.' Her face was suddenly older. Careworn. 'It's just a long time since I've had it like that.' She turned to Alice. 'I'm glad that your physio is helping. And I'm glad it's not *quite* as bad for you as it was.'

'Thanks, Sally. It's just difficult to know where to go from here, how to improve more. Living like this is no fun.'

The two women hugged each other, and Alice relaxed into the comfort of being heard.

'Let's go join the others,' said Sally.

They walked through to the lounge room, to a sideboard where the four women hovered, shuffling food and mugs around. Alice accepted a piece of proffered orange and almond cake and, before her courage could fail her, voiced the other question that had been niggling at her over the last few months. 'Has anyone else seen the gyno at the pelvic pain clinic?'

The visit to the clinic in Murdoch had been on Sally's recommendation. It wasn't perfect, she'd said, but the best option for now, if only to be better informed. At Alice's initial appointment – her 'Assessment' – the female gynaecologist had moved her pelvis around and plunged a hand into her body. The fingers had poked at knots and ridges while the gyno and pain specialist talked about a nerve block, *for diagnostic purposes*, over her chilled legs. Nerve block: it's a forbidding term, a terrifying thought, but what else can she do? *It'd be a shame to fall at the last hurdle*, said the specialist as she left the last appointment. Easy for him to say, she'd thought.

'Oh, that gyno!' Denise's tone was scathing. 'What the fuck? Does she enjoy hurting us or what?'

Alice decided to tell them the rest while they milled about, each grabbing a plate with their chosen cake. It might be easier while they were distracted.

'When I didn't have much pain with that point test,' Alice began, 'nowhere near as much as I used to, she thought I would be able to have sex again. She said, "Do you think you might be dragging this on a bit?"' Her throat gripped. 'She didn't seem to understand that the pain is everywhere and all the time.'

'Oh, she's not as bad as that GP everyone used to go to,' said Maria, flicking her black hair over a shoulder as she leaned forward. 'Remember? The one who said to Fleur that she just needed a good root?'

'You're kidding!' Was it insensitivity? Alice wondered. Was she jollying this Fleur along; trying to establish some kind of 'we're all women here' rapport? It was surprisingly consoling to hear that other women had borne the brunt of such insensitivity.

'I hate the way people think they can make these assumptions.' Denise's indignant voice. 'Like that doctor I saw: "Do you think he's the right man for you?" Really? And you know me, how?'

Atikah was quieter. 'The GP I saw at the beginning said I was indulging it.'

'What about Janey?' Simone asked. The others all nodded and she addressed herself to Alice. 'Janey was in the group a while back, then she just stopped coming. Anyway, she'd been told by a "healer" that she'd been sexually abused. It took her years to get over it. And it made her whole family second-guess themselves and each other, all the family's old friends.' Simone's eyes were shiny with tears. 'It was a disaster.'

'I'm so sick of people acting like they know what will cure me,' spat Denise. 'And when I don't try their bloody spiritual realignment or their miracle-working chiropractor or their fucking affirmations, they decide I really don't want to get better. Doesn't matter what you do, there's no way to win that argument.'

'They just want to help,' Sally said, trying to calm her friend.

'I don't give a shit. Make your suggestion then leave me alone. I'm in the best position to decide what quack treatment I'm going to fork out my dwindling financial reserves on. Don't they understand how scary it is to try another useless "solution"? The hope you invest in it, then how it crushes you when it doesn't work?' Alice saw Atikah and Maria exchange a glance, but nobody interrupted. 'And while I'm at it, what about the people who think that if you smile or laugh you must be bullshitting about the pain. As if we don't work so hard to try to be normal. To be a good person. Don't they know what it costs us?'

The sudden tears were a surprise. But Sally seemed unfazed. She put her arms around Denise while she sobbed. They ate their cakes soberly, and soon Denise was wiping her face with tissues and laughing ruefully. 'Sorry, guys.'

*

Here you go, the quotations from the Gaillard Thomas book ☺ :

> *... an excessive sensibility of the nerves supplying the mucous membrane of some portion of the vulva ...*
>
> *... The slightest friction excites intolerable pain and nervousness; even a cold and unexpected current of air produces discomfort; and any degree of pressure is absolutely intolerable ...*
>
> *So commonly is it met with at least, that it becomes a matter of surprise that it has not been more generally and fully described.*

The 1800s. Ironic, hey?
Sally xx

A shiver rippled over Alice's back. She shot a quick return email from her laptop: *That's it exactly, intolerable. Amazing it's from the nineteenth century. What happened between then and now? Freud, I guess! Ali xx*

It was an ongoing conversation between Alice and her new friend: the western history of vulvar pain. The way it had been detailed so accurately so long ago, its virtual disappearance from the literature, then its resurgence as 'psychosomatic' in medical articles of the 1960s and 70s, often from the States, littered with Freudian ideas and terminology: 'psychological causation', 'unconscious conflict', 'sexual dysfunction', 'secondary gain'. And this purported gain? A way to avoid intercourse. Ha! She'd laugh if it didn't rile her so much.

What is Somatoform Disorder? The question had burst from Ashleigh on one of her rare visits to the support group. *Is it the same as 'psychosomatic'?* And Sally had talked about physical symptoms that couldn't be explained by a medical condition, about how 'psychosomatic' is often used to suggest that psychological problems are being expressed through the body. *That's just not correct,* Sally had said. *Mind, body – it's a complicated two-way thing.*

Alice joined her hands behind her shoulders and stretched. Returned to her own body, the here and now. Her place at one of those high tables that suited her so well. Instead of sitting on a bar stool she stood in the café, her head at the same level, and did not stand out.

Waves of chat swelled and broke around her. Two older women in matching blue greeting each other with shouts of delight; a little boy running around tables and barging into a waitress – his mother remonstrating, 'Now look what you've done!'; a tattooed couple turning to their phones, desultory, egg yolk and baked beans congealing on their plates.

The sea beyond the café's glass was slick and clouds banked on the horizon. It would be sticky out there with no sea breeze. She drained her cup of its last cold gulp of coffee, focusing on its tang in her nostrils, its rich roundness on her tongue. The small acts of abstinence she'd tried seemed about as effective as attempting to put out a bushfire with a bucket of water. Why punish herself unnecessarily when there was so little joy in her life? Now she tried to build the deliciously bitter taste in her mouth and the expansiveness filling her thoughts so that both wrestled with the more demanding sensations sweeping her genitals. She would have to take it easy when she got home. Allow the deep, dragging ache to subside. Rest her intractable body.

She still wasn't sure about Freud: so spot-on with some ideas, so ridiculously off-track with others, his theories twisting themselves into such strange shapes as they slipped into other cultures and languages, into medicine, into the mainstream. And what about Charcot? How did his ideas fit with the times? Or that terrible Isaac Baker Brown with his 'hatchet-shaped' cautery iron – how could his operation be condoned at a time when vulvar pain was also described in surprisingly modern ways? Why, it was in 1866, she'd discovered, that Baker Brown had published his book on clitoridectomy, yet it was in 1861 that gynaecologist J. Marion Sims – male, of course, despite his name – approached with insight, with understanding even, the spasms, the mysterious hypersensitivity experienced by his female patients. Alice had looked up Sims's article and read about the woman that could be her, pictured *herself* lying on the couch as the gynaecologist examined her, imagined him writing later, by the light of a lamp – or was it candlelight then? – about *her*: *The slightest touch with a feather or with a camel-hair pencil at the reduplication of the hymeneal membrane produced as severe suffering as if she were cut with a knife*.

It was reassuring to know that once upon a time physicians were less suspicious, more … trusting of their patients. It gave Alice a strange and surprising kind of hope: maybe, one day, doctors and gynos would again take women at their word and treat them with increased understanding, even empathy. Because there were plenty of them, women with this pain: sixteen percent, Sally had stated baldly during their very first phone call. And when she herself, unbelieving, had finally looked up the articles mushrooming in medical journals – researchers, now absorbed in this enigma, spouting statistics and depressing words – she'd read the words herself: *a lifetime incidence rate of 16% for burning, knifelike* – there was that word again – *pain in the genital area that lasted 3 months or more*. Why, then, weren't there newspaper articles? Letters to agony aunts? How was it possible that GPs and specialists in Perth didn't seem to know about vulvodynia?

It wasn't the first time she'd felt angry. At the bloody inefficiency. The appalling injustice.

'Affection', they called it, those nineteenth-century gynos. Their word for affliction: *this affection has been encountered, doubtless, for all time*, Sims wrote. As if there could be any affection towards this disorder! And her mind snagged on the image of Baker Brown again and on his radical, brutal surgery. Would there be answers in his writing? Some believable rationale for his extreme decisions, some comprehensible purpose for his barbaric actions? She'd find out soon enough. The thought of picking up the book she'd ordered through the uni library and the idea of reading about the cutting and the searing and the terribly mangled women brought with it a thrill somewhere between anticipation and dread.

And still, beyond the words from the past and the present, beneath the feelings that tossed her back and forth between fear and fury, there was that other thing. The *something* of which she could hardly conceive. The pressure that came with creativity – she knew it so well – the sense of compulsion without an outlet; all the time the pressure growing, growing … a domain distilling, characters finding inchoate form, a fictional narrative taking invisible shape …

The jangle wrenched her back to the café.

Alice pulled the mobile from her silk purse. *How are you today? X. Penny*. She thought for a moment, then: *Same old … Just working in caf. Ena coming soon x*. Pen's reply, *Hope it's still easing. Damn nerve block! :-(Will call later xx*.

Alice replaced the phone in her snug silk purse, which was only big enough for the essentials. Keys, coins, mobile, a card or two. Usually the precious gift sat on the bedside table, close enough for her to touch in the night, but she had brought the purse today to find out more. Little bigger than her spread hand, it was dwarfed by its mystery.

She logged out of her uni emails and shut down the laptop, her head cottonwool. The caffeine effect was waning, speedy thoughts and associations stalling. Maybe she would have to limit her coffee intake. Drinking it again brought marvellous aha moments, but it also made her body race along with her mind, as if there were a finishing line she might cross first, if only she ran fast enough. And the prize? It could only be recovery, these days, not career ambitions satisfied or acquaintances maintained, when all she could do was say no to teaching opportunities, no to parties or lingering lunches; no, while she researched and thought and wrote, searching for a way to pick the lock of suffering.

Deeper relationships sustained her now – Ena, and now Sally, Denise and the others. Her illness had shattered the circle of friends who knew her mainly as the Alice in 'Duncan and Alice' and, in the aftermath, only these confidantes remained. And Penny, of course, though even she'd shown a hint of impatience lately. Did Pen wonder about Alice's inability to regain health? Did she question it silently or with her snooty executive mates, who took meds when struck by fleeting ailments and, pinstriped, soldiered on?

Before I discovered this group, I felt alone, Alice told Sally and Denise when the three met for a picnic. *Like I was the only person on the planet with this, this* thing. They'd both felt the same, they said, and Sally had gone on to talk about the 1980s, before she even had a name for her suffering, and how crazy that had made her. It felt good, now, to share these feelings with these other women, to know that they understood her and she them.

And Ena? With Ena, Alice felt accepted, just as she always had been, and just as she was. Small wonder she visited her mother-in-law more often: donning one of Ena's array of aprons, faded over the years of baking for income then pleasure, choosing a recipe from her scrapbook, trying to make out pale ingredient lists through layered splotches, melting shortening and stirring pudding mix. Then texting Duncan with the invitation, *Ena's tonight!* and settling into an impromptu family meal where she could sit, briefly, having stood all afternoon. Just the three of them, talking literature and culture.

But always, always, Duncan holding his mother ever so subtly away. Did he blame Ena for the traumas of his childhood, those sorrows beyond her control? Somehow, yes, it seemed he did. And Alice had the impression that Ena had stopped trying to persuade her son otherwise years ago. That she understood whatever grudge he held against her she could do nothing to remove. Or was it all just his excuse for carelessly cruel behaviour? Alice chased the traitor-thought from her mind.

'Alice!' Right on time.

'Hello, Ena.' She relaxed into her friend's embrace for a long beat.

'It's lovely to see you, my dear.' No-one else she knew could use the epithet without sounding old-fashioned or condescending.

'You too.' Alice scanned the room and spotted a small table against the glass, the ocean only long steps away. 'Let's grab that one, hey?'

'But what about you?'

'I can sit for a bit. I have my cushion.'

It was hard not to sound slightly bitter: that disastrous nerve block, the pinching sear, newly alive and all over her buttocks, the fresh incentive for a 'special' cushion. Well, she'd thought, I might as well make adjustments, find relief wherever possible, even as bowing to the dictates of her disorder brought gall to her throat, to her thoughts.

Alice gathered her belongings – laptop, cushion, purse – and followed Ena's lurching steps. Was reminded, again: the car accident in 1972 that had left its mark. Her friend's inability to walk far or stand too long. *We make a right pair,* Ena had said at their last outing.

Maybe, she thought, there was more for her to learn about acceptance, about good grace.

Alice put the silk purse on the table and placed her cushion on the chair so the shape faced as it would on a horse's hoof: the 'shoe' opening at the back. As she sat, a tear of sweat trickled from between her legs, tracing every little skin bump and flesh fold. When would autumn come? It was a hot day out there. Another forty-plus, by the looks.

A quick twist of pain between her legs, then a slow, tingling subsidence. She was gradually returning to her pre-procedure self, but even with the new seat – even with her fanny and the inner cheeks of her bum suspended in air and only touched by pure, organic, undyed cotton – her capacity was still measured in minutes. The cushion was merely special, after all, not miraculous. She shuffled against it, nudging it into some small comfort.

'How have you been, Alice?'

Ena already knew about the 'procedure'. The cancellation of another year of teaching. The clawing back to what she thought of as 'the plateau': that endurable state she only now realised she'd achieved in the months before the nerve block. *Be careful,* Sally had warned when Alice decided to go ahead with the procedure in February. *It's hard to improve and so easy to slip backwards.* But the gynaecologist had assured her, *It can't do any harm.* And she had listened.

In the weeks after, Sally had made repeated visits – *Just a quick one to see how you're doing* – and held her as she sobbed, inconsolable. As she wondered aloud if the gyno, the same woman who had thrust a rough hand into her vagina at her first pain clinic appointment, had used the anaesthetic needle the same way, jabbing it like a weapon through the wall of her vagina while she lay there unconscious. Defenceless.

'I'm okay,' said Alice. 'Heading back towards how I was in January, I reckon.' She'd spoken with Sasha about what her reaction might mean. *Let's just talk while you're flared up,* the physio had said at the last session, putting her hand gently on Alice's arm. 'Sasha wonders if the nerve block irritated the pudendal nerve. Maybe other sacral nerves too.' Had the gyno twisted her pelvis roughly on the pivot of her sacrum? Or had she herself developed a version of Charcot's 'dynamic lesion' in her brain? 'I'm wondering, though, because it's spread over such a big area now, whether it's more a central nervous system problem. The people I see at the clinic reckon it's a combo of pudendal neuralgia and central sensitisation.'

'What, a local problem *and* a brain problem?'

'Yep. The pain dude thinks the nerve isn't trapped, but maybe stretched and irritated. And now the brain can't forget the pain; the sensations have become normal to it.'

She had resolved since, privately, quietly, to listen to her body and her dreams more closely. She thought of the slippery-dip dream she'd had just before the nerve block: dream-Alice's shattered legs and empty, echoing home.

The naked late-morning brightness sheeted the room and turned Ena's white hair into dandelion seeds. As if she could be blown away by a single breath. Not like the early days, over a decade ago now, when Ena's hair was still auburn … *and once a brilliant flame*, the older woman had told her. *Ena means passionate in Celtic*, she'd said. *Fiery*. Then she'd told Alice how she'd been born with wisps of fire on her head. How even her maiden surname told the tale. Reid: red hair or a ruddy complexion. *Both of which I had, for my sins*, Ena had laughed, and said how she could never keep a secret back then: *My red face always told the truth!*

Now her face wore a delighted smile. 'You have the purse. I'm so glad you're using it.' Ena put on her glasses and peered at the front panel. 'Look at that courtly couple. And the colour of the rose.'

Alice could see the rose reproduced in the medallion on the back panel, surrounded by flowers in ivory and peach. The embroidery so fine that the antique blossoms surrendered coloured nuances to the modern light.

'Yes – oh, I love it, Ena!' She could still remember the unwrapping. The post-present sex. A different Alice. 'I was wondering if you know anything about it. Duncan said you might.'

'Well, I know a little. But not much, I'm afraid.' A sapphire flash as Ena rolled the rings on her finger. 'My aunt Elspeth was a very careful woman, so she'd looked after the purse well. She was given it by my grandmother Aileen, who married into the Reids.' Her eyes turned upward, recalling. 'Elspeth said to me, *I wish I'd written down everything*. Her memory was not so good by then, you see. All she could remember Nanna saying was that it had been a gift of love in times of trouble. And that it had come sideways through the Reid family and was passed down. I'm not sure what the "sideways" means.'

Ena swept wisps of hair back from her face. It was hotter in this part of the café, the air-conditioning faltering against the day's savage, wet heat.

'My aunt had no children and we were very close, so she gave it to me. That's all I know, I'm afraid.' When Ena smiled, her face shone. 'Except that I am thrilled Duncan gave it to you, my dear.'

Alice's hand briefly grasped and squeezed.

The tale was filled with so many gaps. She would have to use her own imagination to create stories for the silk purse.

Maybe the lady who had first owned it – she saw a figure, a face turned half-away, a coil of strawberry-blonde hair – had given the purse to a dear daughter, or a treasured cousin, who had put it, for safety, in a display cabinet. There it had sat, half-forgotten for years, in that elaborate room. Then, perhaps, it had been remembered and hung from a wall, no-one noticing the gusset facing the window fading slowly, imperceptibly, as the seasons and years rolled over. Until it was rediscovered and given to Ena's grandmother, the purse and its history firing Aileen's passion, drawing her back into life.

'I've been thinking a lot about purses lately,' she said. 'It must be all the Freud I'm reading.'

Ena laughed. 'I can guess what Freud made of purses.'

Because of her approachability, perhaps, or the aroma of warm biscuit dough that seemed to travel with her, it was easy to underestimate the breadth of Ena's knowledge, the keen intelligence that she had also bestowed on her son. So Alice could talk about Freud's 'Dora' case. She knew Ena would understand its appeal, given the site of her own suffering.

'He loved the jewel case in Dora's dream,' she said. 'Female genitals, of course. Freudian gold.' She'd been re-reading the case history recently, scribbling ripostes in the margins. 'When Dora bucked up – she was quite feisty, really, for her age and the times – he just gave further interpretations. But he was hard to argue with. The ideas sound ridiculous, but they slot into this impenetrable kind of monolith.' What was it he'd said about Dora's purse? 'He reckoned Dora "confessed" her masturbation to him by playing with her reticule in an analytic session.'

Maybe Dora's small bag had been beaded. Or embroidered, like hers. What was inside Dora's purse? What was inside her own? Only fragments, it seemed. Disjointed body parts and ideas, rubbing and sliding against each other. Pain stitched through seams and pleats.

'He did understand metaphor pretty well, though,' Ena said, 'from the bits and pieces I've read.' They had discussed Freud and his lingering influence before at dinners, Ena and she laughing and challenging each other back and forth, Duncan animated, joining in and then, impatient to get back to his writing, jingling the keys in his pocket. 'The way dream images and bodily symptoms act as stand-ins. Even if his interpretations were skewed by culture, and by his own history of course.'

Alice looked out to a rising wind, the icing of the sea flaked and swirling, as if spread by an awkward giant hand. 'Is anyone not limited by their own baggage?' The question had been on her mind. She turned to Ena, not really sure what she was asking. Or why she was asking it of her husband's mother. 'Sometimes I think about how the past lives on in us, in ways we're not even aware of.'

Ena thanked a waitress and took grateful sips of coffee. 'Have I told you the story about my grandfather, Aileen's husband?'

Alice remembered some of Ena's tales of the past. Her proud family, with its roots deep in Scottish history. The pressure on her grandfather, as the last person carrying the family name in the area, to produce sons. *He and Aileen, who was a tiny little thing* – Ena had drawn the petite figure with her hands – *parented thirteen children, the last two born after he was paralysed from the waist down.* Elspeth had been born before his accident, Ena's father after.

'Nanna had a visit from several local church ladies. They let her know that the church disapproved of these last births.'

'How come? Because he was meant to be paralysed?' Where had she read that men who were paralysed could still have erections?

'Because she must have had to mount him, you know ... The missionary position was the acceptable thing: him mounting her. But he was paralysed. Anyway, legend has it that she said to the church ladies, *Them that are lashed to the post must take the strikes*.'

'What, make the best of a bad thing? Continue to find pleasure where you can?'

'No, more that it was her duty,' Ena said.

'Her duty to procreate?'

'Yes, that's right.'

Maybe, Alice thought, she was too used to the women in the support group and their references to desire and pain. At last Saturday's meeting, in Atikah's spick-and-span inner-city unit, Denise had said, *I miss pain-free sex. Does anyone else?* Maria had started crying, which had set off Jack, Simone's tiny baby. Many of them still seemed to get horny – a wonder, really – and some seemed able to voice this, to make jokes about big penises and little fannies, even with the pain. Did Aileen imagine pleasure? Did she long for her husband to reach for her or dream of a forbidden touch – her own? a lover's? Was her role of wife and procreator a prison for desire? Had duty, not lust, overcome Aileen's Victorian modesty?

Alice imagined Duncan responding to all these questions: 'It's just history, Alice.' Saw her challenges, bright and bold, that darkened his face.

She must leave. Calm the pins and needles that now striped the backs of her legs. The end point, as always, came on suddenly and without the possibility of negotiation.

Ena read the moment in her eyes. They stood and looked out over the sea together. The depths were darker now, and roiling in anticipation.

'An autumn storm,' said Ena. 'The veggies will love it.'

The air was heavy with the expectation of rain.

Alice had the urge to pull off her sweaty clothes and wander the house naked. Why not? The curtains were closed and no-one else was here.

She put her purse on the bed along with – carefully – the fragile book, just picked up. Then she stripped off her top and skirt, unclasped her bra and stepped out of her undies. There, in the full-length mirror: her body. Its long, lithe paleness. Symmetrical, whole, cohesive. The only signs of disorder the dabs of blue, green, yellow and brown along the sides of her bum: marks of the measured violence she enacted against her body to distract it from the thoughtless violence it did itself. The pinches sometimes shifting the pain for a moment. What else to do?

She assessed her body. The curve of her hip, softer than a year ago. Breasts, pert and keen in the cups of her hands. The bush of hair still startling yet, increasingly, pleasing to her. She wondered if she'd ever wax again: define the edges cleanly, groom the small strip neatly. What a lot of fuss for what, these days, served no purpose. More tempting to repel rather than allure. Keep it to herself.

She grasped the hair and tugged fondly, then pressed her fingers through the strands and past the pleats of flesh, her touch hesitant, then surer, the warm softening overpowering that stubborn ache. She'd been able to touch herself recently without triggering the paralysing rawness that self-pleasure had brought in those first months. And, weirdly, the nerve block, by causing her bum and thighs to prickle and buzz, had helped, distracting her body, it seemed, from her clitoris. Though sex was still out of the question – for her, at least.

Perhaps she should consult the male physio Sally had told her about, once her body settled. *He appears to understand about desire*, Sally had said, explaining how Ashleigh had taken Ryan for a few sessions and how they were now able to have sex again. *Ash is over the moon!* Alice wondered if Duncan would be open to the possibility. He was not good at taking instruction from others, but hope might be a big enough – she surprised herself by laughing – carrot to dangle.

Who would she make such efforts for? Herself, or him?

The book caught her eye in the mirror and she twisted to it, walked towards the unassailable authority of its title: *On the Curability of Certain Forms of Insanity, Epilepsy, Catalepsy, and Hysteria in Females* by I. Baker Brown. The cautery iron. That poor woman. Alice laid on her tummy and slipped the tattered volume from its elastic band. Was Isaac Baker Brown the demon carried by her imagination? Would he detail the atrocities carried out in the London Surgical Home?

The yellowing pages fanned and settled.

> *Long and frequent observation convinced me that a large number of affections peculiar to females, depended on loss of nerve power, and that this was produced by peripheral irritation, arising originally in some branches of the pudic nerve, more particularly the incident nerve supplying the clitoris …*

Pudic nerve? Maybe that was the pudendal nerve. Peripheral irritation? Probably masturbation. She had been reading other nineteenth-century texts that expressed moral horror over the practice; had seen that, on occasion, women themselves acquiesced to certain forms of treatment, even operations, wanting to be rid of a lust that troubled Victorian society's notions of what a gentlewoman should be. Docile, modest. Asexual, somehow.

She flicked through some more pages: *the clitoris is freely excised either by scissors or knife – I always prefer the scissors.*

A sympathetic stab in her fanny. She rolled onto her side and pushed a pillow between her thighs. So the operation was Baker Brown's solution for hysteria and all the associated downward-spiralling conditions: *spinal irritation, hysterical epilepsy … idiotcy* – a spelling mistake here, perhaps? A hint of the farmer behind the surgeon? – and the last, *death*. This was how he fixed them. By removing the problem.

By removing the clitoris.

She kept reading, thinking. Stopping each time words snagged her.

> *… I have been met with many objections, such as unsexing the female –*

Protests from physicians and also other surgeons, from the looks, but no give in Baker Brown's certain, almost strident, voice.

> *… irritation about vulva, perinaeum, and anus … sometimes she has to pass her water every half-hour … for the last three years the act of coition has been accomplished without the least pleasure, but with pain –*

Vestibulodynia? A recurring UTI?

> *… subject to fits of violent excitement … 'she would fly at him and rend his skin, like a tigress' … became in every respect a good wife –*

What choice did she have? What else might they do if she didn't behave?

> *… six years she had been confined to a spinal couch … so forward and open in her manners, that she was generally avoided by gentlemen.* Never had an offer of marriage –

The phrase italicised, emphasised, as if it were out of the ordinary – a terrible, shameful thing.

> *… she complained to my son, Mr. Boyer Brown, that I had unsexed her –*

A family affair then … And the woman *herself* insisting, this time, that she had been 'unsexed'. Alice could have told her that if Baker Brown was not chastened by his colleagues, he was certainly not going to be moved by a woman.

> *... a great distaste for her husband ... managing to free her hands ... jacket substituted –*

A straitjacket? So, not only hacked at, but also restrained. Moral education, it seemed.

She flicked back a page or two. Stopped suddenly. Here, finally – finally! – the words of the woman. If the note-taker – a nurse? a doctor? – could be trusted.

> *'Last March, instead of sliding down a slope, I jumped. This caused displacement of my womb ... I was fomented with hot water ... I am obliged to relieve the irritation by rubbing ... felt as if I did not care for living. I would like to have my hands untied; I will be very quiet ... I am very rude – I beg your pardon ... I had a baby two years ago: it was not born at the full time ... My brain has been affected.'*

All this, seventeen hours after the operation: the clitoris excised, the patient bound and tied.

Scissors. Knife. Cautery iron. Which did he really use against these unknowing women? And did the instrument matter when, after all, the horrific outcome was always the same?

Alice closed her eyes and waited for ... what ... an image? Some kind of clue?

She could just make out the shape of the room that came to her. In a house? a hospital? Anyway, a consulting area where Baker Brown might see the fathers and the husbands, furnished to impress and with an undercurrent of musty velvet. Empty, for the moment. A few dreamlike strides, then an examination room: a lady lying on a narrow bed, her eyes wells of suffering and, perhaps, accusation. Alice turned from the woman's unspoken appeal. A sweet, pungent scent caught at her and carried her down a passageway and into some wards. The scent now a stench. Chloroform? A woman in a ward bed. Her body trussed by bandages and straitjacket, eyes flicking – left, right. Baker Brown's hand clamping her shoulder. *I would like to have my hands untied*. The woman's whimper. *I will be very quiet*.

An angry rumble. A heavy patter against the roof. Jerked back into her naked, modern self, her skin suddenly goosebumped.

Alice scrabbled for her underclothes, skirt, top, began to pull them on, fingers fumbling with urgency.

Chapter 16

London, February 1866

Two weeks hence.

Isaac Baker Brown's door shuts behind them and Arthur takes his wife's gloved hand as they step onto the footway and towards their carriage, slows his pace to match her stuttering gait. It is dreadfully chill and her hand in his feels inert, lifeless. He looks to her face for tears, but there are none. She looks dishevelled, though, the fall of her cloak crooked, her chignon mussed; the little hat skewed, its feather tatty.

It is a day of hard frost, and coal smoke shrouds the houses of Connaught Square, wraps itself around the naked trees in the centre garden. All is weighted by the leaden sky. The east wind drives a few drifting snowflakes against them.

"Are you all right?"

"Yes." Her voice is inert, too, her body stiff, like a wooden figurine whose parts are moved into awkward poses that it holds without volition.

He looks closely at her, his wife. Tries to imagine how she would seem to him if they were strangers, wonders what it is about her that has changed. She is no less beautiful than she was on the day they wed, but her slight figure and listless face carry a sense of tragedy, a feeling of separateness so different from her old joyful response to life. He would like to break through to the sadness beneath, warm her back to life, but he does not know how.

Euripides and Herodotus are stamping their shod hooves and gusting white from their nostrils. It was their little joke, his and Emmie's, once upon a time: his Rugby School favourites; the fascination with all things ancient Greek. *Hero and Euri*, they used to nod to each other, like a secret language.

He helps Emily up into the carriage and makes the decision without her. "Marble Arch, Harry." And at their driver's nod: "Thank you." He needs open air just now, and they need somewhere private to talk, if she is able. He waits for her complaint or refusal—"I must go home, Arthur, lie down"—but can see from the emptiness of her eyes that she has not even heard him give the order.

Once, they would have walked to Hyde Park from here, tossing their words and laughter back and forth, but it is too far for her now. Instead, she stands in the carriage, hands braced against its sides, her back curved, knees bent, her neck angled awkwardly. The carriage lurches into movement and Arthur rounds her waist with his hands, reading the reluctant assent in her eyes. As they jerk and bounce along, he tries to hold her steady, and the terrible and inevitable advance Baker Brown has painted for him—hysteria, epilepsy, idiocy ... death—floods him, and the consultation returns to him in bits and pieces: *a certain coarseness ... enable procreation ... moral duty ... good wives*. Then, before he can naysay them, he hears the words that so shocked him rising like shouts in his mind: *unnatural practices*! *persistent excitation*! *your wife herself*!

Your wife herself.

The separate bedchamber. Is there another reason she has shut her body away from him? Does she draw on her own troubled resources? Seek pleasure at her own hand? Senseless, surely, when she cannot tolerate his amorous attention, when she winces at his touch, even in the daylight, even when light and accidental. Ridiculous! But still the images form, make him want to push her away, even as he yearns to draw her down and onto his lap, wrap his arms about her body, a safeguard against all that might further injure her.

Two weeks hence.

Is this the right choice? Would it be better to return with her to Herdley, after all? Consult with Morrison and see who can take on his case load? Or find someone to be with her while he continues in the city? But what would that achieve, when rest at Hierde House has so far seen no improvement? And when she continues to turn from him, as if *he* is the enemy? Shut herself away, as much as she—

The wheels come up against the kerb, jarring them to a halt. She sways against him, then pulls herself away. He lifts the ermine muff, gently pushes her unresisting hands into its centre and steps ahead of her onto the footway, helping her down, noting the grimace of pain.

When he sees the hot-potato man near Marble Arch and when that familiar warming, starchy scent reaches him, his mouth rushes with juices. But the old queasiness has returned these last months and he never knows whether to starve it or feed it. Besides, it seems greedy—almost unseemly—to be scoffing food when he knows she will not. So he moves away from the hot-potato man, turns his back on the organ-grinder playing Mozart, and the Punch and Judy show just beginning—Punch's red and yellow motley a touch of sunshine on this grim day—takes Emmie's arm and walks slowly with her into Hyde Park, trying to forget how they once would shout at Punch's wicked crimes, find themselves chuckling at his outrageous antics, talk afterwards about just which politician he was mocking this time.

Ten months with the worst of it. Only ten months, but it seems like months without measure when he remembers Emmie as she used to be, thinks of her here, in Hyde Park, riding along Rotten Row with Beatrice, her red-gold hair, netted in black, catching the light as they canter towards him. Or just over a year ago, skating with other pleasure-makers along the Long Water by torchlight, ignoring the board marked *Dangerous*, her dress hitched up to show her fancy Balmoral boots and scarlet petticoat—*magenta*, she'd corrected him, eyebrow arched—her cheeks and lips flushed with cold and excitement. She'd called him onto the ice on the evening that comes to him, travelled backwards holding his hands to secure him, the poorer skater, then once he was sound on his blades she'd flown off, skates hissing, under the Serpentine Bridge and round the snake's curve, red ribbons streaming from under her Scotch cap, those "follow-me-lads" testing him, teasing him, drawing him on. And then later that same night—how it hurts to remember—he had placed her above him and they'd rocked and swayed to the same rhythm, and afterwards curved into each other like a blessing.

The sky is turning pink and the air sharp, like glass: a real snowfall can't be far away. On the path ahead a rook stabs at something with its dagger beak, scrapes at it, muscular neck working, then flies off to the west, its beak clamped on the unknown treasure. To its rookery, no doubt; to confer with the rest of the parliament there.

He guides her to a space just off the path, a wooden bench where they can sit a little way removed from other walkers. He takes off his overcoat and folds it into a cushion, but she shakes her head, leans against the side of the bench and closes her eyes.

Perhaps … but, no, they must talk.

"Did he speak with you about the operation?" he begins. "About what it entails?"

"Yes—I think so. He spoke of removing the cause of the irritation."

He has watched her wrestle with many feelings—sadness, fear, anger, despair—but never seen her like this: so utterly devoid of emotion or animation. As if she has given up; as if she is already dead.

But they must continue. "And you feel that this is the right course?"

"I do not want an operation, but I want to be better, so if Father and you think it is the right thing to do, I cannot find it within me to refuse. I must trust you." But her face is dreary as she speaks the words. "If it will take away the pain then I will go against all that tells me to not do it."

For a moment, his heart leaps. "There is something that tells you not to do this?"

But she sighs and shakes her head. "My thoughts are no longer to be trusted."

He plunges on. "And do you understand what he says has caused this?" Speaking the words quickly. "And why you may need to be watched closely afterwards?"

She turns her face to his and, for a moment, he sees her eyes flash. In anger? betrayal? She looks away and over the park.

"If you would think this of me, then you must go ahead and believe it," she says dully.

He does not want this, he does not! But what *is* he to believe? What are they to do?

Oh, how he would like to turn her face to his again, say the words that are in his heart: "Emmie, Emmie, my love! Where have you gone? How can I return you to yourself? How can I return you to me?"

He shivers and stamps his numb feet. They must go home soon. He will ask Millie to warm Emmie's bed and see if Mrs Fennell can whip them up a hot toddy. They will talk more tomorrow, this time in the comfort of their home.

A man and woman push a perambulator up the path. Closer they come, and closer. The man's hair is silky brown under his top hat; the woman's hair is golden, her attractive face rosy. Now, only yards away, they stop and lean over the little blue bundle in the perambulator, then debate something briefly, a little crossly, their faces worried and their eyes on the sky, their hands overlapping and plucking at blankets. Then they smile fondly at the baby and each other before hurrying up the path and out of sight.

"It could be us." Her voice is desolate. "Oh, Arthur, why isn't it us?"

His own tears spill and freeze on his cheek. He slides along the bench towards her, puts his arm around her waist and sighs as she leans into him, just as she used to. There is warmth under her clothing, beneath her crinoline, and he turns his face towards it, into it, feeling for who she is, seeking that place where they might meet within her, whispering, "It will be all right," reassuring her, "It will be all right," telling himself, surely, surely it will be all right.

Perth, June 2009

After the appointment, the air had been thick with anger and uneasiness. The drive home as bad as their journey there – even worse, what with the throb and sting of intrusion and the lingering image of Duncan's folded arms and unreadable face in that stark, white room. Then, at home, there'd been the blistering argument, both of them striding around the lounge room, flinging accusations, using the secrets they'd shared over the years – their own vulnerabilities offered as gifts, delivered with trust – as weapons. But finally, after nights spent at opposite ends of the house, days in taut silence, they'd come together and reached a truce, of sorts – for theirs, she observed, seemed to have become *that* kind of marriage.

So, the truce: she would continue to see Sasha alone; they would see Paul together and find out whether he could help them – help her? help him? – have sex again. And if she wanted to see Paul beyond that – beyond having sex, that is, Duncan had clarified – *well, you can see him alone*. Then he'd given a strange half-smile, her husband. It was understandable, the establishment of this deadline and Duncan's territoriality, a kind of testing of her, she supposed, but the ticking of the clock made her mind rebel, made resentment towards him leak from her, even as they edged closer and closer to the goal, even as she continued to stretch and massage the area, rub oil in gently, think on it with kindness. And, yes, she had now fully recovered from the nerve block; yes, she was back to 'the plateau'; yes, she could contemplate intercourse; yes, they were pretty much there. But *where*? And at what cost?

Still, she honoured the terms of the truce and so did he, visiting the physios through May and into June: she, Sasha; both of them, Paul. And Paul told her to trust herself and her body, told Duncan to attend to his wife's body as it opened to him. And Sasha listened when Alice shared her fears and her hopes, urged her to be strong for her husband too. And Paul and Sasha both assured her, independently and with firm compassion, that she was ready.

So, when Duncan reached for her in the weeks that followed, she turned to him. Allowed him entry. The payment was a savage rawness later that night or over the next day, as if the lining between the inside and the outside of her was too thin. The rewards were caresses and loving looks, and the lifting of that constant, heavy, unspoken pressure. Duncan smiled at her again; doubt and guilt no longer pressed the words they spoke into flat pleasantries.

At what cost?

She sighed and rolled over on the sofa. Lifted the slender book from the coffee table, testing its weight in her hand, in her lap. *On the Curability of Certain Forms of Insanity, Epilepsy, Catalepsy, and Hysteria in Females* by I. Baker Brown. Such a slight heft for such an important-sounding title, for such dark contents. All those silent women, and that man pontificating about them, deciding, cutting, 'curing'.

Men, and what they do to women's bodies; these were things that would not have interested the old Alice. Sure, she'd considered gender relations and their imbalances, theorised about them too, but that's exactly what it had been: abstract notions, ideas drifting in the air. And now? Now the subject gripped her, registering in every muscle, every tissue, every cell, and in all the entries to her body, finding its way back out again in moments of piercing recognition. It inveigled its way into her essays too, her research into hysteria confirming the lopsided history of what men did to women in the name of medicine, her own experience exposing breaches and faults in modern knowledge when it came to women – to their bodies, their sexuality.

And yet ... and yet ... the more she read and the more she wrote, the more dissatisfied she felt. It was something to do with the words that had burst into her mind during that anxious, angry drive to the appointment with Paul, the images that had come with them: pain that pierces your bones, that shoots through your thoughts, frightened birds taking flight. More, it was to do with that pressure and urgency – somewhere below her thoughts or somewhere within her body, in that strange geography of creativity – a story, no, a *life*, demanding to be written. Because she didn't want to be in her head anymore, she knew now, didn't want to write in that formal, academic way; she couldn't, not anymore, not while this demand to make a life, to ... discover a life, really – but whose life? *whose* life? – remained unfulfilled.

Whose life? It could only be a woman, couldn't it?

Maybe someone back then, in that place and time she was beginning to know through reading, through research: England, the nineteenth century. And a *lady* felt right – yes, a gentlelady, all wealth and comfort, yet felled by pain.

How might such a woman make sense of this mystifying pain? What choices might a girl on the cusp of womanhood – or, more realistically in those times, her father – make? How might a man and a woman in love deal with it? She thought of the gentlewoman on her silk purse. The peach gown, the golden hair, the red rose in her hand, the expression on her face … and an answer to her silent query in the lover's countenance: tenderness and desire. She imagined the woman, the man, drummed by pain out of desire, out of love. The impossibility of speaking the suffering and fear in those times – or was Victorian repression a stereotype? The taboo of marital lust a myth? She imagined the married couple like Ena's grandparents: the woman, *lashed to the post*, taking the strikes of lust, fulfilling the duty of procreation. She pictured them like she and Duncan: stumbling along, knocking hard against each other as their solitary paths crisscrossed. Could it be any different?

Was there another way?

She stilled her racing mind, swept the flickering images and questions from it and brought herself to that quiet place again. Felt, over the slowing seconds, the slower minutes, the breath moving in … and out of her, the subtle sweep of blood through her body, its decelerating throb in her fingertips. Sensed that pressure, that coiled urgency that had been building for months, now rising, rising, and holding it … holding. And again, rising, rising, and then … thrusting up and into light – like a buoy, bursting to the surface of the ocean, like a deep-sea creature heaved from darkness into light.

And then, just like that, she saw him and felt the shock. A man! And it was almost frightening how quickly he rushed to her then, fully formed and garbed in tweed trousers, frockcoat, top hat, as if he'd been wandering alone in blankness, waiting for her to see him, or tapping the toe of his boot in the wings of her mind, listening for his cue –

Arthur. His name was Arthur.

Hair a soft, fine brown. Eyes dipping at their outer corners.

Arthur with his wife. She has *that* pain – her very own. They are suffering, both of them, and need to make a critical decision … Isaac Baker Brown! An operation?

How to help her!

Arthur a doctor. No … a lawyer? a politician?

Arthur a boy, sitting on a heavy oaken bench at his lessons. She felt him – the silk of his hair, the wriggle of his legs; she felt it – the softness of his cheek against her lips.

She wondered how she would begin his story.

Chapter 17

London, February 1866

Chimes reach him from the library, then the striking of the hour. One, two, three, and the thoughts and images are still dashing around his head, keeping him from sleep. Emily, her face wrung with suffering and her sore, depleted body. Baker Brown's prognosis—hysteria, epilepsy, idiocy … death. And his own useless self.

His own. Useless. Self.

Stop.

Think on what might help. Steps to take in readiness, for after the procedure: Millie to tend Emily, he and Beatrice to distract her from the pain. Then, after some months, as she improves, how to engage her, bring her out of herself … Herdley from July—short runs in the brougham, the life of the country, the pure air and warm summer sun, and then short walks, the village …

And here the path between Hierde House and the village comes to him and he sees the elm thicket near Herdley, recalls all the times he scaled the biggest trees in his hunt for rook eggs, all the times he raced past the copse as a lad—back from the tomfoolery of the village gang, back from the hustling busyness of the marketplace, with its fragrant dung of cattle and sheep, its shouting hawkers and spiced pies; back to Mother, always to Mother. Later, walking past the elm thicket stolid and unwavering, feet moving, left, right, left, in a sombre march.

And now he is sinking heavy in his bed … then changing … shape-shifting … turning to air and floating away flying away and … *the path beside the elms opens before him again, the same as always, yet different too, the grass a fluorescent green, its softness cushioning his bare feet. The elms wave him into their midst and sway above, stately guardians, their branches closing around him like giant arms, the wind through his hair like a woman's touch. He senses knowledge moving through the sap of the trees like blood, feels it filtering through the veins of their leaves. "What is it?" he cries. "Please tell me!" But their leaves fold in on each other. They will keep their counsel.*

The world is utterly, horribly silent.

February 13th 1866

Dearest Bea,

Thank you for offering to have me in Westminster afterwards. I would appreciate this—Mam says I can stay with them, but I don't think Father has told her a great deal about what is ahead & I don't want to upset her. It is all very difficult. The operation will be carried out on February 26th, then Father says I will have to make "progress" before I can be released. Are you sure it will not upset your household too much & that you yourself will not be too drawn upon? I do not wish Father Rochdale to be at all inconvenienced, especially when the proposed Reform Bill is causing ruction.

I am trying to be practical & trusting, & to think of how much better life will be after; I try to imagine a time when I will be able to be as I once was & how wonderful that will feel. But I am terribly scared, Bea, & uneasy. When I allow this fear to take hold I feel dizzy & panicked, yet when I think of how it might be not to go ahead, I panic then too. It would be impossible to continue as I am—I just can't go on like this, I can't. It might be hard for you to understand & it is hard for me to even think it, but I would rather be dead.

I'm sorry, dear Bea, if this upsets you, as I'm sure it must. I will continue to remind myself of how reluctant Arthur was to proceed & how he now thinks it is for the best, & calm myself with that thought.

Love Emily

February 16th 1866

Dear Bea,

I know you think you are helping, but ~~please don't~~ I don't think it does any good to disagree with Arthur at this point. It only upsets him, & me. I'm not sure how I can defend this decision—I hardly even know how to think about what is ahead—but you must see that Arthur & I are talking more now, & deciding things together—he is very tender & caring—& it would help us to have your support. Father says it is only a little procedure & then I will no longer have these troubles, so this is what I am imagining now & counting down the days.

Em

February 20th 1866

Dearest Beatrice,

Thank you for your visit. I want to thank you also for your concern & to agree that you have every right to argue with Arthur, or to persuade me otherwise—I know you mean well & only wish the best for us. As for me, I still have these topsy-turvy moods. Right now I do not know whether to berate you or ask you to save me; sometimes I feel sure & resolved, & then I falter & doubt everything. Can you support me whatever happens? Oh God, I hope we are making the right decision!

Pray for me, sister.

Your Em

February 23rd 1866

Bea,

Arthur looks dreadful—sick with worry—& this makes me doubt us, doubt everything. I think his fears, like mine, will vanish once Monday has come & gone—once it is all over. Can you help distract him in the meantime? Please come to All Saints with us on Sunday, if you can, & then back to our home for a quiet afternoon, the three of us together.

Emmie

Chapter 18

Perth, August–September 2009

It was a source of wonder to her, a sweet miracle the way Arthur had formed a personality, decided on a setting, consolidated a history, in that same strange independent way in which he'd first presented himself. The childhood scenes came quickly too – more like remembering a story than creating a character, the recollections like sudden shards piercing her thought, insisting on being recorded.

But now she was suddenly, and without warning, stuck.

Part of the problem – yes, she knew it – was how much she'd fallen in love with the young Arthur, how affected she was by his despair, how she longed to be able to help him. And so, lost in him and with him, she visited the same early chapters over and over again in a reverie, a growing nostalgia for what she'd created. She edited and tweaked, swapping one word for another, moving a paragraph and then shifting it back, seduced by pride and a kind of sensual pleasure.

There were other reasons for the halt.

One was her awareness that having the one narrative voice didn't work. Arthur must be the central character, this much was indisputable. The story demanded this of her and, she'd gradually realised, for good reason: having a male protagonist was consistent with the times, but having a male character who was compassionate, more 'modern' in many ways, might contest knowledge, might redress something of the imbalance that had carried right through to her and to how this disorder was seen now. Yet Arthur's voice alone was not enough.

A bigger part of being stuck, though, was her palpable reluctance to write an adult Arthur. She didn't want to deal with the crisis waiting for him ... didn't want to fast-forward to the time when decisions must be made. When she thought about this, her resistance was like stiff connective tissue cladding the front of her body.

She sighed. Looked through her study window at the wind-thrashed trees. Turned to her Victorian paraphernalia – books and pictures and medical articles and photocopied pages scattered over the desk. All those words and all, *all*, from men. How did they feel without voice, those Victorian women? Did they find any words for their nameless horror? Or was their torment only expressed through the pens of their physicians? Were these gentleladies, these mad, bad inmates, these hysterical crying girls, able to speak of their pain to a close friend? a loving sister? Or did it remain a terrible secret, a 'female complaint' that imprisoned them and kept them from the world? If so, what part did men play in their captivity?

What part did *that* man play?

She plucked the slight text from its place at the peak of her paper stack. *On the Curability of Certain Forms of Insanity, Epilepsy, Catalepsy, and Hysteria in Females.*

Would it be possible to write about the women who, once cut, once burned, were tucked away into respectability? Whose wounds disappeared into the fog of history?

I. Baker Brown.

Could she really write about this unfathomable surgeon? Work through her fascination? her distaste? her terror?

She'd started to dream of them, moustachioed men in worsted trousers and jackets. In one dream, an upright physician demanded, with old-fashioned words like 'decorum' and 'diffidence', that dream-Alice behave herself; on the wood stove behind him, an iron heated. In another, a handsome young man in a frockcoat wielded an antique razor against a trussed Victorian girl-child. Alice could still hear the screams. In the most disturbing one, dream-Alice was menaced by two men with identical sideburns and shrewd mouths. One was Isaac Baker Brown and the other was called Arthur but, horrifyingly, resembled Duncan. The two men operated by night on bound women. They followed dream-Alice with slow, dogged steps, their arms hanging like weights at their sides. She woke with her own arms pushing at the doona, thrusting away these determined zombie-like men and her own question: why Duncan?

When Alice had such dreams she ignored her journal and walked quickly to the shower, distracting herself with daytime thoughts. Where to submit the hysteria essay, now it had been honed; when to contact her uni colleagues about teaching in 2010 – would there still be a place for her after two years away? She scrubbed briskly at her nails and feet. Turned the hot water to high and lost herself, for a moment, in the flood of warmth over her bum and thighs.

Why Duncan? She knew why.

She thought about the support group. She'd been to all their homes several times over now, but not one of them had asked her when she would host a meeting. It was tact, she supposed, an awareness of the tension in her marriage – mainly because she barely spoke about Duncan, had managed to keep the two worlds apart, did not know what she would do if those worlds met. Would Duncan welcome the women or be icy? Would he criticise them after? No, she couldn't deal with that, not on top of everything else. She didn't have the strength to choose. Not yet.

A gust pummelled her study, lashed its corner with a ghostly wail. No walk today. Not when the wind would run at her from all directions like a wilful child, pinching and smacking, whipping up the griping soreness that lurked in her, that still needed to be placated, that still categorically *remained*. No other bodily grumble could compete with that constant complaint: not her legs and feet, weary from standing at raised platforms and against walls and … wherever she went, really, or her knees, aching from kneeling when she could no longer hold herself upright.

Ache. Hurt … throb … sore … sting. The words people used for pain felt empty. Without force. Nor did they garner sympathy from Duncan. He'd had enough of her pain, it seemed. And he'd had enough of her essays. He found it repugnant – that was the word he'd used, repugnant – her determination to write about vulvar pain, was resentful about the possibility that he too might be found out when dots were joined: Alice … painful sex … Duncan. She got it, she truly did, his distaste at her self-exposure, his fear that he too might be tainted, but she also sensed that his focus on sex was a mask, or some kind of smokescreen. Another way of him refusing to believe that this pain – what this ghastly, lingering pain had made her become – was to do with the whole of her, not just her genitals. And, yes, it was scary to risk being identified as a woman with this particular pain, of course it was. But readers must understand, they *must*. That you could be sensual, even uninhibited, ordinarily, yet still have sexual pain. That you could be smart and insightful, yet still be utterly disabled by seemingly senseless, never-ending symptoms. That you could be creative in the midst of it.

Because, what would he say if she told him the rest? Arthur, Emily and Isaac Baker Brown, the couple's fateful encounter with the surgeon, a long narrative devoted to this 'repugnant' thing –

'Alice.'

She jumped at Duncan's voice. Came back to the buffeted room and the notes scattered over her desk, the laptop screen in hibernation.

'Hi, babe,' she said. 'You okay?' Then swore silently at herself. She'd been working on this, her sweetness, and the self-effacement and appeasement that fed it. Maybe it was the habit of her old self. Maybe it was guilt at her furtive movement away from him. The story that called to her and the quiet but discomfiting self she was becoming. The self that hovered beyond his reach.

'Just wondering when you were coming out. What you wanted to do this afternoon.'

Duncan leaned against the doorframe, arrested by the unspoken rule: entry to each other's study only by invitation. He had guarded his workroom jealously when she first moved in and showed her to her own separate room without discussion. She'd gotten the message.

Lately, she'd been escaping to her study on Saturdays. The strategy was partly to avoid Duncan, to delay the momentous talk she sensed they were teetering on the edge of. But it was also because she was a little besotted with it, the story that was slowly, slowly revealing itself, and because that story seemed intertwined with who she was herself becoming, or ... no, making possible who she might become – first here, in her study, shaking herself free from her old self in the words she wrote. She wanted to protect this new Alice, shield her from Duncan's categorical appraisal, and was glad, now, that his insistence on private spaces provided the freedom for her uncertain form to coalesce. Because it was clear who he preferred. The former Alice: the young, diligent, smart-as-a-whip Alice. The – yes, she must admit it – submissive Alice.

Now he lingered on the threshold as if requesting entry.

'I wouldn't mind just reading a bit more on those women,' she said. 'The ones I was telling you about. At the Salpêtrière in Paris – you know, Charcot.' It was a lie, but a convincing one. That was what she had been doing, after all, only months before.

His sigh was heavy. 'All those people are well dead, Alice.'

'So is Hemingway,' she shot back.

'Yes, but his literature is still read. It's an extraordinary cultural heritage.' His lecturing mode. 'The writing is alive; it still affects us. And it's about all the big questions. Mortality. Love and loss. Redemption through nature, the wilderness.'

'It's also phallocentric – all about the male project.'

She'd almost said, 'He also hated women.' Duncan might be an expert on Hemingway, but she too knew the material. Her husband had been an effective tutor all those years ago.

'That's beside the point.' His chin had that stubborn set to it. 'Those Victorian doctors are outmoded, and the women in that hospital may well have been frauds, from what I can see.'

She felt herself reducing. Her conviction ebbing.

'All those women with vulvodynia aren't like Hemingway,' he continued, his voice confident. 'They've been forgotten.'

He'd already rehearsed this conversation, she realised, considered every response. Thought he had her covered, when all she had was heart and conviction. But she drew on that now, and found the truth.

'Exactly. They've been forgotten, and they shouldn't be. That's part of my work.'

'What, resurrecting dead people?' It was his incredulous tone, the one that usually silenced her.

But not today.

'Yes. Absolutely. Because they need to be resurrected. Remembered. Taken account of.' She felt the heat rush into her cheeks. 'Don't you get it? Women are suffering unnecessarily and alone. Don't you understand how unfair that is? How angry that makes me? Something has to be done!'

'But by you?'

'*Yes*, by me. Women are scared to speak about it.'

'And that's your responsibility – to speak for them?'

'Well, yes. But it's more than that. I'm excited by this work and where it's taking me. I can't even imagine going back to who I was, or to the things I used to write about.'

'But what about us?' He rushed on: 'What about me?'

What about me? The words were stones flicked into a pond. In the silence she felt the ripples. Watched as the water settled into a new form.

'Can you make half of the chapters hers? So you have both Arthur and Emily, maybe alternating?'

Alice scrolled through the pages. Imagined Emily's words in them: her joy, then her confusion and despair.

'I could, but I don't really want the reader to be in her consciousness too much. I think it'll be stronger if the reader sees the challenges to Arthur's mindset – sort of … through Arthur.' Alice considered for a moment. 'I want Em to have some kind of voice, but a voice that also suggests a lack of agency, because of the times.'

Silence for a moment. Alice could almost hear Pen thinking. Then her voice through the speakerphone: 'What about having chapters from Bea's perspective, but focused on interactions between her and Emily?'

It was a good suggestion: Em might feel more able to express what she could no longer enjoy – even tolerate – to another woman, and the strategy would have the added advantage of giving Beatrice some kind of voice, presenting her as a feminist of sorts – an early suffragette, perhaps. But would that detract from Arthur's voice? Dilute, too much, the effect Emily's pain has on him, a man? Wasn't that itself a feminist manoeuvre – having this different kind of man? Teasing out what had changed since then, but also what hadn't?

'Hmmm, maybe. It would be good to have that relationship between Em and Bea foregrounded … I'll have to think about it more. Good idea, though!'

'How's it going otherwise?'

'Good. I guess it helps that Arthur and Emily are so happy in the bit I'm writing. You know, newly married and all that. Arthur's cock-a-hoop!'

They both laughed.

She didn't really want to talk about what was to come in that world, especially not over the phone. And she didn't want to tell her friend how the happy scenes that sprang to life in her imagination threw her own marriage into relief. What would Arthur do when he was tested? What had Duncan done?

And deeper even than these questions, others arriving as whispers at the edges of sleep: will Emily have the operation? Will Emily recover?

A knock reached Alice through her mobile. 'Shit,' Penny muttered. A man's voice in the background, Pen's response to him sifted through her fingers, then a muffled door closing. And Pen, her voice clear again: 'Have to go, sweetie. Bloody work! See you on Saturday?'

'Yep – and thanks, Pen.'

Alice saved the writing and turned off the laptop. Stretched her arms up and back, rolled her head on its base. The tension and ache below and within the same – always the same. But now she had another treatment to try. An acupuncturist. *I thought you might be interested,* Pen had offered, *cos of the material on the net about some women responding well.*

She was grateful, and not only for her friend's thoughtful ideas. It helped to share Arthur and Emily's fledgling world with someone who could quietly hold it.

A meaty aroma rolled through the air. Six o'clock. Time to baste the roast, to tease dainty thyme leaves from their stems and fry dark-lipped mushrooms in the pungent leaves and butter. Maybe add a hint of lemon zest to cut the richness of the meal.

Duncan would arrive home with only enough time for his shower. Then, at dinner, they would make conversation.

'How was your day?'

And, 'How was yours?'

'How are the new units going?'

And, 'Did the plumber call?'

Not, 'How is your writing going?'

Not, 'What is happening to us?'

Two worlds: the present and the past. She could no longer tell what was about the world she had entered and what was about her own daily world, about Duncan and her. The two worlds were intertwined, each weirdly affected, she sensed, by the other. And with Emily's pain still to be written, Alice felt constantly on the verge of crisis. Power was about to be wielded, compromises made, but in which world? Disquiet permeated her thoughts, gave her the sense that their new coming together – hers and Duncan's – had been a false beginning, had been at too great a cost – had elevated his needs above hers, his concern for himself above what she needed from him. Which was what? Some kind of unequivocal support. Some kind of trust. So now their love faltered, or so it seemed to her.

And what about Duncan? In his mind, it seemed, she had already abandoned him. Swung the spotlight of her attention away from her husband and onto subjects that didn't interest him: pain, female bodies, Victorian medicine, hysteria. More, she had found a new guide to living: herself. Her body, her dreams, her desires. She saw that for him this was a rejection, an abandonment that, perhaps, echoed his mother's 'abandonment' of him all those years ago.

But, she protested – silently, futilely, as if she were her husband's own tardy conscience – he had sworn to love and cherish her, hadn't he? He had promised to be on her side, to listen to her, to share her troubles? Hadn't he? Well, he'd broken that promise. He'd let her down. He'd closed himself to who she'd had to become in order to survive and then thrive. He'd shut the door to her and become the same person he was with his mother: guarded. Untrusting. By this she understood that if he had betrayed her, he believed she had betrayed him too.

She lowered the blinds against a faint outline of clouds, dense in the darkening sky. Closed the door on her study. Pulled her jacket from the back of a kitchen chair and slipped it on. Basted the roasting meat and stepped back from its angry spit. Flicked on the lounge light. Turned on the heater.

The sofa was hard against her hip, its cushions cold, unwelcoming. God, she was sick of this protracted winter, its stubborn intrusion into spring. She remembered Duncan's arm, warm and heavy along her shoulders, when he first showed her his home. Recalled again her brazen words: *It's a mausoleum!* Nineteen ninety-eight. She, an undergrad and he, her former tutor. Their giddy laugh on that sweet January morning, then their confident stride into a sunny future.

Oh, the arrogance. The naivety. Because now, look, it had come true. The deathly chill and closing walls. The realisation that she had been buried alive. The only warmth to be found in the new Alice. The only light, her writing. The only air, Arthur and Emily.

Chapter 19

February 26th 1866

My dear Beatrice,

No, we did not go, nor will we ever! Something has changed & I hardly know how to speak of it. It's not the pain—well, not directly, in any event. I'm not being deliberately mysterious, Bea, it's just that I feel Arthur & I have entered a new world, & I am overcome by what I find here. I have no words yet to describe it—I don't want to describe it, because to do so would be to spoil it.

I will write again soon. Don't fret in the meantime: all is well.

Your Em

February 28th 1866

Dear sister,

Thank you for not asking questions, for just saying you are relieved & glad! I can tell you, now, a little of what happened, even if I am still unable to make complete sense of it.

On Sunday night, in the earliest hours of the morning, Arthur began crying & tossing about in his sleep. I tried to wake him, but he would not be stirred at first. It was as if he were in a place distant to me & could not hear me, so it took some minutes until he was fully restored to himself,

& even then he cried & swept his hand through his hair, over & over. I begged him to tell me what was wrong, what I could do to ease his feelings, but he told me these were not tears of pain. He said they were tears of joy mixed with sorrow that could find no words.

I held him—we held each other & cried together—& when he could finally talk, he said he had been in a place to which he was drawn often in his dreams. The elm thicket along the path to Herdley? He said, "It is a place where I suffer & am lost, as I was after Mother died." This time, he said, it was different, but all he would say of his dream was, "I heard the quiet voice that tells the truth" & something about your mother & fending for those unable to fend for themselves. He said he knew then what he should do.

Does this mean anything to you? Arthur says it might. Please come to us this evening, if you have no engagements—we can talk more then.

Love Emmie

March 1st 1866

Dear Bea,

I am so glad, so sincerely gladdened, that you & Arthur could share your memories of your mother & who she was, not only with each other, but also with me. I would have loved to have known such a kind & wise woman.

Would it surprise you to know that I have felt James with me more since this happened, & that it is a good & a comforting feeling?

Your sister,

Emmie

March 2nd 1866

Bea,

I must tell you, we received a telegram from Paris this morning:

AVOID THE PROCEDURE BY ALL MEANS POSSIBLE. LAWLER

Thomas returns in two weeks & Arthur wished to reassure him straightaway, so he has gone to the telegraph office on his way to work. He says he will write a letter to Tom this evening so we can find out why he is so definite. Thank goodness we did not go ahead!

Emmie

March 9th 1866

Dearest Bea,

Father is cross at me for not having the operation, but Mam is her usual self: loving & docile. She wonders if I would like to take the country air for a good, long spell & Arthur thinks this an excellent idea, though he would rather have me with him, he says. At all events, the three of us have decided on it & Mam says she will hold firm, even if Father grumbles & thinks me silly for not doing as he wanted. So Mam & I will go to Almsford very soon & I will stay there until you all leave London in July. Arthur will visit me when he can & we will be reunited with the rest of our Rochdale family at Hierde House for the summer break, just when Father joins Mam at Almsford. How does that sound?

Beatrice, it is a strange thing, but I feel better already, even though the stabbing & burning are unchanged. The disorder still plagues me, but I feel friendlier towards it. Why does this cheer me, I wonder?

Your Em

March 16th 1866

My loving sister,

You ask what has worked the change in me. It is to do with trust, I think, & being listened to properly. Arthur had stopped believing in me & me in him, but really it was the terrible affliction that turned us both from each other; I see that now.

Arthur says it was the appointment with Baker Brown that helped open his eyes, & the looming surgery. That when it came to it, he could not countenance inflicting further harm on me. And when I turned to him & leaned on him once more—when we began to draw together again after that horrible consultation—he says that he could no longer believe I was irritating the nerve in the way that Brown suggested, if I did not confide this to him—that he trusted me. And then that final thing: the dream that came to him in our darkest hour … It was then that he placed me above him, when I was no longer able to do this for myself; then that he considered me & believed me over all others.

I am still trying to work it out, but there is no hurry, not when we both hold true to the best in each other, just as we once did.

Love Em

Chapter 20

Perth, November–December 2009

Alice flicked the switch as she came back into the lounge room and Penny's hair sprang from blonde into gold. Once it had been a glitzy shade of red, Alice remembered, and she saw Pen's crimson hair and dress again, the birthday party where she herself had laughed with strangers while Duncan glowered in a doorway – *Not really my bunch*, he'd said as they drove home. At the party Alice had chatted, flirted a little, sat on sofas and kitchen chairs easily, comfortably, without thought, not knowing that very soon this would be impossible, sitting. Over two and a half years ago, that night. Such a short time, really, in which to become a new person. And, somehow, Pen was also different. Softer, perhaps. Or was that just her own changed eyes?

'Here you go,' she said, and put Penny's glass on a coaster, sipped from her own as she slid onto the sofa, bunching cushions to support her back and head.

Afternoon was darkening to evening; their cups of tea had segued into glasses of wine. Basil and garlic filled the house and the charred sweetness of roast capsicum drifted from the kitchen. Alice's mind drifted for a moment too, and Arthur and Emily rushed in just as they always did, given an opportunity. She'd already spoken about it with Pen, that compulsion to write – words coming to her now in torrents, and scenes erupting out of chronological sequence, raw and higgledy-piggledy, leaving great narrative holes. She felt the pressure of them, these stuttering blanks, their demand that she fill them with the missing pieces of story.

'So, they're supporting you then? The uni?' Penny, picking up the conversation where Alice had been forced to interrupt it with one of her more prickly dashes to the loo.

'Well, they're supporting me, just not financially. It's an honorary post – not paid.'

Her last meeting with the head of school had helped counterbalance that, given her a sense that she was valued, even valuable. She'd realised he knew about her pain, though she could only imagine how those collegial conversations had gone: 'Yes, well, she has some kind of disorder ... there, you know, in her ... reproductive area, I mean.' Yet he'd treated her without doubt or judgement, and with a careful kind of respect.

'Unis love publications,' she went on, 'and I've had another of my family stories accepted – the cabbage patch doll one. The other stuff's doing well too. Those essays, you know? Two have been published and there's one in editing.' She shifted her body around on the sofa. 'I thought it might be tricky at uni, writing and publishing about vulvodynia, though it shouldn't be, of course.'

It's important that you've taken something so ... difficult and created strong work from it, the head of school said at that meeting. She'd felt herself expanding at his words. Found herself saying, without thought or reflection, *Well, I guess you gotta make a silk purse out of a sow's ear!*

And that's exactly what you have to do, she'd thought afterwards: take this ugly fleshy ear and make of it something beautiful. Join its panels together with strong threads. Place in it the jagged language of pain, the snippets of her life, the bits and pieces she'd been reduced to. Work with these fragments, listen to them, feel them heating and shifting like alchemy into the soft-spun words of narrative. She didn't see how there was any other way. Not for her.

Now, she continued, 'But without the sessional teaching I'm earning nothing – just small amounts for publication.'

Duncan had begun making the odd comment. Never an overt, 'When are you going to teach again?' Just gentle digs. Pulling the Visa statement from its envelope, *This is a biggie*. Shading his eyes and surveying the roof, *It'll be good when we can get that guttering done*. Making a fist and pushing it against their mattress, *We'll have to wait for the new one*. And she felt it, she did, her inability to contribute to their lifestyle, even if his income was more than enough for them both. Still, she wouldn't complain about such pettiness, not with things always just that tiny bit stilted between her friend and her husband.

'But there's talk of me taking one of the old units in semester one.'

'Oh, Alice, that's fantastic!' Penny's smile shifted. 'Do you think you'll be up to it?'

'I think I'll be okay. It's almost manageable, with the physio and the exercises. And I'm learning what to do and what not to do, other than sitting.'

It had been so long now, that daily waking litany: biting vulva, stinging urethra, aching buttocks, tingling thighs. The lament less intense than it once was, but still depleting, and part of a conversation that went nowhere, really. But at least it felt like she and her body were no longer enemies. Felt like even, at times, she *was* her body.

Thunk.

Duncan. His tread along the hall and into the lounge.

'Penny!' The delight in his voice seemed genuine.

'Duncan.' Penny up-tilted her head. 'Great to see you.'

'You too.' He squatted next to the sofa and gave Alice a quick kiss. Then, moving back to take both of them in, 'It's been way too long.'

They all nodded in the moment's silence, while Alice thought about all the catch-ups with her friend, delicately and silently timed to include just the two of them. Would he notice this new attempt to bring her separate worlds together?

'How's work?' Duncan filled the silence.

'Oh, it's fine. You know, unruffled waters, plain sailing, all that. I could really do with a holiday, though. Just some cruise where I can lie down and do absolutely *nothing* for a week.'

'Yes, well,' said Duncan. 'I think we'd all like to take a break, if we could.'

Was it a crack at her?

'You've been busy, Duncan. Alice tells me the new book's a success.' Pen, saying just the right things.

'It was a long haul, but I finally made it.'

He looked like a success, standing there. Broad-shouldered, fit in his tennis garb. Emanating, as always, that easy sensuality. Would he tell Penny that while the publication of his Hemingway biography had received good reviews from other academics, even experts in the field, book sales had been a little disappointing? Comments like 'historical' and 'competent' a little off-putting?

'That's great.' Penny flashed her wide smile at him. 'And what's next?'

'Well, we're having a bit of a restructure at the university at the moment, so I need to put some time into that. A couple of new units …' He trailed off. 'But on a Saturday,' he mimed the swing of a racquet, 'it's all about brushing up the game for summer.'

Laughter. They were behaving well.

'Speaking of which,' he continued, 'I'd better have a shower. Make myself presentable for you lovely women.'

'Take your time,' Alice said. 'Dinner won't be ready for another half hour or so.'

'Okay.'

He loped off to their room – the other end of the house.

'Gee, he looks well, Alice.'

'Yes, he does.' But she wanted to communicate something of the shadow side. The side he didn't present to anyone but her, not even his own mother. 'It's been a hard year for him, though. The changes at uni, and the book. Promotion – a little travel for that.'

'Has it put pressure on you guys? Having him away, I mean.'

'No. Well, not for me, anyway.' Her voice had dropped. She felt bad saying it, but she needed to speak the words, so she continued quietly, 'I feel like I'm more myself alone.'

'Shit, Alice, I'm sorry.' Penny's voice held genuine regret. 'Is it because of the sex?'

How good it was to be with Pen: the cut to the chase a relief.

'No, cos we can have sex now. Not heaps, but enough.'

How to explain how it started?

Perhaps with her realisation that the younger Alice had shaped herself to Duncan's desire. Reduced herself and the woman she might become, willingly, even eagerly. Then, his disappointment in her, her … inability to open herself to him. And how that mistrust of her – that he didn't understand that she would have him inside her if she possibly, possibly could; that she would put him first, if only he could continue to believe her and believe in her, place her somehow above him – was a betrayal of sorts. Of loyalty. Of faith. Of *them*. And when they began, it should have been wonderful to hold his sweaty, satisfied body against hers and see that body restored to itself, proud and full, to feel the stirrings within her of what, one day, she might be able to call pleasure, even passion. It should have felt good, no, *right*, to join properly with him again. But for all their heat there was also a certain coolness, a strange distance their bodies couldn't bridge. What else? Oh, yes. How he seemed to resent the research and writing she'd been brought to. *This obsession*, he'd said one night, spitting the word, *this bloody obsession with vulvodynia and sick women*. That sweeping motion he made when she tried to share something of her world – her excitement at discovered papers and historical artefacts, her new words lush with pain – as if his hand were a brush flicking the dust of her away. And finally, finally – this the most hidden thing, hidden even from herself over all their years together – the sense that there was something about him, something fundamental, that was missing. Or flawed. The word that came to her the other morning as she woke from a dream ... the Roman statues, the empty eyes ... her hand on cool marble ... as she opened her own eyes to his sleeping, undefended face ... the word she wrote ... semblance, that was it, the impression, the feeling, though she did not know, exactly, was still finding out, what she meant by the word. What it meant to her. What it meant to them.

It began over the fridge, of all things. Her inattention, when they arrived home with the shopping, to his preferred method of division between the two crispers. One for salad veggies, one for cooking veggies: one of the unwritten domestic rules she'd signed so many years ago, back when she didn't understand how foundations determine what's built upon them.

So, Duncan objected to her carelessness, which led to *regret* at her *new, sloppier habits*. And then, surprising them both, complaint leaping to blanket grievances. To accusations already curdled by constraint.

'But that's what people do, Duncan: they change. I might have changed now, but I changed when I met you too. I changed who I was to be with you, to be who ... what you wanted.'

She closed the neatened fridge. Stuffed the shopping bags inside each other and held them to her chest.

'That's rubbish, Alice. It's *you* I met. *You* I wanted.' He leaned back against the kitchen bench, regarded her frostily from his side of the kitchen. 'Nobody asked you to change anything about yourself.'

'But that's what women do, or what young women do, maybe. Women who aren't certain of themselves, who can't know ... people who don't trust their own judgement. Maybe you didn't see it was even happening back then. I didn't – or ... I didn't let myself.'

'Well the changes must have been bloody tiny, because I didn't know about it, I can assure you. And I never asked you to make them.'

Her heart juddered into her throat, but she couldn't stop herself now: 'Not in words, perhaps.'

'Oh, bullshit. And if you did have to adjust, so what? You think I didn't make changes? That I didn't have to accommodate when you moved in? Make compromises in my own life? This is entirely different, this bloody vulvodynia and who it's made you become.'

So, it had returned to this: his repugnance, her defence.

'People change when … because they have to.'

'Not like you have. Not so radically, not across the board. Not if you're fundamentally happy with who you are. And it's just …' His eyes softened. 'You've lost something, Alice. Like … sweetness. A kind of lightness and generosity. Just who you are.'

She swallowed the lump in her throat. Tried to close herself to the unexpected appeal in his voice.

'But what if you start seeing things differently?' she said. 'I thought I was happy with who I was, but when my body changed … when I had to adjust to this new reality … And, look, I don't – I didn't, anyway – want this reality, I hated it! But everything about me had to change, just to keep living and –'

'But if you hate it so much … You don't have to change everything, surely, not everything. That's just wilful and … bloody-minded.'

Maybe she should back down. Give him something – anything – to break this impasse. But she felt herself shrinking at the thought. It was him or her, now.

'Duncan, that's the thing. I realised I wasn't happy – or at least I couldn't be happy anymore with how things were, how they … are – not as this new person, anyway.'

'So, what are you saying? That you don't love me anymore? Is that it?' His face was white now, tight with hurt or fury. 'How fucking predictable you are – you know that, right? It's pathetic.'

'Oh, Duncan.' She watched her hand reach out to him. 'I'm –'

'You're what? Sorry? For deciding things without telling me? Cutting me out of your life?'

He turned his back, paced to the window and leaned over the sink. She saw his shoulders shudder.

'But I haven't decided … I'm just trying to tell you … You act like I had some choice in it –'

'You did *and* you do – of course you fucking do!'

'No, I fucking don't! And don't fucking yell at me!'

They faced each other across the kitchen table, panting. Then he lunged at her and she stumbled backwards, fell against the wall, her arm over her face, only to see it was the table he was aiming for, the heavy bowl at its centre, its clear glass blushed with fruit. He lifted it, held it up high, looked at her for a long moment and then slowly, very deliberately, loosened his grip.

'Alice.'

His voice was soft. So, she knew it was over, the argument. The pieces of it swept up and emptied into the bin with those sticky, crimson shards of glass.

'Come here.'

It was the way he said it – so gently, as if she'd been a naughty girl he was now forgiving – that invited her to curl up in his lap and rest her weight against him. To forget what was happening to them. To forgive him. Forgive herself.

'You know I love you.'

But did she? She looked at him in the armchair. His long, straight legs, crossed at the ankle. Chinos and deck shoes. And when he walked, that slow roll of the hips. He was as he had always been. Why, then, did he look different to her?

'Alice.'

It was a promise. It was a command.

How long would it take her to no longer love him?

CHAPTER 21

March 28th 1866

Dear Beatrice,

Just to let you know we arrived safely in Almsford.

I had a peaceful sleep & will rest & recover today. The staff are very welcoming & Millie is enjoying being reunited with old friends from amongst them.

Mam is keen for us to have a short walk tomorrow & to show off countryside I have not yet seen. It's not as hilly as Herdley—there are thick patches of forest broken up by lovely dells & a pretty river that flows through it all.

Your Em

April 3rd 1866

My dear Bea,

Mam & I have had a thorough assessment of my daily habits & we are determined to make some changes.

First, clothing: On Friday we went through my wardrobe, & the first items to be ejected were those horribly tight corsets—no more will they cramp & suffocate me. And I am fortunate society is deciding the mighty crinoline is passé, because then it was the turn of the cage: out it went, along with my several big, heavy dresses—to the joy of the parlourmaid, who we spotted parading proudly along the main street of Almsford on Sunday! I have taken over one of Mam's dresses for now (which flops on me terribly) & some flounced muslin petticoats, & we are about to visit a dressmaker in Almsford that Mam swears by; we are thinking a morning dress, a tea gown for special occasions, & a shortish walking skirt & blouse should be enough. Mam says I must pick bright colours to brighten myself up, & light poplins & merinos & such, to give me ease.

Next, <u>medicines</u>: We decided to slowly reduce my dependence on all the tonics & tinctures recommended by the London physicians (Father does not know). I have found a change already with the lower doses of laudanum—I can <u>think</u> again, Bea, & the pain has not worsened. And Mam has a further plan: Rosie, in the kitchen, has a mother who is an old "healer" & we have organised to visit her. All hush-hush, of course.

Then, <u>exercise</u>: I have begun to take daily walks—<u>very slow & short</u>, to start. Without stays I can breathe in the scent of bluebells as I enter the wood, & I feel my spirits lift when I round a bend & see their blue carpet before me. Oh, & the cheery wild pansies & daisies & buttercups dotted about & the apple buds springing open: I had forgotten how such beauty sustains me.

Mam is also encouraging me to eat more & build up my strength so I can take longer walks. She is being a perfect angel in all affairs & becoming known to me as her own delightful person away from Father. And that devil that tortures me? It is difficult to hope these changes might help me—might help <u>us</u>—when my hopes have been dashed before, but this all feels <u>right</u> to me. So, dear Bea, I will ignore the terrible pains as much as I am able & <u>continue on in hope</u>.

With my love,

Emmie

April 10th 1866

Oh Bea,

I have slumped. I did too much after February's crisis & in the elevated spirits of our arrival & now must pay the price. "Some days of rest will see you right," Mam says to me. Will it? I must not think, & just endure.

Em

April 16th 1866

Yes, we have visited the healer—Ada, her name is—& been given several home-brewed cordials that I must take each day. I cried & cried when we talked of my pain & its recent resurgence, though I didn't mean to. She comforted me & said, "You mustn't worry yourself, my dear: it will pass." Bea, she sounded so completely without doubt that I almost believe her. She says we are doing exactly the right things & that I must avoid the city if I can, & too much excitement—that I am sensitive, so my spirit & body are easily troubled.

We visit the parish church most days, which is restful, & attend at least one service every Sunday. I stand at the back & hope that no-one notices me. The wee building has been restored recently & a small organ installed, & on Sundays the church swells with the voices of an enthusiastic choir. The clergyman, who has been vicar here for many years, knows only that I have been unwell. His wife has come to call several times, but we are not too encouraging, as I am not yet ready for regular visitors.

Em

April 30th 1866

Dearest Bea,

Arthur writes that he has read Baker Brown's book on his operation, just published, & discussed it at length with Tom. Arthur says I shouldn't read it—that it would only upset me where there is no need.

Now that the possibility of this operation is completely gone, I feel as if a noose has been taken from my neck. How could I countenance that most precious part of me being cut? How could I allow Father to think, Arthur to wonder, at the possibility of unhealthy practices on my part? What was I thinking? Do you know?

Love Emmie

May 4th 1866

Bea,

No, no improvement yet. I try to remain hopeful & trusting, & I take joy in the serenity around me, & I wait.

Em

May 21st 1866

Dear Bea,

Arthur left early this morning for London & says he will come again very soon. I must confide that almost two months away from each other has given me respite, not because Arthur is demanding in any way—he is not, at all—but because I have had only to think of myself for many weeks & not really take another's feelings into consideration. Yet I have missed his presence, too, so it was with a full heart I greeted him, & with sorry hearts that we bid each other farewell.

I feel that I have been blind to Arthur for most of our short married life, with this disorder, & now I am left to consider the many ways that bind me to him & make me grateful: he is tender & caring, he is merciful to those reliant on his good graces, he avoids topics that irritate people unnecessarily, he is unobtrusive in company & humble in general, he takes no part in idle gossip, he is patient & prudent, he takes unfair advantage of no-one.

I am so very fortunate to have my dear husband & you, my dear sister.

Your Em

June 1st 1866

Dear sister,

Some news: I am able to walk further & with greater ease. I hardly dare say it, I hardly dare believe it, but I think the pains do not bother me quite as much as they did.

My love,

Emmie

June 8th 1866

Dear Bea,

I am "middling, middling", as Father says. The improvement is so slow as to be almost invisible, but if I compare the pain to what it has been, yes, I do think it might be waning.

Bea, I'm scared. Scared to hope or believe recovery might be possible, & for hope & belief to be crushed again.

Emmie

June 22nd 1866

Dear sister,

Every day I have my quiet walk with Millie or Mam. We call in at Ada's wee cottage or at the parish church: both help me feel more at home with myself & give me the sense that I am in some way making peace with God, after feeling so much anger & despair. It is precious solace.

Emmie

July 2nd 1866

Oh B,

It is as if I am waking from the sleep of one hundred years. I see that the world around me has changed; that people have gone on with their lives in the meantime. I realise the pain & my determination to survive it left room for nothing else, not the fortunes of my family, nor the fate of our nation. There is so much to catch up on: Cissy's courtship & now her engagement—how exciting. The defeat on the proposed Reform Bill, & Derby & the Conservatives back in power—how upsetting for Father Rochdale & the party. I know I am meant to be kept calm, but surely a little news will not hurt?

Arthur & I are very happy when he visits. What a trial this has been for us & how grateful I am for my understanding husband. He has given me the most perfect gift for our new beginning: a silk purse. Bea, apart from their old-fashioned clothes, the couple on its front panel could be us. Arthur says it was this semblance & the love in their faces that compelled him to buy it. So now the purse sits by my bedside at night, & I take it with me on our walks, like a friend. I am looking at it right now. You will see it when we come to Herdley—what date do you think you will arrive?

Your M

July 20th 1866

My dear B,

I do appreciate why you must stay in London, for the moment, whilst Parliament is all in flux, & reformers agitating so on the streets. Arthur says that Gladstone will need to curb his irritable & imperious manner in Parliament if he wishes to lead the Liberals when Russell has had his day. And he tells me that Gladstone is become quite the hero with the press—& with the masses, though they do not know how ambivalent he is about reform … Please write me the political news, Bea, so I can think about it properly & from Father Rochdale's perspective—but only if you have time.

I am doing quite well, thank you. Now that I have it less, though, I find I am haunted by the pain; now I am not fully in its grip, I understand that its severity was even worse than I could admit to myself or show others. Why must life hold such suffering, I wonder?

Enough! It is a beautiful, hot day & Mam & I are about to walk the shaded tracks to Ada's, a visit which comforts us both.

I miss you, dearest B, & anticipate embracing you, walking with you & sharing all our hopes & fears again soon, with great pleasure. How wonderful it will be to see my sister again!

Till then,

Your M

London, July 1866

The yellow calf is sleek under his fingers. It might be a thoughtful gift for Emmie, a handsome journal for her new beginning, but is it too much, straight after the purse? God knows he would like to celebrate his wife's improvement—sweep her into his arms and twirl her about, yodel to the moon and stars—but it does feel like tempting fate to be *too* happy. It is only weeks, after all, with progress, not yet complete recovery. And what if it were to rebound, the sickness? Best to leave well enough alone, for now, to tamp down the happy mood that has recently surprised him.

Arthur edges his body around the legal almanacs hanging from wooden poles, slides past the shelf of law lists in their coats of bright red leather, nods to the aproned stationer and steps out into Chancery Lane.

It is dust upon dust in the street—the air around the hustling clerks and barristers and solicitors is crammed with it—and Arthur's brisk pace drives its own grimy swirls and eddies up the plate glass of shopfronts. Through them he catches glimpses of the wares and in each glimpse his phantom wife: guiding her pen at a little leather-topped writing table; assessing skins of parchment, lips pursed; peeking, all wonder, into the pigeonholes of a handsome mahogany desk. Emmie as she once was, as she might be again: smiling, attentive, grave, laughing, pensive, teasing ...

Arthur dodges a youth with bundles of red-taped papers, strides through a dense flurry of men in black gowns and powdered wigs, and skips up and through the doorway of Button's, doffing his hat and brushing the grit from its brim, peering through the haze for Tom. The dining house is heaving with bodies and food, and great wafts of sweat, beef and yeast sweep over him. He can make out, on the sideboard, hunks of meat sliced from steaming joints, platters laden with roasted turnips and carrots, bowls of broad beans, boats thick with gravy and, at the other end, pies that shed pastry and ooze sauce. Saliva floods his mouth—and without queasiness. Something else to be grateful for, the abrupt disappearance of that old problem along with his fortunate decision: when he'd realised, and put her first.

There's Tom at the bar, surrounded by noisy customers. Arthur claps his friend's shoulder and they edge along with the queue, make their orders of roast dinner and stout, pile their plates high, make their way to a table, and shout questions and answers at each other between mouthfuls: yes, Emmie is still in Almsford and, yes, still improving; yes, Tom has been welcomed at the Hospital for Sick Children; yes, the Rochdale family are thrilled at Cissy's engagement; yes, the Drury Lane homeless refuge has benefitted from an anonymous donation; yes, the law is still a dunce; yes, it's hard to find good lodgings for a bachelor physician; yes, Sir George is encouraging the switch to politics—has said, *You should consider it, Arthur*. Yes, yes, yes and yes.

They finish mopping gravy with hunks of bread, swig remnants from their tankards, push to the bar for a refill and then, without discussion, make their way to the little reading and chess room where they claim a small table in the corner and let themselves down with sighs.

It's a weekly ritual now, luncheon in Chancery Lane—close to Lincoln's Inn and to the hospital too—and trusting conversation afterwards in this quiet room: their worries, their fears, their hopes. They've talked about Baker Brown here, of course, shared their dismay at such wrongheadedness, their relief at disaster averted: Thompson, a colleague in obstetrics, sharing his misgivings about the surgery; the dream that brought light and clarity to Arthur. And they still debate Baker Brown's book, shocked at the gusto with which the surgeon has speculated, cut and burned.

"The mood continues to turn against Mr Baker Brown," says Tom now. "Thompson tells me, of course, but it's also becoming public. Letters to the *British Medical Journal* and such."

"What, complaints?"

"Objections to Brown's self-advertising and exaggeration, his lack of ... sensitivity towards ... regard for female sensibilities, the reckless and unproven practices and so on." Tom pulls on his stout, wipes the froth from his moustache. "Who knows where it will all end, unless the man can rein himself in."

It is strangely satisfying, Arthur finds, a daydream in which he indulges: driving to the home of Isaac Baker Brown, lifting him by his snowy shirt front, punching him in his smug, self-satisfied face. It's a blood-heat that swarms Arthur's body, shooting out to his limbs and bringing memory with it: the day his foot rested on the throat of Rattlin Rowlands, and the moment he was almost overcome by the blind urge to destroy the youth—this almost-man who would use his power against the defenceless. And Tom next to him, calming him.

"Are alternatives presented? In the case of such complaints?"

"Not yet," says Tom. "Most are voices of caution, and reports that several patients Brown described as cured actually received no benefit from the operation. And many of the women who present at consultations have diverse maladies of mood, just as much as physical ailments. But Thompson tells me the disorder, almost exactly as Emily described it, has been isolated before. Here." He opens his jacket, pulls a folded piece of paper from the pocket.

Arthur squints at Tom's scrawl, sees the inky heading, *Sims 1861*, and, below it, a few scribbled quotations in words that jump out at him: *severe suffering, knife, for all time.* He shudders as he reads out loud,

> *"Notwithstanding all these outward involuntary evidences of physical suffering, she had the moral fortitude to hold herself on the couch, and implored me not to desist from my efforts if there was the least hope of finding out anything about her inexplicable condition."* .

"Poor Emily. She was so brave, and I doubted her."

"Well, maybe … But so did I. You made the right decision in the end, remember."

"But what if I hadn't?" And with these words fear rushes at Arthur in a mighty wave, swamping his buoyant mood. If he feels this frightened, with what terror must Emily have contended? Must even now contend?

"There's no reason she should deteriorate."

"There's no reason it should have developed in the first place. No reason about any of it that I can tell." Arthur looks away from his friend, wondering if he can share the rest. But if not with his knowledgeable, stalwart friend, then who? "It seems selfish to talk of my doubts, when my wife has been living through hell, and when I feel that I should only present her with conviction and …" He stops.

"What is it, Arthur?"

He thinks, tries to shape his fears into something he can describe.

"In some ways," he goes on, "it was very simple when Emmie's pain was at its worst. I needed to look after her, protect her if I could, and natural … impulses were kept in check by this concern." He hesitates, then the questions come in fits and starts: "How do we begin—start over? How will we express this feeling, this … I mean, our love for each other?" He lowers his voice. "How can I know that my … desire—our desire, if we can ever reclaim it—will not raise the pain again? That the natural passion and *vigour* of love-making will not hurt her? Was he right? Baker Brown? Was it true? Will my touch, my … my attention to that part of her body—my encouragement of *her* attention to it—set off the problem again? Do you know? I don't know this, Tom. I can't!"

Tom glances at the men playing chess at the next table. Angles his chair so its back faces them. "I feel it unlikely," he says, his voice slow, careful, "that it will happen again in Emily's case, if you … tell … I mean, *ask* her if she has physical discomfort, then—any hint of a recurrence—at that time when … you two …"

How he wishes they could find straighter words for such conversations! More than this language that only circles the nub of the problem: its causes, its manifestations—all the untidy, troubling, battling feelings that throb at its heart.

Chapter 22

Perth, January 2010

The world looked tougher the further north she drove. Wilder. White limestone irrupted at the crests that bordered the black road. Wattles and banksias riddled the bush with crazy angles, branches scarred by wind and sun and salt. Blackened stumps of grass trees were a memory of fire. Soon she would come across the stand of native Christmas trees, their incandescent orange like a celebration.

The trail was becoming familiar to her – only her, not Duncan – a weekly journey that she covered with a lie: she was going to go shopping then on to a late appointment. What did he think when she returned as stars came out, that the acupuncturist worked into Friday evening? Would he even care that when she drove out of their street she immediately turned from the nearby shops, headed north to the acupuncturist in a new 'city' as empty and disconcerting as a display home and then after, instead of pointing the Toyota south, swung the car onto the coastal highway and, solitary, dreamed her way to her destination?

That place in the sun.

She turned off the air-conditioner and opened the window, propping her elbow on the frame and diving her fingers through waves of heat.

The first time was a whim. Leaving the appointment, altered body and mind, she'd surprised herself by turning north at the highway entrance. Four or five turn-offs to the beach passed before she'd taken a left – who knew why? – at the sign, *Wrigleys Point*. Now it was a weekly fixture. Sometimes she came home to dark windows and hollowness.

She shifted her bum sideways on the worn 'special' cushion. This time, madly perhaps, thinking what the hell, she'd pulled bathers on under the t-shirt dress, and their grip was less friendly than the usual soft cotton undies. It would be early evening by the time she got there, but still warm enough to swim, if she dared.

Ah, the Christmas trees. About ten minutes to the turn-off now and her bum insisting she must stand up.

It caught at her, this secret journey, being built, as it was, upon other secrets: Arthur and Emily and Isaac Baker Brown, her covert research and writing, the attempts to understand, to work out what motivated the women who assented to that terrible mutilation, what drove the man who carried it out.

They'd tried, she and Duncan, even if it hadn't gone well, that last conversation in the garden, face to face. Some kind of honesty, they'd said. An attempt to understand each other properly, they'd agreed. But when he'd complained that she hid herself away these days, never showing herself to him properly, and she'd replied, *What choice do I have when you don't like what I show you?* she'd known this was only a partial truth, where once it had been the whole; understood that she doubted his ability to know the compass of who she now was; realised she might not want him to try anymore.

She braked for the turn-off. Pulled down the visor to shield her eyes from the dipping sun.

It was only that … sometimes, when she and Duncan smiled at each other, when his hand brushed hers as they passed in their hallway, when she was reminded of what they had been to each other, she wondered if she was making a terrible mistake. It was ridiculous; she loved him. Why couldn't she continue to show herself fully to him, make him accept who she was now, try to make him change too? Why did it have to be this way? But then a quiet voice said, *no* – and she was torn again, as if parts of her were travelling in opposite directions, one into the future and the other clinging on stubbornly, desperately, to her love for her husband.

She thought she'd known everything about grief. Thought when she'd wrestled with her body over dragging, agonising months that she would never know pain like it again. And it was true that this different kind of pain, this new form of grief, didn't threaten her very survival, didn't make every second of her life a feat of endurance. Still, though, her chest ached as if a blistering rock split within it.

Fragments of sun hit her eyes. She pressed her towel against her face with one hand, pulled on her sunglasses. But still the tears ran and still the ache grew, saying that something inside was lost forever.

Over the brow of the hill and Wrigleys Point laid out beneath, a little coastal town shaped by dunes and feet into a maze of narrow roads. She threaded her way through bits-and-pieces fishing shacks and brick-and-tile houses, around the occasional new-Australian monolith, blurred by her tears.

Then, the ocean.

A family played in the small park that overlooked the shore: a man, a woman, two little girls. Last swimmers were clearing the beach. A couple of barefoot boys dragging sandy bodyboards. A woman yelling to her Jack Russell as he bit the frothing waves in high-pitched yaps. Two teenage girls, foreheads almost meeting as they climbed the steps, shorts slung hip-high, bellies and breasts sumptuous, light and water a glistening patina.

The breeze cooled her damp face as she stepped from the car. The sun was heading towards the sea, growing as it approached the horizon. Nearer, waves formed choppy lines. Not too much swell for her – not for the swimmer she'd once been, anyway. She hesitated, remembering how long it had been: almost two and a half years since that holiday with Duncan, twining in the pool and the ocean, and the beginning of it all. But she was sick of her timid life, weary of having to refuse the world. She grabbed her towel, mobile and keys, popped her silk purse in the glove box and walked quickly down the steps before she could change her mind.

The air was heavy with seaweed and the water bit like winter. She squatted into the remnant of a wave and breathed into her belly, allowing that nagging part of her body to adjust. The swell was bigger than she'd thought, but she stood and strode towards it, only quaking a little as her feet were buoyed from the sand. When she slid under the first wave it felt like the touch of grace, and when she came up for air she asked herself why she'd waited this long.

She was upset before she even reached the door. As always, Ena seemed to understand before hearing a word.

'It's alright,' she said, and opened her arms. Alice leaned against the smaller woman for a moment. 'I know you have to do it. And I know you don't want to hurt me.' She took Alice by the hand and led her into the house.

How she would miss all this: the sweet, buttery aroma, the promise of cinnamon and nutmeg, the welcoming kitchen, and Ena's limp drawing her on. The things that had never changed – and the things that had. Because she saw vividly now, bringing fresh tears to her eyes, Ena's decline: the list evermore to the left, the hollowing below her cheekbones and clavicles, the jutting angles of the frame beneath the skin – a gradual withdrawal from the busyness of the world, the slow surrender to mortality. If ageing meant coming to terms with the finitude of possibility, she understood that she herself was still very young.

'You know, he was always a particular child,' Ena began without preamble, filling the kettle from the water-filter jug, lighting the stove, pulling a favourite coconut slice from the fridge and placing it on the table. 'Jealous of toys, easily upset, that sort of thing.' She sat down heavily on her chair and Alice stood her own raw body at her friend's side, needing the closeness while avoiding sitting. Wanting no extra pain to mar this farewell. 'I said to myself, he's an only child and he's lost his father. Always ready to excuse the behaviour, as mothers do!' Ena smiled at the memory of her younger self. 'He's always been quick to blame others for … well, his own shortcomings and dissatisfactions. And I know that he believes he was abandoned as a child and that that somehow justifies this sort of … mean-spiritedness.' She sighed deeply. 'He's a good man, Alice. And loving, to a point. It's just that there is a limit to it, his love for others. An end point.' Again the sigh, as if she were bone-tired; as if she needed to unload some of the burden of these thoughts, carried alone, Alice saw, for years. 'I hoped his love for you might change that, might make him open his heart – properly, I mean. But I can see that when he was tested, he failed. And I can understand why this might not be enough for you, even when it might have been for someone else.'

If she talked now, Alice knew, she would sob. She reached out and took Ena's hand.

'I'm from a generation that stuck with marriages where there were inequalities – even cruelties,' Ena continued. 'But I know things are different now: sometimes both of the people in a relationship must grow or it will fail.'

Alice nodded. The concession brought the tears. 'I'm sorry, Ena. I didn't want to have to …' She held her hands to her face.

The older woman shook her head vehemently. 'Alice, I do not blame you. I will never blame you.' She hesitated, then, 'I hoped that Duncan would be able to love you enough, but I feared that he would not. And I saw that one day I might lose you.'

Ah, she knew. Understood that Alice couldn't allow herself to be the wedge that drove mother and son further apart, couldn't be that further reason for sourness – not when they only really had each other. If there was a time when he would need his mother, and the possibility that he would reach out to her, it was now.

Jealousy shot through her, then faded.

The heating kettle ticked.

'Will you stay in the house?'

'No,' Alice said, though already she worried about where she would go. 'It was his home before it was mine. And I need the change – I think without changing where I live, I'll struggle with what I need to do.'

'And what's that, my dear?'

'Oh, Ena,' she laughed through the tears, 'I don't know exactly!'

The kettle began its whistle.

'Here, I'll make it,' Alice offered. She knew the way Ena liked it: the blue-wash teapot from the shelf, boiling water from the kettle to preheat pot and cups, the loose-leaf tea canister, a strainer and cosy. 'I've been writing something longer. A novel, it seems to be.'

'A novel, Alice. How exciting!'

'Well, yes – yes, it is. But I really don't know how it fits into the rest of my life. Whether it's some kind of delusion, whether I'm even up to what it's asking of me. And I'm only at the beginning, cos there's a lot I don't understand … about the characters, about what they need. Oh, Ena, I do love it, this writing, but there's all these gaps I'm not sure how to fill – there's so much work to do!'

'You'll manage it, Alice.' Ena smiled warmly. 'I see a strong future for you. I always have.'

Tea streamed darkly into their cups, swirling the milk, and Alice thought for a moment about that future, which seemed so bleak sometimes, when – she'd discovered from her test of the ocean – she couldn't swim. When she couldn't sit without her cushion or wear tight pants or dance with abandon or pull Duncan onto her, into her, right when she felt like it, her skin and bones loose with desire, heart aching with need and sadness …

Would she stay, forever, just like this?

It was possible to recover: she'd seen it with her own eyes, Atikah's 'tickles' dissolving slowly into nothingness; heard about it from Sally, group attendees coming once, twice, then putting the dark time behind them; read about it online, women quietly returning to their normal lives. It *was* possible.

It was just … She wasn't sure if it was possible for her. Wasn't even sure, yet, if it would be possible for Emily.

'I've been thinking a lot about the future,' she said. 'Wondering about the larger ... I guess, patterns in life – wondering if there is even such a thing. Patterns, I mean.' She topped up the teapot and drew on the snug cosy. 'I guess because vulvodynia has brought me to a point I would never have reached without being forced – and, look, I'm fine with who I am now. I'm more assertive, more ... incisive, I think. More satisfying – to me, anyway.' She carried the cups to the kitchen table. 'So, even though I have this crap pain, I wonder about the meaning – like I said, the patterns in a life, the themes, why I am where I am. But then I feel like a callous idiot and like I'm ... missing the point.'

'What do you mean?'

'Oh, you know, how I'm one of the privileged few who have food, water ... shelter. It's easier to see purpose in pain when your life isn't under threat.' A bracing tannin smell wafted from her cup. 'And then I think,' she went on, 'if there *is* meaning in any of this, then the engine behind that work – whatever drives such patterns – is completely unresponsive to human suffering.'

'I know what you mean,' said Ena. 'And I know you and I have had the God conversation before.'

Alice remembered the friendly arguments over crisp salads and robust casseroles, seasons skimming past. Duncan laughing, *God is love, Mum? Is that the best you've got?*

'I don't know,' Ena continued, 'that I can speak for anyone else except myself, or even approach an idea of the kind of love I feel. Because if there is meaning and purpose behind life, if there is a love that holds us all, then it's a love that's bigger than any suffering or any evil we could possibly conceive.'

'I'm not sure that I can see that – that I have the same understanding. I think love is tied up with being creative for me, but I'm not sure I even know what that means. I guess I'm still working it out ... how that kind of love works. Maybe all I can do is find purpose in what has happened to me. How I can write meaning into my life, and hopefully help other women through that.'

Ena smiled, then hugged Alice against her. 'Isn't that more than most, my dear friend?'

For a moment Alice saw the baby of her imaginings, felt its mouth tugging at her, its head nestled in her hand.

*

It caught her as she set off on the return drive to the city after a walk along the shore, swinging her car, for a change, through the puzzle-like streets: a homemade 'for lease' sign, the mobile number fading on cardboard. She braked, then pulled onto the verge. It was like many of the old beach shacks at Wrigleys Point: faded and stumpy, humble. Greying draperies laced each square window, listing verandah boards suggested neglect. But the curtains had been drawn neatly, and a brick-and-concrete garden bed abutting the side of the house told her this had been a home once. *Our Place*, declared a wooden placard hanging from one rusty nail head.

A break from each other, just to see, she'd said to Duncan a week ago, and he'd agreed. Then he'd taken his pillow to the spare room.

Alice stepped towards the verandah, the squawking of gulls and the ocean's heave filling her ears, her feet squishing remnants of a conifer, toes rubbing the old needles into the warming sand and massaging them back to life. The resinous scent brought Rottnest with it: the hairy, pooey scent of quokkas … bathers stiff with salt, rubbing red … the stinging welt of a stinger and the pungent slosh of vinegar … steamy buttery bakery bread … Mum sipping an 'adult' drink, gazing out over Fays Bay … somewhere, fish being fried …

The verandah boards were loose and rubbed smooth by the tread of countless feet. When she perched herself on their edge and looked towards the last of the sunset, the warmth of the wood radiated up through her body. A light sea breeze lifted the hair around her face.

Would it be like a holiday to live here, in Wrigleys Point? Might it bring a kinder beginning?

She allowed herself to imagine it, living in a shack by herself, driving to uni to teach that one unit each week, pulling some of her old life into her new. She saw Sally and Denise and the others parking their cars here, on this crack-crazed driveway. Pictured herself laughing freely with Pen right here, on this deck. Imagined ringing her mother and speaking the hard words, seeing if they could get past them. Saw herself conjuring the courage to push into the world again, making the attempt to find a home for her collection of stories, her slumbering motley families.

And she imagined herself waking, each day, to the writing. To Arthur and Emily. Working their torment inside her, listening for the moment when Arthur would decide, discovering whether Emily would recover.

But what about Duncan? How might he fit into such a life? *Could* he? Did she even want him to? For a moment she saw his face, closed to her; the moments when he'd refused to believe in her, in them.

Maybe it was a particular aptitude, the ability to protect someone weaker or with a greater need, this love that put someone else first when it mattered. To defend them, even to *fend* for them. The word seeming right, somehow: old-fashioned … gentlemanly; kind and good.

Anyway, it was not the kind of love she had – she'd had – with Duncan. She knew she couldn't call him a narcissist, or deeply damaged, or anything of the sort; she was no longer sure of her judgement on this, didn't even know whether such labels helped anyone. What she did know was that he did not, at least, have the capacity to put her first when it would have made the difference. And though it made her sad, with a deep, tired sadness – another letting go, another loss – maybe it was for the best that the baby with Duncan she'd imagined into being – it felt so very, very long ago – would never now breathe life.

The sun had dropped away. Time to return to the city. Time to talk properly. To decide.

She opened the car door and lifted the silk purse from the passenger seat. Thought for a moment about the purse and how it had changed, the way she saw it: the contents still fragmented by pain, with loss and suffering, but threaded now with creativity, with possibility. She pulled her mobile from the purse and keyed in the numbers. Perhaps she would claim this place in the sun.

CHAPTER 23

LONDON, JUNE 1867

Arthur stands, and wriggles to shuck the shirt from his back. The room is stuffy with heat, all odours oppressing—wax, charcoal, the men themselves.

"Yes, it's sweltering." Charles pulls at his necktie. "I have struggled to sleep this week."

"The days are no better," says Arthur. "The stench from the Thames is enough to stymie reason in the courts."

"I read that the politicians are struggling too." Tom sips languidly at his brandy.

"Father says Parliament has almost lost sight of the reasoning behind extending the male vote," Arthur says. "The heat and stink make all of them irritable—Liberals and Conservatives both—what with amendments to Disraeli's bill being proposed and defeated, members of Parliament no longer knowing what they're voting for—"

"It's chaos on the streets too," Tom adds. "The demonstrations in Hyde Park, the weather becoming hotter and hotter, the stench affecting breathing ..."

"The heat poses a threat to the health of many," says Charles. "My young and elderly patients struggle particularly."

"As do the impoverished," Tom inserts.

The physicians chat on and Arthur leans against the cool wall and allows his mind to float, relaxed in the company of his friend and his father-in-law.

It's a regular occasion now—just like his weekly luncheon with Tom—this evening appointment. "The three bachelors", they sometimes laugh over late supper, before taking brandy in his Portland Place library and sharing news and opinions. Tonight it's been easy talk: Cissy's approaching wedding with the Earl of Whatley—*A fine match for her!* pronounced Charles; his own niggling concern for his father's wellbeing; Beatrice's support of votes for women—Tom's disbelief, *Did she tell you she signed the suffrage petition last year?*; Edith's letters to Charles, reporting on their daughter's progress …

It's the second year now, Emmie with her mother at Almsford for spring and summer's beginning, his own hurried visits to her there, letters back and forth, the planned Rochdale family reunion at Hierde House in July. Once Disraeli's bill is settled—and it must be settled soon, one way or the other—he will escape from the city and travel with his wife to Herdley.

It's not ideal, this separation, and he chafes against it at times, but he is prepared to suffer it for her sake, if the countryside has helped heal her and continues to provide comfort. He could endure almost anything for her sake. And they will be together for several months, soon enough, then they can explore their rediscovered passion for each other, even if both are still hesitant, even if she is still haunted by a pain he cannot begin to imagine. Nevertheless, they are already able to share the new words that come slowly, like a language both must learn, at night, in their bed—he asks her where he can place himself; she tells him where he might touch.

And now it returns to him—her words, her hands, her opening—and his body aches with longing.

"… since he was expelled from the Obstetrical Society."

Tom's words catch at him. Arthur calms himself, returns to his armchair to listen.

They all feel it on these evenings, the pressure to discuss Isaac Baker Brown—the desire to account for, and maybe leave behind, that terrible time—though Arthur can barely trust himself to speak on the matter.

"Yes, I hear of the decline in his fortunes." Charles speaks tersely. "I'm not sure that expulsion was the best outcome, y'know, yet the ill-feeling made it inevitable."

"And with good reason," says Tom. "It must be admitted that he conducted himself in a most ungentlemanly, even criminal, manner. The advertising and promoting, the failure to protect the sensibility of the weaker sex, the operating on women of unsound mind when his Surgical Home is not even licensed, the … demeaning of women's reputation with this claim about their purported practices—never proven, of course."

Charles's eyes shift about as Tom speaks; he shuffles his feet and resettles his compact, cocky body in the chair. "It is plausible," he says, "that excessive … that overstimulation plays a part in causing the disorder in some women, or maintaining it, once established."

"Plausible? Perhaps, perhaps not. This is not proven. And, even so, all these women acting thus? And then so many 'cured' by the barbarous excision, as Brown insists?" Tom shakes his head. "I have little sympathy for the man at this juncture."

"Baker Brown is prone to exaggeration," says Charles, "but I remain convinced of the benefits of surgery in the case of severe hysteria."

Arthur sees it again of his father-in-law: Charles must be right. Having argued for Emily's operation, he has no choice now but to stand by his guns, to make concessions only when it comes to Baker Brown's character—and even then only small allowances—not his surgical "solution".

"We must disagree on this"—Tom making his point—"even if we share concern about his future and, more so, that of his family."

"Yes, it is wrong that his whole family must shoulder this shame. But I do feel for the man, y'know, and I cannot imagine his career will recover." Charles's expression is uncharacteristically pensive. "It's a tremendous cost for ambition and rash, misguided action. But does that make Mr Baker Brown a bad man? You are not yet fathers … do not yet know what pushes you on as the head of a family." He looks down at his hands. "In some ways, y'know, I believe Baker Brown to be an ordinary person. He loved his children; he struggled—as we all do, yes?—through doubts; he made mistakes, yet hoped to better himself. Should we punish him further when he has already fallen? When he might be already broken?"

So, Arthur sees, it is not just about being proven right: Charles can see himself in the aspirations of Baker Brown—in his pushy self-promotion, his desire to insert himself in society. But, in possession of all the facts, would Charles have countenanced inflicting harm on his own daughter?

"These are difficult questions," Arthur begins, "yet I find it impossible to think kindly on the man." He falters for a moment: "It is difficult … It frustrates me that I do not understand the medical details more fully and that I am unable to comment with authority. I am no physician or nerve specialist, just a husband whose wife was endangered."

"Which makes you more entitled than anyone to have an opinion on the matter," says Tom. "You have seen the situation from the inside—comprehend the implications of the operation more than most." Tom plays his fingers on a side table, considers. "If you wish, though—if you *do* want to understand Brown's unravelling from a more ... medical perspective—I have articles you might read. From last year and into this."

Arthur feels a pulse of resistance. "Perhaps," he says slowly. "I wonder though. Do I really want to know the whole palaver? Make an effort to fathom the man and his actions?" He stands. "Still, I appreciate the offer, my friend. I'll think on it."

He walks to the window; peers through it as the meandering conversation of his companions resumes; wonders if Emily is looking out into a clearer, cooler night, and missing him.

Herdley, August 1867

Arthur's eyes flick over and through sentences, wanting to leave the words behind as quickly as they leap from the pages into his mind: *regrettable spirit of exaggeration ... moral questions ... erroneous physiology ... completely unjustifiable ... removal ... without the cognisance ... highest degree improper ... even left worse ...* and whole paragraphs filled with high-minded censure—

> *the disgust which reasonable and thinking men must feel at the public discussion, before mixed audiences, of sexual abuses. It is a dirty subject, and one with which only a strong sense of duty can induce professional men to meddle; and then it needs to be handled with an absolute purity of speech, thought, and expression, and, as far as possible, in strictly technical language.*

Sexual abuses. Dirty subject. Arthur thinks back to the appointment with Isaac Baker Brown: the insidious suggestions and the slurs cast on his wife—all in her absence and without the capacity to defend herself. How does Emily feel now, reading words about women meant only for men? Is she offended by the intimate language? Made angry at what might have been, had they gone ahead? Should he have kept them to himself, these articles? Emily had thought not: she'd been insistent when she noticed the *British Medical Journal* papers piled on his study desk, apprehending their content before he could stop her. *I need to understand the matter more fully*, she'd said, and went on to challenge him by asking how he could have assumed she would not take an interest in the surgeon's fate, when theirs had been intertwined with it—*almost disastrously so*. He'd felt sheepish as he brought the medical articles into their own private Hierde House drawing room and away from the questions of Beatrice or Father, but reluctant too, that impulse to shield her from harm still adamant.

Now his wife looks up; says, "It is unequivocal, Arthur," and reads out loud,

> *Both of them declared they had not practised self-abuse. They were not in any way benefited by the operation. They further stated that the operation was performed without their being at all aware of its real nature.*

She turns several pages one-handed and scans to where her other hand has fixed a passage. "And, look here," she says. "This poor woman was operated on in July of 1865, but it says that by January 1866, *she was worse than ever*. January 1866, Arthur. It could have been me; it could have been us!"

The image comes to him again—his Emily lying unrobed in a narrow bed in Baker Brown's "Home", her eyes wells of despair, accusation. He shudders as he thinks of their alternative fate: of her alone, without his defence or protection; of her insupportable pain, stretching into the future. What if reading this reminds her too? Brings back the old, paralysing terror, just when she is regaining trust and reaching for him again, her body restored to itself? Should he not continue to fend for her? Encourage her to plan for the future; to leave the past well enough alone?

He studies his wife across the drawing room table. She is reading again, her finger moving across the page, emotions passing fleetingly over her expressive face: surprise, dismay and then, unexpectedly, an ironic twist of the mouth. It reassures him, the fleeting smile, reminds him of her cleverness—a resilient intelligence that seems to have only strengthened through her ordeal, when it might have faltered, or become bitter. She is becoming her own person, he sees now; is no longer the girlish woman he fell in love with and married.

He turns more pages of the article before him, picking up the tone and trajectory, the playing out of the whole sorry affair in reports and letters from medical men, the pages brimming with righteous indignation and contempt: *her firm determination … promised it would effect a cure … lamentable failure … wives and daughters … unjustly taxed with filthy habits … wantonly exposed … worse than futile operations … theories as wrong as they are filthy—*

He stands and strides to the window, unable, suddenly, to contain his revulsion.

How had Baker Brown been allowed to carry out these operations? And for so long?

The Naze is solid and certain against the vivid blue sky. They should walk Hierde Hill after luncheon, he and Emily. If he strides on ahead, perhaps he can exercise the fury that has suddenly gripped him. Exorcise it from his body. Return to her, hold her hand, feel calm; reclaim—

"Here it is!"

He goes to her. Looks over the netted and beaded gold of her chignon.

April 6, 1867

The Obstetrical Society

MEETING TO CONSIDER

THE

PROPOSITION OF THE COUNCIL

FOR THE REMOVAL OF

MR. I.B. BROWN.

He places his hand on her shoulder as they take in the words, feel the gravity of the occasion. Then they slowly make their way through the pages, her finger tracing the names of the eminent men gathered from all around the country to determine the fate of this one contentious surgeon. *[A]mong women … we have constituted ourselves, as it were, the guardians of their interests,* he reads, *and in many cases, in spite of ourselves, we become the custodians of their honour.* Then the interjection of the mass of men—their hearty approbation: *hear, hear*—and the words that follow:

> *We are, in fact, the stronger, and they the weaker. They are obliged to believe all that we tell them. They are not in a position to dispute anything we say to them, and we, therefore, may be said to have them at our mercy.*

Arthur squirms a little as he reads, uncomfortable in a way he would not be were he alone. It is reading the words through Emily's eyes, he realises; understanding how close being protected is to being patronised—even, perhaps, controlled. He flicks the thought from his mind.

"And here, Arthur. About operating on lunatic women."

He takes the chair next to his wife and reads along with her: Baker Brown finding himself *on the horns of a dilemma*, trying to win … recognition? acclaim? while disavowing wrongdoing—*he took credit with the public of having cured cases of insanity, yet to screen himself from legal proceedings he denies it before the Commissioners*. And then the surgeon's response to his accusers, page upon repetitive page of it—*common fairness … fair play … common fair play as an Englishman … open and honest worker … painful position … not kind … fair opportunity … honest and open worker … honest man*—without properly addressing any of the charges against him, and all the while, the wandering, plaintive, even wheedling address interrupted by cries of protest, of indignant men rising in judgement against him.

"He only made matters worse for himself by conducting his own defence so ineptly," Arthur says. "Still, they were divided. This one"—he points out the passage—"defended Brown's right to speak—to be uninterrupted. And here, the suggestion that he acted out of ignorance, not malice. But the remainder? I think they'd made up their minds."

"Perhaps they hoped he'd change after the faults in his action and behaviour were pointed out. And when he didn't, he became the enemy, or the buffoon." She indicates: *I must admit Mr. Brown, no doubt, is "owdacious."*

It is a relief to laugh along with the *roars of laughter*, but he can sense the men's dismay too—their fear at this chaotic intrusion into that principled world—just as he can feel their own, his and Emmie's. And he can feel the desire to be done with it, this impossible subject, in the men's demand for a vote and some kind of reckoning that would settle the matter, especially here, in these words. "They're right, you know," he says.

"Arthur?"

"He took up the role of good Samaritan voluntarily and yet he appeared to have no remorse. No compassion at all for the women whose lives he affected. Ruined, in some cases. As they say"—he runs his finger under the words—"*our sympathy should be with the women in this position and their friends, not with those who are instrumental in producing such unhappy results.*" He scans the next column of print, is brought up abruptly at the words *an account of the operation*, thinks to warn Emily. But she is reading it already, they both are—*the pair of hooked forceps … and a cautery iron—*

"Oh! No … Arthur …" Her words are choked with distress.

He picks up her hand, squeezes it. "You don't have to read it," he tells her.

"I think I must." Her voice trembles, but is resolute. "I had an escape; the least I can do is acknowledge their suffering and allow myself to be affected by it."

She turns the page and they read together,

> *After the clitoris and the nymphæ were got rid of, the operation was brought to a close by taking the back of the iron and sawing the surfaces of the labia and the other parts of the vulva [cries of "Enough"] which had escaped the cautery, and the instrument was rubbed down backwards and forwards—*

"You're right," she says. "And so are they. It is enough." She turns from the pages and he wraps his arms around her, his brave wife. "What follows, Arthur?"

He looks down the column, leaning his cheek against her head. "Brown defending himself"—he reads aloud the clumsy, fumbling words—"*there was no terrorism, and no large fee taken; for I think I only had ten guineas—certainly not more than twenty [a laugh]—for the operation.*" He scans the columns. "More skirmishing over details of letters and statements—the surgeon's denials—and then the vote. For the removal, 194; and against, thirty-eight. Only five non-voters."

It would be pitiable, really, if it were possible for him to feel pity for the man.

But no. He will not understand Baker Brown—will not excuse his behaviour, or forget the damage he has done to those most vulnerable. The surgeon's book returns to him, and the woman's words: *I would like to have my hands untied; I will be very quiet.* No. He will not forgive the man, even if others might.

He stands, drawing Emily up with him, and folds her in his arms. They sway and press against each other, and he feels the comfort of it running through his body.

"Do you ever worry about it, Emmie?"

"Hm?" Her voice is muffled against his chest.

"Do you worry that it might return?"

He holds his breath, waiting for her reply.

"Oh, of course, Arthur, but less and less all the time." She lifts her face. "And I know it wouldn't be the same if it did recur. I would know what to do—and what *not* to do—straightaway."

"And our love-making?"

"I have thought about this, Arthur, and tried to remember the very beginning." She fixes her eyes on his; lets him know, in this way, that he must attend closely. "I do not know that the pain was to do with pleasure, with excitement. Not solely, in any case. It was there constantly … only made more severe with any touch or pressure." Her hand is warm against his cheek, her touch tender. "It is true I could not tolerate anything that made it worse, but it was Mr Baker Brown, I think, who channelled our thoughts in this singular direction, who momentarily fed the distrust which had grown between us." She smiles at him. "But we know better now, don't we?"

Arthur senses something stretch, rise within him. Like a bird that has been grounded, remembering it has wings.

"Indeed we do," he says, and kisses the top of her head. "I will always put you first, my love. I will always care for you above all others."

They walk to the sofa and sit closely, arms about each other.

"I wonder, Arthur."

"My dear?"

"Will sense ever be made of such an illness?"

"Surely one day," he replies.

What else can he say?

Chapter 24

Perth, February 2010

'That's it, then.'

He put his pen down, her husband, and they tidied their sets of notes; money and belongings anaesthetised and sliced in two.

Alice couldn't imagine what came next. 'So we'll hand these over to lawyers?'

'Yes, they'll need the information. You'll need to find your own, of course. Lawyer.'

Would she? Did it have to be like this, two opposing teams?

She felt his hand briefly on her shoulder, its absence when it was lifted away. 'Will you be alright, do you think?'

'Oh, Duncan, you're being more than generous.'

Alice went to the kitchen sink, leaned over it, splashed water onto her swollen eyes, over her puffy face, combed it through her hair.

'Well, it's not just that. You're very alone here.'

'I know,' she said. 'But I need to be.'

His face was older in the stark electric light, wrinkles pronounced, hair dull. He'd be forty-five this year, she calculated, and suddenly he looked every day of it.

She picked up their mugs, rinsed them out.

'And what about the pain?' he asked. 'Is it any better?'

'Oh, look, it's okay. Well, it's not – it's still there all the time – but it's manageable. I'm cobbling together all the things that help.'

She wouldn't tell him that the acupuncture wasn't making any difference – not that seemed to last, anyway. She wouldn't tell him about what had turned out to be her final session with Sasha and the physio saying that Alice was doing well, that she might be able to manage on her own. About the panic that had flooded her, the sense of abandonment and defeat, and her own words: *You think I might never get better, don't you?* About Sasha explaining that, no, it was just needing to think about it differently, the vulvodynia, *ironing out the highs and the lows,* and that, maybe, over time – *it may be months, it may be years* – management might lead to improvement, even recovery. She wouldn't tell him that she knew, now, she was not to be one of those lucky ones with an uncomplicated trajectory – better, better, best. That she was trying to accept who she was right now, taking charge of her own body, finding whatever was good in her life and making it enough, otherwise she'd be miserable. Bitter. Resentful.

'And uni?'

'I'll only be in the one day a week.' She laughed ruefully, 'I think we can be civil? And I don't think it's anyone else's business, the details. But I'll leave that up to you.' At his nod: 'I'm going to keep an eye out for postdocs at other unis. Maybe something will turn up closer to here – even some sessional teaching.'

'It would help if you got that collection of stories published. Make you a more attractive proposition.'

'I know that, Duncan.' Did he still think he had to manage her? Give her permission?

'No, I don't mean just that. What I'm saying is that your writing is good. It really deserves to be published. And that will open doors for you.'

'Oh, thanks. Thanks, Duncan – I mean it.' She thought for a moment. 'And you? Are you okay?'

'Not really.' For a moment, he looked angry. Then he spoke again through a sigh: 'It's a lot to adjust to – but I was alright before and I'll be alright again. And I think you will be too. At least, I hope so.'

Why couldn't they be this honest with each other before? This kind? The graciousness, she supposed, was a measure of their defeat. But he wished the best for her and that was something – that was important, she supposed.

The tap dripped. Dawn entered the window. She turned off the kitchen light.

'Okay, then.' He stood slowly, lifting his bag. 'I'll ring you, Alice. We'll sort out the rest. It'll just take a bit of time.'

'Yes.'

On the deck, she slid her feet into thongs. The sky had that pearly dawn glow and the air was parched. Families would make their way to the beach later, once they'd rolled themselves from their Sunday beds.

Duncan stepped down to the path and she walked behind him to the car, making a memory of that loping walk. Something to keep.

He put his bag on the back seat, started the engine and raised his hand.

Then he was driving down the road.

Then he was at the bend.

Then he was gone.

She turned her feet towards the ocean. In the eucalypt at the corner of her street, a magpie carolled and, further along, the casuarina was a conversation of rousing pink-and-greys. She followed the path through the patch of scrub with its tiny, hectic birds. A jay rearranged itself as it darted up from a bush, its wings the sound of ruffling pages.

She crossed the front road and passed through the bank of melaleucas, their tops angled by onshores, a punch of green in the lee of each stunted shrub. She slipped off her thongs, slid a finger into their loops and stepped onto the path that led through the dunes. Against her feet the sand was cool and she dug her toes into it, feeling its soft squeak against her skin. Then around the last bend and the beach stretching like a woman's flank to the north and south. She walked over its sweeps and curves and stopped at the water's edge. The sea was on the verge of waking, each small wave gathering, hovering, momentarily stilled, as if the world were holding its breath.

She closed her eyes and felt froth between her toes, her feet sinking deeper into the sand with each rippling eddy. She tried to fill her mind with that sensation, tried not to imagine diving deep and floating, feeling the joy of the ocean against her body. She opened her eyes and the sky was lighter still, the beach flooded in pastels. She scooped up a hank of seaweed and burst its tiny brown bubbles as she walked along the shore.

Near the old boat ramp she cut back through the dunes, meeting the path that went to the tiny beachside shop. The car park was empty. A crow stabbed at some paper beside the bin, gave a short, rusty cry and lumbered away over a stand of banksias.

She headed inland for the loop back to the shack. The narrow zigzag roads were empty too, each house still. Even the birds hushed themselves as the sun edged over the hill to the east.

She walked through the quiet streets until she reached her home. She nudged a nail jutting from the verandah. Another thing to fix. She upended a terracotta pot over it to remind herself and walked to the bedroom. She lowered herself into the impression their night-time bodies had made, felt the ghost of his arms around her. Felt fresh tears on her cheek. Felt the reminder of her constant companion, clamping, stinging and aching; turned herself inward with that, through that, to the fragments inside: her life in bits and pieces, and all of it shifting around. And as she cried, she felt them again, Arthur and Emily, all the fragments of their lives milling inside her, too, all their possibilities – for good, for evil – jostling for position, jagged words forming phrases, the scattered scenes of their lives weaving around each other, threading themselves together into some kind of sense.

But she couldn't force it, she knew that. And there was something important, she could feel it – something almost … necessary about being in this in-between place, purged by sorrow yet brimming with uncanny expectation. Something was being demanded of her. Something was on the verge of happening: hope, a world shaping itself, a future.

So she would hold them, Arthur and Emily, in the midst of their pain and suffering. Believe in them. Trust that the writing knew what needed to be done.

She stood and smoothed the night from the sheets. Pulled out fresh undies, bra, shorts and t-shirt. Looked out of the window with her clothes in her arms, watching the sun rise. The 25th of February. A date to mark. Her new life.

The bedroom was luminous in the moonlight. Was it this that had woken her, or Emily and Arthur – their lives, their stories? She rolled the sheet off, let the fanned air whisper across her skin, tried to breathe herself into drowsiness, but the tightness in her chest and belly told her sleep would be impossible.

She padded to the kitchen, pulled the hanging cord. Her papers, scattered over the table in the evening, switched into life, the pen sitting on top.

It was Arthur, she could feel it – his confusion tying the knot in her gut, his wavering that was a leaping pulse, unsettling hers, his distress and despair sitting in her bowel like stone; his decision that must be made, about Emily, *for* Emily. And for her, too, she understood. He must make the right decision for her too.

Alice leaned forward onto the bench, closed her eyes and slowed her racing mind with deep, long breaths. And when her body was quiet enough and her mind still enough, she took herself to him.

Here he was, her Arthur, asleep in the bed he shared with Emily. The embers of the small fireplace highlighted the shadows of weariness on his young face; his eyelids fluttered and his mouth worked. *No,* he said, throwing his body around. *No!*

She sat on the bed next to him and smoothed his cheek. She felt her way into his fears, his confusion, his anger, his sorrow. She imagined herself a rook and flew into his dream. The elm trees, their crimson flower-bursts. The nest. The egg. Then she bent to his ear and whispered the words that might help: *Sometimes, Arthur, we must fend for those who are not able to fend for themselves.* A sweep of her hand through his hair. *And sometimes we must listen for the quiet voice that tells the truth.*

And then it was gone, that world, in a rush, in a backward plunge that left her dizzy and alone.

Chapter 25

Herdley, December 1868

He is brought to a gasping halt at the sight of them: Kettle Peak and the knolls, solemn and majestic, just as they've always been. He turns in a slow circle, breathing in the expanse, filling his lungs with it and hearing, just for a moment, a phantom Taffy panting at his leg. Eleven years ago, he calculates: striding through the chill with Taffy—taking stock of the world he strode through too. It returns to him. Family. What to protect. How to protect it.

Smoke threads from one of the Hierde House chimneys. Emily will be with Mrs Simpson, little Lou leaning from her mother's embrace, arms waving, as if she could catch the smells that cram the kitchen—yeast, cinnamon, raisins—in her tiny fingers. And when Lou becomes too heavy, Emmie will see if Bea can tend to her squirming niece and sink with a sigh into the nearest chair.

He feels the smile on his face, and it reminds him that he could, if he wanted, think as a child might—as he once did—on the failings of guardians, on the loss that scarred his childhood, on that interminable span of time when he and Emily were cleaved from each other, battling something they could not even name. But he is a guardian himself now. A husband, a father—maybe soon a politician under Gladstone, if Father's retirement opens the way for him to stand, represent the constituency; one day, a baronet. And so he will do what he has done for years now: stay calm, be patient; quietly support any legislation that continues to improve the lot of the poor, the uneducated, the homeless; take comfort in these little steps; cherish thoughts of the future—the influence he will have, the plans he will set in motion. He is only twenty-seven, after all.

He stamps his boots against ground made rock-like with cold, wiggles his toes in their woollen socks, whacks his jacketed arms across his chest, rubs his gloved hands hard against each other, turns again to the ascent, slipping on heather, skirting spills of rock, feeling the air race raw into his lungs. A cow lows in the distance as he climbs, and rooks cry harshly overhead, making their way north. Heading for the elm thicket, no doubt, the rookery there.

There was one in that dream that came at the darkest time, the dream that is now only wisps in his mind: entering the thicket, the cradle of elms, and a glossy rook egg. Black, beating wings. His own form reflected, whole and good, in the eye of a rook. Then Mother's voice, and the egg's dark tracings settling into a language he could finally, finally understand.

Here it is, the outcrop of gritstone. The craggy tumble, the gaps and crannies. And now the skull, a bare summit. The vista of villages and ranges. The feeling of being on top of this whole vast, multitudinous world. And again the sense of Taffy alongside him, their breaths hanging white in the chill air, the press of the terrier's hard nut of a head against his leg. Then that urgent bark. It comes back to him, this memory, with clear, bright edges: the downhill run, the fierce moorcock, remembering Harris and Rattlin and the fight. His own defence of something he could not put a name to, then. Mother. And fending for those not able to fend for themselves. Fighting for others. Fighting for love.

His feet lead him off again—to the east this time, along a path he rarely follows. And then that cry again, like a rusted lid forced open: another rook, a straggler making its solitary way to the rookery.

How wonderful to be able to fly. To see the world like a story unfurling below you. To see him, Arthur, brown cap of hair and feet beneath. To see him, Arthur, striding into his future. To see him, Arthur, becoming smaller and smaller until, finally, he disappears.

AUTHOR'S NOTE

In both narrative timelines, geographical locations are generally intended to replicate real places, but there are some exceptions.

In Western Australia: the university where Alice teaches is a composite of a few Perth campuses, and her home with Duncan is in a nebulous setting; Sally's home in Claremont and Simone's home 'in the hills' are fictional, as are the details of the streets that lead to them; though pelvic pain clinics can be found in capital cities in Australia, this one is made up; the café where Alice and Ena meet is imaginary; and Wrigleys Point has similarities to coastal communities north of Perth, but is not identical with any one place.

In England: Isaac Baker Brown may have practised in Connaught Square, London, but his surgery there is imagined; Herdley, its buildings and surrounding landmarks are fictional, but inspired by Chinley in Derbyshire, England; and Almsford is a fiction.

All the characters in the Perth timeline are fictional, including the women in the vulvodynia support group. Isaac Baker Brown was a real person, as were the Victorian-era politicians, headmasters and published physicians referred to, but all other characters in the Victorian timeline are imagined.

On vulvodynia: informational and self-help books were useful in the writing of this book, as were articles in medical journals; the *Journal of Reproductive Medicine* has published material on the subject since the 1980s. The Gynaecological Awareness Information Network (Australia), the International Society for the Study of Vulvovaginal Disease, the Australian and New Zealand Vulvovaginal Society, the National Vulvodynia Association (US), The Vulval Pain Society (UK) and a number of Facebook groups provide information and support to women and their families.

An earlier version of chapter one was published as 'That Hand' in the anthology *Other Voices* (Peter Cowan Writers Centre Inc., 2013).

A small amount of material in the novel has been previously published in the following of my personal essays:

- 'Affectionate Love'. *Peripheral Visions*, special issue of *TEXT*, no. 57, October 2019.
- 'Mark My Words'. *Southerly*, vol. 76, no. 2 , 2016.
- 'A Conversation with the Enemy'. *Outskirts*, vol. 32, May 2015.
- 'Vulvodynia and the Ambiguous Between'. *Axon: Creative Explorations*, vol. 3, no. 1, March 2013.

In visualising Arthur's walks through 1860s London, I relied on the 'Map of London 1868', by Edward Weller, sourced online at Mapco (london1868.com). Quotations in the novel have been drawn from the following publications:

- Baker Brown, Isaac. *On the Curability of Certain Forms of Insanity, Epilepsy, Catalepsy, and Hysteria in Females*. London, Robert Hardwicke, 1866.
- Briffault, Robert. *The Mothers*. Abridged ed., George Allen & Unwin, 1959.
- *British Medical Journal*: Issues for 28 April 1866, 24 November 1866, 15 December 1866, 29 December 1866, 12 January 1867, 6 April 1867.
- Charcot, Jean-Martin. *Clinical Lectures on Diseases of the Nervous System: Volume 3*. Translated by T. Savill, London, The New Sydenham Society, 1889.
- Charcot, Jean-Martin. *Lectures on the Diseases of the Nervous System*. Translated by G. Sigerson, London, The New Sydenham Society, 1877.
- Dodson, Melvin G., and Eduard G. Friedrich. 'Psychosomatic Vulvovaginitis'. *Obstetrics and Gynecology*, vol. 51, suppl. 1, 1978, pp. 23s–25s.
- Frazer, James George. 'Part I: The Magic Art and the Evolution of Kings'. In *The Golden Bough: A Study in Magic and Religion*. 3rd ed., vol. 1, The Macmillan Press, 1911.
- Harding, M. Esther. *Woman's Mysteries: Ancient and Modern*. Harper & Row, 1971.
- King, Leonard W. *Enuma Elish: The Seven Tablets of Creation; The Babylonian and Assyrian Legends Concerning the Creation of the*

World and of Mankind. Vol. 2, Luzac and Co., 1902. (Note: some lines from the translation of the prayer to Ishtar have been omitted.)

- Moore, Bruce, editor. *Australian Concise Oxford Dictionary*. 5th ed., Oxford University Press, 2009.
- Sargeant, Hilary A., and Frances V. O'Callaghan. 'The Impact of Chronic Vulval Pain on Quality of Life and Psychosocial Well-being'. *Australian and New Zealand Journal of Obstetrics and Gynaecology*, vol. 47, no. 3, 2007, pp. 235–239, *Wiley Online Library*, doi:10.1111/j.1479-828X.2007.00725.x.
- Sims, J. Marion. 'On Vaginismus'. *Transactions of the Obstetrical Society of London*, vol. 3, 1861, pp. 356–367.
- Plutarch. *Plutarch's Lives: Translated from the Greek, by Several Hands*. Vol. 1, London, Jacob Tonson, 1716.
- Thomas, T. Gaillard. *A Practical Treatise on the Diseases of Women*. 5th ed., London, Henry Kimpton, 1880.

A full listing of texts used in the research and writing of this book can be found on my website.

Acknowledgements

I'm fortunate to live by the wardan on Whadjuk Noongar boodja, and I wish to pay my respects to their Elders past, present and future. Country sustains and informs my writing in ways for which I continue to be very grateful.

My thanks to Whadjuk Noongar Elder Len Collard, for providing information on the land where I write and for generously offering me language for it.

Fremantle Press has proved to be a fabulously supportive and cohesive team, and a wonderful home for my novel. I thank especially my editor, Armelle Davies, for her care, clarity and elegant solutions; Naama Grey-Smith for her meticulous proofreading; Georgia Richter, who 'got it' immediately and with delight; and Claire Miller, for her warm and tireless can-do attitude. I'm also grateful for the inspired design work from Nada Backovic.

I am indebted to Lee Kofman, Donna Mazza and Susan Midalia for endorsing *Eye of a Rook*. It means a great deal to have my writing understood so well by three such fine writers.

Thanks to the Department of Local Government, Sport and Cultural Industries, who have funded the Four Centres Emerging Writers Program (EWP) through their Culture and the Arts division. The program has directly aided the publication of this novel. We are fortunate to have a government body that invests, culturally and financially, in WA writing and writers.

I'm very grateful to the Peter Cowan Writers Centre (PCWC) for delivery of the EWP, and for providing me with writing and teaching opportunities over many years, including a residency in 2018. Special thanks to Keith Melrose and to the other EWP writers.

Thanks to Edith Cowan University for assisting my efforts through the position of Adjunct Senior Lecturer (Writing). I'm grateful to the team at *Westerly* Magazine and the University of Western Australia for their ongoing support. The editorial board at Margaret River Press has proved a sustaining dwelling place for matters writing, editing and publishing. Of many individuals within these bodies, I am especially indebted to Danielle Brady, Jill Durey, Tony Hughes-d'Aeth, Ffion Murphy, Catherine Noske, Marcella Polain and Caroline Wood, for research, writing and/or vocational support.

Personal assistance from Jo Outhwaite at the Temple Reading Room, Rugby School, was gratefully received, as was information from librarians and other staff at the State Library of Western Australia and Edith Cowan University – a shout-out here to ECU Library's document delivery service.

Feminist reading group Magdalena Talks Back provided a safe and nurturing space in which to present my writing. Special thanks to Lekkie Hopkins and Julie Robson, for founding the group, and to Amanda Gardiner and Rashida Murphy, for their attentive and sensitive feedback in Mags and as part of the PCWC Advanced Writers' Group.

I'm so very grateful for the support I've received from the West Australian writing community. The vigour and camaraderie of local writers, writing-related organisations and publishers is something to behold and to celebrate. I'm especially thankful to Holden Sheppard for expert guidance on the business of being a debut author, and to Ken Spillman for useful suggestions in the early stages of writing.

Several friends and family members have at times gifted valuable writing spaces, for which I'm grateful. Many thanks, also, to Anna and Pat Luca, for allowing me to write Alice in your 'beach shack'. In responding to copyedits, Phillips cabin at Katharine Susannah Prichard Writers' Centre proved to be a delightful, quiet place to find focus and clarity.

I am grateful beyond words to the women with vulvodynia and related conditions with whom I've had contact since 2003. To Annette, Catherine, Justine, Kath, Melissa and the two Nics: thanks for being there for me in the hardest times. Through this writing, I would like to honour the memory of Yvonne Wallis, as well as my friend 'the other Josephine'.

To my non-writer friends, too many to name, too wonderful to single out any one of you: we all know how much you've helped me over the very long haul!

The men I've shared my life and home with over the writing years – my husband and our four sons – have provided unwavering encouragement. Thanks, guys, for your patience and belief! John, I'm so very grateful for your steadfast love; Ben, our epic conversations prompted more breakthrough writing moments than you'll ever know; Ash, I've felt your support no matter how far away you might be. I've also felt the unconditional affection and acceptance of my whole family: siblings, cousins, nieces, nephews … Thank you all, so much. I'm indebted to my sisters Judy and Philippa, who have offered countless listening hours; you two have helped me find the strength to write on this topic. Thanks also to Mel, for fruitful conversations on Jung and feminism. This book wouldn't have been written without the inspiration of my mother, passionate reader and writer Ena Taylor, who said to me right from the start of it all, 'There's a story here!' You were right, Mum.

My dictionary defines a mentor as 'an experienced and trusted adviser'. I've registered my mentor Susan Midalia's experience through every facet of her response to many drafts. She recognised the intent of my writing immediately, saw the large picture of the work throughout, and applied astute, rigorous and encouraging editing. I trusted her from our first meeting, but that trust only grew as I understood her belief in and commitment to this novel and to me. It's been a privilege, Susan.